ONCE AGAIN ASSEMBLED HERE

Also by Sean O'Brien

Poetry

The Indoor Park

The Frighteners

HMS Glasshouse

Ghost Train

Downriver

Cousin Coat: Selected Poems, 1976–2001

The Drowned Book

Collected Poems

The Beautiful Librarians

Essays

The Deregulated Muse

Anthologies

The Firebox: Poetry in Britain and Ireland after 1945
(editor)

Short Stories

The Silence Room

Novels

Afterlife

ONCE AGAIN ASSEMBLED HERE

SEAN O'BRIEN

PICADOR

First published 2016 by Picador
an imprint of Pan Macmillan
20 New Wharf Road, London N1 9RR
Associated companies throughout the world
www.panmacmillan.com

ISBN 978-1-4472-1971-2

The extract on p.165 is from *Collected Poems* by Louise MacNeice,
published by Faber & Faber.

1 3 5 7 9 8 6 4 2

A CIP catalogue record for this book is available from the British Library.

Printed and bound by CPI Group (UK) Ltd, Croydon, CR0 4YY

For Paul Harrison

Lord, behold us with thy blessing,
Once again assembled here;
Onward be our footsteps pressing,
In thy love and faith and fear...

Break temptation's fatal power,
Shielding all with guardian care,
Safe in every careless hour,
Safe from sloth and sensual snare;

Thou, our Saviour, thou, our Saviour,
Still our failing strength repair,
Still our failing strength repair.

Henry James Bucknoll, 1843

'Why', he asked himself, 'am I always lost?'

Derek Marlowe, *Nightshade*

'There should have been fictions to be real in.'

Peter Porter, 'Story Which Should Have Happened'

Prologue

2010

This is a story about murder. I think I can safely tell it now, but it's never possible to be quite sure, so the manuscript will go to a safe place – that is to you, for you to deal with as you see fit. Dispose of it if you think it wisest. I will not be around to comment on what you decide.

In those remote days, in the 1960s, when this story took place and when I grew up, peacetime was by some means always wartime. It should not have been surprising that there were casualties. I remember the day before, and I remember the day it happened, when I entered another world, adjacent to this one but impossible to come back from, the one where everyone lives, death notwithstanding. I say I can tell this story, but, as they still used to say then, you had to be there to get the benefit.

History, in a statement whose own provenance is disputed, is said to be 'one damn thing after another'. It's an idea whose unreasonableness can at times seem rather satisfying. Hurl the stupid newspaper aside, switch off the idiots on television, or, perhaps more likely nowadays, click to be somewhere else on your laptop. But I don't believe it: history, at least as it presents itself to my imagination, can be any number of things taking place at once, however dispersed in time they may originally have been. When I try to tell this story straight, I stall; therefore, in order to get anywhere, to get started, I have to digress, folding one incident inside another and another as though inside the brackets of an interminable equation of the sort I never properly understood.

I sleep badly, in small episodes. Nowadays what sleep I get

is dry and thin, but to be wakeful by night is worse. Somebody once recommended that thinking of a walk through a familiar setting was a cure for insomnia. Not for me. More and more often I find myself lying there and repeating the following episode.

I cross the railway track and open the gate into the grounds. It seems to be November. If I stay here, I think, nothing will happen. The leaves will fall. The fog will persist, with occasional damp birdsong and the faintest sound of traffic from the city. But nothing else. I cannot be compelled to go either forward through the wood past the lake, where the raft is tilting and slightly adrift of its mooring, or back across the track to where I should never have been in the first place. With luck, if I stay here long enough, I will simply vanish, one more cloudy breath dispersing in the frosty air. But this is not true, and as ever I will walk on, and events will take their course. Carson will still be dead, and others will follow.

The dream-walk is, I suppose, a kind of advice: insofar as it is in your power, tell the truth.

The subject matter follows me into the waking world. I sit at my desk in the window of my flat, looking across Fernbank Avenue, through the trees and into the grounds of Blake's. And I find myself back in the woods by the lake once more. When the reverie fades I am still at the desk, my pen put down beside the creamy manuscript book in which I am allegedly writing volume two of the history of Blake's School, *Wartime and Reconstruction, 1939–1979*.

Progress is slow. The problem lies in some of the facts.

There is no official place to put them. In another of my interior travels, I picture a classroom that everyone has forgotten about, on a high upper corridor, an old part of the library that has been locked and forgotten. I should not have a key, but here it is in my hand as I make my way along the corridor late in the evening when no one's around. I turn the key in the lock and open the door and go in. Once again I am crossing the railway line. Once again I come to my senses and the page before me is still empty and the history unwritten.

But now, in an identical manuscript book, see, I am writing it. This is it, I hope.

How fine it is, to speculate at leisure. Larkin feared the 'thin continuous dreaming' that would occupy the old age he did not live to experience. Less of the 'thin', if you please. If anything, I find that the textures of reverie grow denser. They put the present in the shade. I can sit here at the window all day, if I choose. As far as the here and now is concerned I have no more urgent matter in prospect. One thing is clear to me: the past – every morning on waking I discover with alarm and excitement that my life is now mostly the past – is more substantial and beguiling to me that anything else, despite what it holds. Each day I write looking out between the bare plane trees on to a setting I have known for fifty years, but the place is not what it was. Mere persistence has earned me the right to say that.

Tomorrow it will all begin again at Blake's. If I happen to be strolling in the grounds after breakfast I may hear them singing 'Lord Behold Us With Thy Blessing'. They cannot possibly be real, can they, these people? Autumn term. The whole idea is implausible. I shall sniff the bright September air for the first hint of frost and fog and bonfire to come.

I should explain at the outset that while some people are drawn to schoolmastering, as we used to call it, I seem to have thrust it on myself out of uncertainty as to what I should make of my life. I wanted to write novels – or perhaps it would be more accurate to say *to be a novelist* – but these pages are as close as I shall come to that, and these pages are, of course, not (really) fiction but instead a memoir of a time and a place and some people. Self-destruction; demented antagonism tended with loving care long after its alleged time; some deaths; some killings: all of them were undoubtedly real. I was a witness to much of what took place and a participant in some of it. The school was a killing ground then.

In the daylight hours these events, pondered and rehearsed and rubbed at for so long, have begun to invite my incredulity now, even as they grow more insistent. By night they arrive as with their full original force, no longer as ideas but as invasions of the senses, in three dimensions. A street corner as it stood before it was demolished; a pub with its nightly actors, though it has long since changed out of recognition; a shade of lipstick glimpsed on a woman in the crowded street; even the smell of Belgian chocolate, or of mud at low tide in the creek. Most people say the sense of smell is not available in dreams, but perhaps they do not have the dreams I have. Is there an age beyond which it is no longer possible to go mad?

Concentrate, Maxwell. Focus, as they say.

Schoolmastering turned out to suit me. I had the necessary ability either to excite interest or to impose obedience, but the work also encouraged my tendency to procrastinate. The ritual cycle of the school year allowed for indefinite postponement. In a bleak mood I might say that in the event I managed to postpone my entire life. But I hope I managed to do some good amid the temporizing and despite what may come to seem the larger failure set out in these pages. That sounds like a rather ragged piety, doesn't it?

Let me describe the place. Blake's. The main school building, the tall redbrick-and-masonry ship, a church in light disguise, is still moored against the field, with the various smaller additions, the restored Memorial Hall, labs, a sports hall, the library and even nowadays a theatre (or 'Performing Arts Centre', though the Memorial Hall was good enough for our productions), clustered around its foot like a town about a castle. In the official history I shall note these recent developments as signs of Blake's readiness to meet the challenge of the future while cherishing the inheritance of the past – as if I were writing a script for one of those grim *Look at Life* shorts we used to yawn through at the cinema while waiting for the shooting to start.

The central thing is still there, the Main Hall with the classrooms opening off it on three sides of two floors, beneath a hammer-beam roof. Everything passes through that space, gets its warrant from that cold, high-windowed climate of Victorian medievalism. When I walk through it today it will be empty and silent, the old elongated desks that doubled as benches long gone, rows of grey stackable chairs in their place. I pause by the foot of the wide staircase, then go up to the balcony and along to the far corner to what used to be the history classrooms and the adjacent bookroom where Captain Carson held court. I come here a lot, out of term-time.

Yet now that I am nearly done with Blake's, and thus done with everything else, I find that, when the pupils and staff are on the premises, the place lacks solidity somehow, and authority, and my selfish motive in this is to revisit at least the ghosts of those qualities in the lives of those who moved through this setting, all of them – the major actors and their attendants, I mean – gone now, dead, or vanished, which amounts to the same thing. Which makes me a sort of rearguard.

So I walk the boundaries, around the wooded pond, along the railway line until it crosses the broad creek, known to the boys as Shit Creek because of its dangerous and foul-smelling mud at low tide, where a few decayed small craft are all that remains of the sailing club once advertised as one of Blake's distinguishing features. On the far side the boatyard and the timber yard have long shut down. Beyond them lies the asphalted fairground where no fair has taken place in years. I follow the path along to the fence, where the creek disappears to pass under the main road, then make my way back through the woods that extend down the whole of Fernbank Avenue.

Eventually I find myself emerging from the gigantic rhododendron bushes, among the Portakabins which are serving as temporary classrooms until the new science block is finished. Beneath one of these cheapjack huts is the site of the old Porter's Lodge, where Sergeant Risman and his invisible wife lived. Mrs Risman was barely a rumour, in a place that ran on rumours, but on an early autumn morning, when the chill is coming downriver and across the flat, low-lying terrain, I would not be surprised to meet the Sergeant on the driveway, approaching with a guardsman's bearing and a sceptical gaze directed at the world of subalterns and other daft buggers. But this morning he is not there. Or perhaps I'm the ghost and cannot be seen by the living.

I pass through the gates and return to the flat on Fernbank Avenue which I have occupied for forty-odd years. I make tea and I come to the window and sit at my desk with a view of the woods and the roofs of the school beyond, and I close one manuscript book, the official one, and open the other, the one no one knows about, and I return to writing this. Or I try to, once more. I have accumulated a lot of beginnings, circlings, evasion, evocations that strand themselves among the woods and pathways of this unholy ground.

Yesterday all the past. But tomorrow the current staff and pupils and the terrified newcomers in either category will begin afresh, convinced, as we once were, of a kind of provisional immortality, divided into three parts – until Christmas, until Easter, until the far-off green-gold sexiness of summer. I have not lived in the world: I have lived here instead, in this specialized and surely impossible place. *Yesterday all the past. Tomorrow the struggle.*

To work, to work. My ostensible task – the one to which the school has appointed me in my retirement – is to write the second volume of the history of Blake's, covering the period from the Munich crisis of 1938 up until 1979. I am not convinced that any living person other than myself has ever sat down to read volume one, *A Firm Foundation 1887–1938* (Waterside Press, 1960), though after all it was James Carson who wrote it, and he could actually write; nor that any will relish volume two. Like its predecessor, that will be a book with no conversation – the kind of thing Alice found so boring, though look what happened to her. Like Blake's itself, she was the creation of a clergyman.

Even Carson could not make his opening description seem other than leaden:

> Blake's was founded by Isaac Blake, an Anglican clergyman and philanthropist from the Isle of Axness, by means of a bequest enabling the creation of a school intended for the education of able boys of all classes in mathematics, science and the classics in order that they might serve the nation as Christian gentlemen.

This aspiration must seem almost touchingly remote in its priorities. And an inspection of the records indicates that Blake's wishes have been served only to a limited extent. The school's twentieth-century output seems to have been more typically involved with the law and commerce, to put it mildly. Perhaps the original Blakean spirit was crushed in the trenches. As Carson puts it,

> Men of Blake's – recent pupils, masters and groundsmen – were quick to answer the call to arms in 1914 and saw service in the local regiment on the Western Front and in Mesopotamia. A total of a hundred and forty lost their lives.

Beyond the city itself, the Plain of Axness remains to this day in a more-than-rural quiet, like the patient green graveyard of those vanished into the conflict, a place still waiting for a returning echo that never comes. Carson would have considered that a too-literary way of putting it, though he would have agreed it was the case. And like the Plain of Axness the school has never escaped the Great War entirely, nor the second conflict that shaped so many of the staff I encountered first as a pupil and then as a colleague.

My official history will go straight into the school library – unread, unheard, unnoticed. Its purpose will be simply to exist. Never mind: I plan to finish what I've started. But while

I may feel that it is taking longer than expected to get the official book written, any real urgency is mine. I can take my time. All the time in the world, the present Headmaster indicated. He is perhaps forty. His name is of no importance in this story. He invited me to write the thing and then, I imagine, forgot all about it and me after the leaving dinner and the gift of a complete set of the novels of Graham Greene, which I already possessed.

Yesterday all the past. Today the accounting. If I die in harness, he will declare it sad, but the unfinished book will not be important. The word 'hobby' hangs like a fart over the whole thing: it is a school story, after all.

Like so much else about Blake's, this second manuscript feels like a conspiracy. I first wrote down much of the following narrative forty years ago. At the time, for reasons which should be clear from what follows, it would have been impossible to publish a factual account of the events I recorded. And to be on the safe side I made it into a novel in order to conceal the identities of those involved. I'm sure, though, that they would have recognized themselves immediately. This too would have been unpublishable. Now, after half a lifetime and more, I'm reintroducing the real names, for my own satisfaction.

I am blending memory and desire with the secret writings of others. It's difficult. More than that, time blends with time, recombining events and emotions, awarding a hindsight that may intensify the torment I for one probably deserve. But yes, there is something else. At the time of my central narrative, in 1968, there were those who could not have permitted this story to be told. They may themselves be dead but they were not irreplaceable. When I go, leaving you these pages, perhaps history will undergo a minor adjustment. But nothing fundamental will change. Of course not. How could it? This is Blake's I'm talking about, Blake's and a sort of England.

Enough evasion. I must cease my preparations and open the blocked off-entrance to the forgotten corridor, take my place in one of the chilly classrooms and begin. Begin somewhere, anywhere. Begin in earnest. Life is no longer a preface to itself. Life is over, nearly. Then begin! Everything will lead to the same point, the core. Wish me luck.

PART ONE

ONE

1968

In a while there would be the respite of half term. Eventually it would be Christmas and the conflict would be suspended, for a while. But now it was barely October. Frost and fog, mainly fog. At least it was Friday. For now, there was assembly to be got through.

I still found it hard to convince myself that I was a master, not a pupil. It seemed plausible that Gammon, the Acting Head, allegedly a geographer, could any second aim a dart of reproof at me where I sat on the balcony. And yet my gaze wandered away from his snappish figure at the lectern far below, and out through the windows on to the grounds which I had planned never to visit again after my initial escape from the sixth form. Bellows, who taught classics, had an apt quotation for all occasions. Bellows was dead of a heart attack now, but what would he have found to apply to a prodigal's return? Odes i.iv, perhaps: 'Life's brief span forbids us to depend on distant hope.' Gammon went on talking. I went on looking out of the window.

Private schools have large playing fields ringed with woodland in order that in drizzly autumns, when everything but the churned earth disappears, the pupils will gain an idea of the fog of war. The rugby pitches at Blake's (football is for the juniors) were named after sites of battle – Majuba, Spion Kop – and the pavilion, isolated in the murk, could be a farmhouse suitable for a last stand, or the location at which Blücher's black-clad cavalry suddenly emerges like Death's Imperial Guard. 'On, my children!' cries the Marshal, sabre aloft at the head of the charge. You may have seen the film.

When I was a pupil we used to see all the films. Avoiding games on Wednesday afternoons, we would sneak off to the Cecil, the Regal, the cavernous and ever-empty Criterion and the rest. We used to see some of them twice – *The Guns of Navarone*, for example, *The Dam Busters*, *The Red Beret*, *The Wooden Horse*, and the one in which Jack Hawkins plays a British spy masquerading as a Nazi general. I have it: *The Two-Headed Spy*. Much of this material was already old by the time it reached us, but it was as much a part of our present as homework, as daily spam and chips in the dining hall, or as the streets beyond the school gates where those who were not us moved about their mysterious lives among the weed-grown bombsites.

No one from Blake's pursued us into the flickering dark of the Rexy or the Apollo, though the school knew where we were, perhaps because the cinema offered an education in itself, in, among other things, an idea of Englishness – bravery, endurance, an ironic obedience to necessary authority, a readiness to kill for the cause given half a chance. And, to me at any rate, there were those other things, harder to give a name to. Even now there comes to my mind's eye a scene from *Dunkirk*, in a field hospital where Harry Landis (Dr Levy) looks up momentarily from typing a report as heavy machine-gun fire becomes audible in the distance while the British forces flee for the coast. Nothing is said; he returns to work. I recognized that implacable stoicism before I could understand it.

I imagine that the survivors of those times, Old Blakean lawyers and businessmen scattered around the suburbs of the city, find themselves tuning in to repeats on weekend afternoons when their wives are out shopping and the golf or the tennis grows dull. On an old movie channel, by contrast, Stanley Baker at his most vaunting and demented, playing the parachute instructor, plunges to the earth when his chute fails to open. Those were the days – not our days, clearly, but the days of war and opportunity. It was our birthright we were watching. Although in the event most of us refused to serve, we were a violent tribe. And now there we sat, in assembly, waiting. Waiting for lessons, for the next thing, for the further postponement of life, for orders.

I looked back at the stage below, where Gammon was still talking, with senior staff seated behind him, among them Captain Carson and Major Brand, who gave every appearance of complete attention. We rose to sing a hymn.

When I was a pupil, in assembly, while Dunkerley, the Headmaster before Robert Rowan, delivered his latest instalment of threats to the degenerate and the idle from the podium, I would drift off and read the names listed in gold on the honours board. After the First World War they had run out of space to list the dead. The casualties of Hitler's war and Palestine and Korea and Malaya and Cyprus and Aden had to shift for themselves. They were in no position to object.

In 1968, when I was twenty-three and had returned to the fold as a master, I passed my eye again over some of the names on the boards. Those old boys would have thought of it as the Great War, always supposing that as subalterns they had chance to consider the matter before rising from their trenches to walk out with their men into flanking machine-gun fire, or while they crouched under drumfire, awaiting the shell that would dissolve or bury them a platoon at a time, at an average rate of attrition of three thousand per day.

The last survivor of their generation, a tall, silvery classics master called Pember, had finally retired the previous summer. I remembered his patience with our A-level group's blundering passage through *Aeneid* vi, but especially the time when he covered an absent colleague for divinity and recited, mostly from memory, large sections of Ecclesiastes, the oddest of the books of the Bible, with its wild self-contradictions and its haunting, addictive blend of beauty and despair. He stopped a minute or two before the bell and looked out of the window. We waited, uncertain of what was expected of us. When the bell rang, Pember simply smiled and nodded a dismissal.

People said he was mad, and it may have been true, but so what? It was school, it was Blake's, and it was in part his recital that made me curious in my reading, and for that I am in his debt.

It is tempting to give in and drift, as I did in assembly that day. I must try harder. Get to the point, Maxwell. Less of the flannel.

So. The boards in the Main Hall silently invited successive generations to recall, or imagine, all those who were absent, missing in time's action. There were no prisoners. Age would not weary them, but it seemed that their perpetual absence wearied most of us. In a sense this was a kind of loyalty: imagination, which runs away with ideas or is kidnapped by passions, was for the most part not encouraged in the curriculum at Blake's. The dead lay on us like a protective colouring, proof against the claims of the present.

And now, somehow, I was a master. I looked down into the body of the Main Hall at the current cohorts in their black suits. I wanted to stand up and make a public declaration: *at all costs get as far away from here as you can and don't come back.* And if I had done this, then what? I remembered once during my sixth-form days when Dunkerley, whose mood was soured by episodes of gout and who was in the habit of delivering damning impromptu remarks to the whole school, looked about him from the lectern and said: 'Look how the sea gives up its dead.' We absorbed the comment like much else, with invulnerable indifference. And, had I actually chosen to offer my words of advice, the dead sea of the school would simply have closed over my head again as if nothing had happened.

When assembly ended we made our way to lessons, in my case to address the causes of the Second World War in a double period with the upper sixth in a freezing corner room off the ground floor of the Main Hall. I returned some essays, made comments and set to putting notes up on the board. The use of the Gestetner machine to reproduce material was frowned upon by Gammon as a dangerous novelty, akin to

Cuban-heeled boots. Writing in chalk on the blackboard took time, of course, which could be useful in itself.

'My uncle says the trouble started because of the Jews, sir,' said Arnesen. Feldberg, the outstanding student in his year, glanced up expressionlessly, then looked down and made a note. The others waited: perhaps there was sport to be had. Horobin, my predecessor, had evidently been a hard nut, but he had left to take holy orders. The boys' assessment of me was probably more or less complete by then, but you could never tell.

'Is that meant to be a joke, Arnesen?' I asked, turning from the board. Outside, the two ancient groundsmen in their faded overalls appeared through the fog with the wheeled device like a miniature gun-carriage that they used for repainting the touchlines. The white stripe slowly extended over the mud. The stripe would not outlast the day. I sympathized.

'My uncle wasn't laughing when he said it, sir.'

'Neither am I.' Arnesen was not entirely satisfied. He winked at his neighbour. I suppressed the urge to smash his white-blond head against the pitted lid of his desk. After all, this wasn't the Science Department. 'You're in the cadets, aren't you, Arnesen?'

'Sir.'

'So in time of war you would be expected to be among the first to come to the defence of the realm.'

'Course, sir.'

'The realm which includes all your fellow citizens.'

'Sir.' Arnesen sensed a trap.

'Unless you were a traitor and fought for the other side. At one time that would have involved fighting for Hitler.' There were sniggers around the room. Feldberg looked up again, then made another note.

Sergeant Risman, the porter, loomed out of the fog on the gravelled parterre, a parcel under his arm. Even in his grey-blue portering suit the lean, leathery, iron-haired Risman looked as if he was in uniform. He looked up, nodded and disappeared.

'Never do that, sir,' the boy said, offended.

'Of course not, Arnesen. Heaven forbid. Well, then, what can you tell us about the German reoccupation of the Rhineland?'

From somewhere else in the room came a low chorus. 'Three German officers crossed the Rhine, parlez-vous . . .'

Arnesen looked blank. Outside, a herd of juniors in gym kit appeared briefly before running into the foggy woods, urged on by old Matthews, Head of PE, at his steady lope in his black tracksuit, cigarette cupped in his fist. Given the conditions, there was an extraordinary volume of traffic out there. Ignorant armies narrowly avoiding clashes. Feldberg's gaze had also followed these movements. He caught my eye. His face remained expressionless. He put up his hand. I nodded.

'Sir. The reoccupation of the Rhineland was a means by which Hitler could do three things: satisfy and create a public appetite for evidence that Germany could recover from the humiliation imposed by the Versailles treaty; display a renewed military vigour; and test the willingness of the Great Powers to confront the newly confident German state. In all three respects the occupation was a great success, sir.'

'Thank you, Feldberg. I hope everyone managed to note down that succinct account of the matter. Arnesen, would you like to hear it again?'

'I can manage, sir,' Arnesen said with a sigh, beginning to write. He looked injured now, as if the rules of engagement had been altered without consultation. The others looked at Feldberg, who was making notes again.

'And how should the Allies have responded to this provocation? Anyone?'

'Send a gunboat, sir,' came the unhesitating chorus. Palmerston – now there was a politician they could love wholeheartedly, this group of future lawyers and estate agents, auctioneers and embezzlers. Feldberg, the exception, then an admirer of Disraeli, would, it was thought, be going on to study history at Cambridge. Captain Carson was right about him. Feldberg was marking time in this group. He didn't belong. Lower down the school the rest of these boys would have attacked him like dogs, because they were like dogs.

I imagined a gunboat bombarding the besieged city, under the cover of fog. A bit like *The Sand Pebbles*.

'Were you in the cadets, sir?' It was Arnesen again.

'Yes, Arnesen. In those days we all joined. It was expected.'

'People don't fancy it these days so much, do they? Boys, I mean. The cadets, I mean.'

'So it would appear. Times are changing.'

'My uncle says those who won't join up are communists and conkies.'

'It's a point of view, Arnesen, but I think you mean "conchies".' Laughter. It appeared I could do this, keep these creatures at bay with what I flattered myself was irony. And the other thing, what was that? It bore some resemblance to pleasure. I might enjoy this dreaded outcome, then, this teaching game, though I'd once sworn I would sooner join the Foreign Legion than do it. But as my friend Smallbone remarked, perhaps even the Legion would have looked twice at my record.

Feldberg looked at his watch. At his father's request he had been permitted to leave the cadets when he went into the upper sixth, in order to concentrate on his studies. Feldberg had done his bit of boy soldiering by then, but for the likes of Arnesen the facts were not entirely the point. I turned back to the board and carried on writing. Causes, effects.

Everything was in motion, I see. The story I have to tell was long underway by this time and a crisis was imminent, but I believe that this was really the moment at which I made my entrance. It was during that perfectly routine lesson that I realized finally, as if waking up while already conscious, that much of what I had considered the trivial adolescent dandruff of school life – the name-calling, the prejudices, the ignorant and immoveable opinions – were actually the very substance of that life, and of life in the city beyond the confines of the school, and of the world beyond that, remote though it seemed through the bars of the school gate. It was a disorienting thought. I don't know what I'd been assuming or expecting instead. As it turned out, I didn't know the half of it.

TWO

'Sir?' I turned from the board.

'Are you all right?' Arnesen scented an opportunity. 'You were just standing there, so I wondered—'

'Thank you for your concern, Arnesen. In fact, I was thinking. As you yourself are no doubt aware, that can take time.' Arnesen was not so dim that he could not enjoy this blow along with the rest of the class. It meant that in a sense we were complicit in the conspiracy that was the school.

'Don't want to overdo it, sir.'

Erik Arnesen, Arnie to his friends, was the son of a trawler owner. When he left with his two Es at A-level, he entered the family firm. It was in the nature of the Arnesens that the male child should go to sea in order to learn at first hand how the family made its money. So Arnesen went as a deckhand learner on the *Kingston Star*. The vessel sank with all hands off Iceland in January. There was talk that its nets had been snagged by a Russian submarine, but the long-delayed enquiry revealed nothing; it was widely believed that this was the intention of the authorities.

In a sense, then, Arnesen may, albeit unwittingly, have died in action. I labour this little biographical sketch in order to say, like the paranoid and the conspiracy theorist, that everything is connected; but perhaps where I differ from the conspiracy theorist is in wanting to affirm that Arnesen's life was real, as real as yours or mine: it was not simply filler in someone else's narrative. Arnesen was a bumptious thicko, but he was real. He was there in the room playing the fool in his dim, good-humoured, bigoted way. And then he was gone. I didn't like him but he too was one of us, whoever we were.

This was the kind of lesson that Captain Carson, Head of History, mentor and saviour of my skin, was anxious to pass on.

'In the end, Maxwell,' he once said, 'it doesn't matter what we think of them. They may be brutes or morons, or chancers, or spoilt rich boys who don't need us. It doesn't matter. We have to remember, in the teeth of temptation, that these are actual lives these boys are leading and that they will grow up to be men who must face responsibility. It is very easy to view this place like a novel or a Will Hay film or some sort of overlong comedy skit. I'm sometimes tempted that way myself. Some of our older colleagues appear to be permanently living inside such a performance. And it's clear that at times you yourself are inclined to succumb. Try not to let your facial expression betray you in assembly even though you're sitting at the back of the balcony. Mr Gammon notices such things. We must resist temptation, must we not?'

Carson's slow, melancholy smile at his own remark represented a kind of provisional reacceptance of me: I would obey and learn, and in doing so assist him in his civilizing mission. I would, albeit belatedly, learn a sense of responsibility. If he was prepared to believe it, then I could at least hope that it was true, even if, in the space of a few months since my appointment, I had in a sense already betrayed him again.

He seemed to think I could be somebody else. I did not share his confidence, but it was Carson who made me imagine I might make something of this strange profession. By any measure he was a great teacher, as great in his way as any history don. When I'd returned from a couple of years abroad after making a mess of things at university, he gave me a breathing space in which, so he seems to have believed, I could discover my true direction. I don't think the others on the committee – Gammon and Brand plus a couple of governors – would have chosen to employ me, even though one of the two other candidates with whom I shared the interview waiting room had a disabling stammer and the other, who slipped away several times to the lavatory, was clearly an alcoholic. Carson swayed the committee's judgement: after all, I was to be his man and teach history. It saved me from Gabbitas–Thring, who were offering me a choice between Hinckley and some vegetarian madhouse in Dorset.

After the interview back at the end of May Carson and I drank whisky in the History bookroom. When he had laboured to light his pipe, he looked at me kindly and said, 'Well, Maxwell. Once again assembled here, eh? I've given you my backing, so bear that in mind and try not to go swerving from the path of righteousness again.' He did not refer directly – not that he needed to, given my own cringing sense of it – to the failure of my undergraduate career. At Cambridge I had fallen into a disastrous affair with a don's wife. I was lucky to escape with a Third and a whole skin. After that I had gone to Paris and taught English and failed to write anything. There had been nothing for it but to come home. I admit it was a relief to surrender, to know the password and for the sentries to let me through the barrier.

Carson appeared to understand that I was an orphan in mind as well as in fact, and that the only home I was likely to have was the school I had attended since the age of eight: so he took me in. I should mention at this point that my father never saw me – a captain like Carson, he was killed in the airborne attack on the Rhine, along with the rest of his unit, when their glider was shot down. My mother seems never to have recovered from the loss. I find that I scarcely remember her now. She died – that is all I was told – when I was five years old, after which I remained in the care of distant relatives, a rural clergyman and his unmarried sister near Wooler in Northumberland, until I was old enough to be sent to the prep school at Blake's as a boarder.

My relatives were kind people in their pale, bloodless way,

but seemed vague and preoccupied in their chilly house, and when they sent me away they were doing their best. As time went on our relations became occasional and formal. I tended to spend the holidays at the school, in the library or mooching about in the woods, until I discovered girls, when I began to mooch more widely. In the sixth form I moved into digs nearby, run by Mrs Jessop, and was more or less free to please myself in respect of the libraries, the woods and the girls. Perhaps the authorities thought I was at the pictures. But this story is only incidentally about me.

'I don't want to have to keep repeating this,' Carson had said, back in June when he'd finished setting out my duties and timetable, 'but take the chance to do something properly. Give yourself a start. Work steadily, embrace the routine of this place, and things will become clearer and more manageable. The mind has mountains – who could deny it? But the point – for all we know, the only point – is to keep going. And who knows, Maxwell? You may prove to be good at schoolmastering. I shouldn't be surprised. It's not what I imagined for myself, but it suits me well enough.' He paused to fiddle with the pipe.

'Anything in particular I should be aware of?'

'Blake's is Blake's. As you may have noticed, it desires mediocrity. It sees it as normal and seeks to enforce it.'

'I suppose so.'

'Do you? I should damn well think you do. And we are the loyal opposition, in favour of serious study, enlightenment and so on, against the dead weight of place and precedent. We will very likely lose. You think I'm joking.'

'Perhaps a bit.'

'Well, I'm not. Arnold Bennett was right about this lot, I mean the English, of which this shower are an essential strain.' Carson took a book from his desk. 'Read this.'

'Do you mean now?'

'Of course now. Where the card is inserted. In fact, read it aloud.' I did as I was told. I inherited Carson's copy of the book in question, and I have it before me now.

> Another marked characteristic is [its] gigantic temperamental dullness, unresponsiveness to external suggestion, a lack of humour – in short, a heavy and half-honest stupidity: ultimate product of gross prosperity, too much exercise, too much sleep. Then I notice a grim passion for the *status quo*. This is natural. Let these people exclaim as they will against the structure of society, the last thing they desire is to alter it. This passion shows itself in a naive admiration for everything that has survived its original usefulness, such as sail-drill and uniforms . . . The passion for the *status quo* also shows itself in a general defensive, sullen hatred of all ideas whatever. You cannot argue with these people. 'Do you really think so?' they will politely murmur, when you have asserted your belief that the earth is round, or something like that. And their tone says: 'Would you mind very much if we leave this painful subject? My feelings on it are too deep for utterance.'

'Well, yes,' I said, when I'd read the marked passage. 'I suppose I see what you mean. But if this is how you feel, why not go somewhere else?'

'And admit defeat? Anyway, it's too late. And now I've got you to help me with the good fight, haven't I?' He put the book carefully back in the pile it had come from. 'You'll have Feldberg in the 1914–45 group. He's bright.' I knew Feldberg's father. I had often visited his antiquarian bookshop in the arcade in the city centre. 'The boy's the best we've had in my time. English want him too but we're not going to let them have him. He's a born historian. Whatever happens we have to get him into Cambridge. They don't come along very often, the real thing.'

Carson met my gaze for a moment, as if about to say more, then looked down into the quad, his great Roman head in profile, a head deserving a coin to be struck in its honour. Much later I read of someone with whom he seemed to stand comparison.

> He seemed to me
> Like one of those who run for the green cloth
> Across Verona's field, and in that race
> Appeared among the winners, not the lost.

I assumed he had decided not to refer to the fact that I too had allegedly been the real thing in my time. I was partly right.

'Have you anything to occupy you until the autumn?'

'Not particularly.'

'Then spend time about the place. Help with the play. Help in the library – someone will need to look after it now that Horobin's leaving us. Look as if you belong.'

'Well, I do belong, don't I?'

'You know what I mean, Maxwell. Show willing.'

So I did.

What Carson had managed to do when I went into the sixth form was to make history urgent. I came to care about the reign of Stephen, about nineteenth-century British history and, for some reason, about Italian unification in particular. Victor Emmanuel, Mazzini and Cavour seemed like live presences, their struggles still taking place in some almost-accessible dimension. It mattered that our group were interested. Then there was the First World War and the rise of fascism and I was decisively tempted away from English. Tim Connolly, my English teacher, accepted defeat with good grace, extracting a promise that I would continue to write what he considered promising stories. This narrative will be the only fulfilment of that undertaking.

Carson's sober charisma was a legend in the school. I stayed on into the third-year sixth, prepared for Cambridge entrance and gained an exhibition. Things went well. Then they went wrong, from the moment I was introduced to the don's wife at a party in the summer term of my second year. Causes, effects.

Carson had fallen silent for a little while. We looked out at the chestnut trees surrounding the quad. Then he said he had a favour to ask.

'Of course.' I supposed it was some minor piece of administration.

'I need you to be my executor.' For the first time in my acquaintance with him he seemed not quite certain where to look.

'I beg your pardon? Me?' For a moment I wondered if he was joking.

'It's simply a formality,' he said. He was embarrassed. So was I.

'Yes, but I'm not qualified, am I?' I asked. 'I'm too young, surely. I don't even know what it means, really, to be an executor.'

'Well, look it up, Maxwell, in a book. You'll find some in the library. You're of age and you're employed. I've known you for years. You have your faults but I consider you honest.' He paused while I absorbed the balance of this judgement. The frankness restored his authority intact. 'Besides, I have no family, no one else I feel I could call on. It would be a help to me, and it would mean a good deal, if you could agree to take this on.' He looked away. I couldn't think of any other time when he had struck such a personal note. Was this blackmail? Surely not, though clearly I was in his debt. I put the thought aside as unworthy. If only it had been so simple. Carson must have known it wasn't, which makes me wonder what other hopes he might have had of me, and whether he was, knowingly or not, offering me the chance of a larger vindication. If so, there a dimension of ruthlessness to his request, almost a Roman severity.

'Then, yes,' I said, 'but are you sure? I mean, I'd be honoured, of course.'

'Oh, let's not overstate things, Maxwell. But yes, I am sure.'

'Forgive me, but is there something I should know? Are you ill?'

'Not that I'm aware of. Anyway, all in good time, Maxwell. And I think that from now on, in informal settings, we should use Christian names.' I knew I would never be at ease doing that.

We act as though our motives and even those of others were known to us. Beyond the most superficial and immediate level I have never understood why I have done or not done things: I wanted something or did not want something, or I was afraid, or I did not want to think about whatever was at issue. Carson, I then believed, would have acted on the oracle's instruction: *know thyself*. But perhaps he was drawn to weakness and failure anyway. Or perhaps I really was the only resource to hand at Blake's.

THREE

It was in the natural order of things that after my job interview at Blake's I had gone round to the Narwhal at six o'clock. I rang Smallbone. He joined me at the bar.

'So what are we drinking to?' he said, easing himself on to the stool.

'Success, so huge and wholly farcical.' I indicated the pint that awaited him.

'Who is she?'

'It's not that. You have two more guesses before the floor opens and delivers you to the piranhas.'

'Gammon's died.'

'He was still alive earlier on.'

'So you've seen him.'

'And Carson, and Brand, and the governors.'

'You mad twat.'

'I thank you, my friend. Drink, drink! Nunc est bibendum.'

Smallbone took a leisurely swallow. 'So you're back in. The iron lid has slammed shut.'

'As of lunchtime. I start in September. History, plus running the library.'

'I didn't know there was a library. They never let on.'

'I can tell you're delighted for me.'

'As I said: you mad twat. You're only just out of the place.' He shook his head. 'I thought you were going to be over the hills and far away. Someone the rest of us could envy in our parochial torpor.'

'Events, dear boy. Events.'

'Is that what you're calling her? I hope she was worth it.'

'Don't spoil it, Bone. At least I've got a job.' Small depth charges of horror continued to explode internally when the subject came up. I couldn't believe it myself. I needed many years to have passed.

'It's a job at Blake's, Maxwell. You know what happens to the ones who go back. They grow pale, they dry out, they disappear like chalk off a board, like paint off a touchline.'

'Very eloquent. You speak as one who works in his mother's stamp shop three hundred yards from the school.'

'Think of Pownall. Think of Spurrier. What are they now? Husks, man, husks.'

'I'm not like them, though, am I? I'm me.'

'Well, of course you say that now. But I see the paleness taking hold while you loiter here. Drink up.' He tapped a coin on the ashtray.

'It's a start, Bone.'

'No, it's the end, beautiful friend, the end.' Smallbone began to sing in a grim impersonation of Jim Morrison's baritone.

'Gentlemen,' said Stan Pitt. The landlord, the last known wearer of brilliantine in England, appeared from behind the partition in his best black suit, polishing his gold Albert watch with a blinding handkerchief. His were the photographs: he could be seen in bouts with Bruce Woodcock and Brian London. He had contended, then retired to his pub, bloodied but unbowed and still more than a match for anyone who came through the doors.

'Well, Stan,' I said, 'the hunter is home from the hill,' which was not, on reflection, an especially apt or encouraging quotation.

'So I see, Mr Maxwell. And in the mood to celebrate, it seems.'

'A pint for my ruined friend,' said Smallbone. 'And one for me.'

'Back at Blake's, then?' said Stan, as he stooped at the beer-pull. He straightened up and winked.

'So it would appear,' I said. 'For the moment.'

'You can keep an eye on your friend Mr Smallbone, then.

He's falling into bad ways. Trying to, at any rate. Or have I to tell my friend Jack Risman and have him put you to rights? That'll be three and fourpence.' I gave Stan the money and he disappeared again.

'How did he know?' I asked.

Smallbone made a face. 'You fail to understand. Just because the Narwhal is outside the school grounds doesn't mean it's not Blake's. It's an outpost, a forward position. Blake's is everywhere, man.'

'I've done it now, haven't I?'

'Difficult to disagree with that assessment. Let's have another one here. Then we'll go and find some mucky women. They've been wondering what happened to you.'

'I've been wondering that myself.'

FOUR

And now it was October, and I was back in the belly of beast. It was almost as though I'd never been away. The place was second nature to me, and my first nature was nowhere to be found. The school day ended. Once again I had pulled off the trick of seeming to know what I was doing.

Arnesen alone of the group had attended class wearing his uniform webbing belt. As I left the main building, I saw him among the cadets gathering for parade in the darkening quad, putting on his beret. Culshaw the boy corporal ordered them to fall in. Dr (Captain) Carson, accompanied by Sergeant Risman and Charles Rackham, arrived in order to perform the inspection. Carson, with his massive shaved head and the bearing of a Renaissance soldier-prelate, always looked as if he belonged in, and could actually see, grander circumstances than the rest of us. It was part of what he meant by 'the historical imagination'. The provincialism of the setting meant nothing to him: he would make meaning by strength of personality, there among the oafs and toadies. He would redeem a few and make the rest remember him at least, even if they retained not a single date or fact.

When I was a pupil it had been always been taken for granted that in due course we would join the cadets, so I did so happily enough when the time came, and I enjoyed much of it, camping out in the woods by the lake, a trip to climb on Skye, a hike over the island of Kerrera, off Oban, over its heathery spine to a castle sacked by Cromwell's men and latterly occupied by a few sheep. There was a view southwards, of island after island stepping into the blue glitter where sea and sky fused. It stirred something in me I couldn't begin to identify until I read Keats's sonnet on Chapman's Homer, where a glimpse of the Pacific is compared to the sighting of a new planet. The blue world seen from the island was ancient and immediate, vast and tragic, and I felt a summons to explore it. It looked, then, like a convincing future.

There was also the running about, weapons training, a handful of blank rounds each, the licence to play at death in our scratchy hand-me-down uniforms and the uncompromising boots we buffed before parade nights from fear of Sergeant Risman. I suppose we thought that with our Molesworthian cynicism we were subverting the Combined Cadet Force. The Force, for its part, saw us coming and acted accordingly to make us its own.

For all Carson's commanding presence, on that dimming afternoon in the quad the company parade looked a bit ragged to me. As a veteran of such evenings myself, I found I disapproved. Given the wider climate of dissent and revolt, it was, I wrongly thought, the beginning of the end, although that year many of the incoming fourth form had refused to join the Cadets. It was as if a seemingly immutable organization, a fixed star in the late heaven of empire, might be tempted to explain and justify itself to unbelievers.

This revolt had caught Major Brand, local officer commanding, on the hop when the boys made their views known at the special assembly in the Memorial Hall at the end of the previous summer term. It was not my business, but I happened to be helping out backstage during a free period with Mrs Rowan of the Art Department, wife of the Headmaster, painting flats for the forthcoming production of *Ruddigore*, and we came forward to listen from the concealment of one of the half-finished Gothic arches. I felt like a spy: simply to witness what followed seemed, inexplicably, like a betrayal. But what could I have done about it?

I felt sorry for the kindly, portly, myopic Major, who looked like the object of mild satire in a Giles cartoon and, wholly against the tide of fashion, of which I dare say he was unaware, favoured the Augustans in his teaching, directing his dull and baffled charges to the essays of Addison and Steele. But he was, in the heavily qualified and ironical assessment of the boys, a well-liked figure, decent and fair.

In the way that legends seemed to pass unspoken directly into the pupil brain, it was known that he had several times attempted to escape from a POW camp after being captured in the retreat to Dunkirk. So Major Brand knew what he was talking about. But that didn't, as they say now, 'play' with the generation of fourteen-year-olds in 1968. Like my own quite recent cohort, many of them would have read *The Wooden Horse* and *The Colditz Story*, and seen the films made of them, but their modest realism and matter-of-fact characters had been put in the shade by *The Great Escape* and the exploits of Virgil Hilts, the Cooler King, impossibly laconic and, in 1944, anachronistically hip. There was no room for Major Brand in that world. Whatever dangers he had risked, he was not to be imagined seeking to breach the wire at the Swiss border dressed in German uniform and astride a stolen motorbike. The Major fell into the category of True but not Interesting.

I need hardly add that it would be a mistake – it would be priggish – to expect the boys' attitudes to be coherent. Many of them thought the Major was a warmonger. Many would have watched with appreciation the Paris students bombarding the riot squad with cobblestones the previous May. Where this left Hilts, who devoted his entire effort to attempting to escape and presumably get back into his aircraft and kill some more Germans, was not revealed. Many of the boys might have liked the idea of peace, but to a man they hated the Germans, a sentiment which the passage of a further half century has done little to alter and which indeed the altered balance of power has rather tended to emphasize.

Perhaps the Major's mistake was to ask for a show of hands. Presumably this was to demonstrate the normal unanimous desire of the boys to do the expected thing. Hands were raised, of course, quite a few, but there were significant gaps in the forest, and a certain amount of smirking and muttering among the malcontents.

'Wake up, chaps,' said the Major, blinking. 'Let's do that again. Hands up.' The result was the same. Captain Carson shook his head and stared at the floor. Beside him Charles Rackham, brother of Mrs Rowan, wore his usual expression of private amusement. Sergeant Risman scrutinized the ranks of the dissenters, as though filing their names for future use.

The Major came forward. 'Well, look, you men, would someone care to tell me what the problem is? We've all been in the Corps, or the armed forces, and so on.' He nodded to his colleagues on the platform, who nodded in return, all except Risman, who made no move but was scowling like a military demon. 'Well? What is it? Let's hear it. Speak up.' Another mistake, perhaps.

At length, as though wordlessly selected by his companions, a boy called Weyman raised his hand. He was not, I thought, representative of the actual opinions of the dissenters, which would be herd-like and incoherent, but he drew the short straw by being presentable and articulate and capable of rational thought.

'Stand to address the officer commanding,' hissed Risman.

Weyman rose. He held a ruler in his hands, having learned from the Debating Society that this would prevent him fidgeting. 'We believe war to be a thing of the past, sir,' he began. 'And that peaceful solutions to problems mark the way forward. We hope for an end to the war in Vietnam and an end of all imperialist conflicts, sir.'

Where had Weyman got this stuff from? Hardly from Blake's, where Suez seemed only yesterday. It sounded quite exciting. There was an air of expectancy in the Memorial Hall now. A thunderbolt might strike. Or Risman might leap down from the stage with a terrifying roar and with a single blow dispatch Weyman to the Hell of scrimshankers and barrack-room lawyers. But Weyman resumed his seat, unharmed for the time being. The air of expectancy intensified. In the boys' minds a row would be good entertainment as long as you weren't singled out.

'Well, yes, nobody likes war,' said the Major. Risman looked at him for a moment. 'I myself have no enthusiasm for it, believe me. But the unfortunate fact is that wars do occur, as I and several of my colleagues here today would testify. It is not something we care to speak about very much – and I promise you it is not in the least like the things you see in the films. But we followed the example of our elders who served in the Kaiser's war and in South Africa before that, and now we in turn seek to set an example, to show the way, to young chaps like you. As I say, wars do take place. And regrettable as that may be, in those circumstances all of us – including all you boys – have a duty to something other than our own pleasure and convenience, a duty to Queen and Country.'

By the Major's lights this was an eloquent appeal. But if silent jeering is possible, it took place now. The Major, largely and perhaps by choice innocent of the 1960s, had appealed to precisely the wrong loyalties: he was playing to the wrong crowd, those aspiring to become the satirical, free-thinking awkward squad of the day. They would oppose any established principle as long as there was no personal cost involved. Cut one from the herd, though, and he would probably conform: revolt and self-interest were strangely mixed and adaptable.

I was in some ways of their party, but I recognized their muddled contrariness, and I sympathized with the Major. His hands clasped behind his back, he studied the nearby piano for a few moments, while the silence deepened. At last he went on. 'It may be fashionable to mock these things, these principles, but always remember this – great sacrifices have been made in their name, not least by old boys and staff of this school, among them members of some of your own families. It is because of them that you are here, that you are at liberty to be here.'

Or as Carson's history put it, 'Blake's tradition of service and sacrifice was maintained with distinction during the Second World War, when seventy-three old boys gave their lives in the conflict.' Not even Risman could identify the voice which spoke into the next pause.

'We don't want to get killed.'

The Major nodded. 'No, indeed. Who does? The ultimate sacrifice is not offered lightly. But I think, gentlemen – no, I fear – that many of you may come to regret the decision you are thinking of making today. It seems a simple thing to you now, perhaps a trivial one, a subject for humour and easy, fashionable satire, but I beg to assure you that it is not. These are dangerous times, whatever you may prefer to think. There are enemies, alas, both abroad and here within.' There was an audible snort at this. 'In the times to come there may be a terrible price to pay.' He paused. 'So I would urge you to reconsider in the light of sober reflection, to set aside cynicism and remember the honour of your school and all it stands for.' There was steel in the Major. No one mistook the firmness of his gaze. He was angry now but would not give in to it. 'For now we shall say no more, only that I would urge you to search in your hearts and minds.' I found myself stirred and ashamed and sceptical all at once. The Major, followed by the other masters, made his exit. Risman held the silence for a long time.

'Now,' he said, eventually, 'those of you gentlemen who intend to join up, form a line at the foot of the stage so that your names can be taken. The rest of you – the rest of you little conchies, think on. And don't come crying to me when the Reds are interfering with your sisters. Dismiss.'

There was a mood of palpable disappointment as the meeting dispersed to lessons. This was a hollow victory: the pacifists had failed to get a row out of the situation, and the authorities had made a tactical withdrawal while claiming a moral advantage. A good many of the boys rose and straggled out into the yard. They wore an air of frustration. The bell rang.

Maggie Rowan whispered in my ear. I could smell her perfume. 'Place needs shaking up.'

'Anarchist,' I whispered in reply. She smiled in the backstage shadows.

So much of authority depends on consent and conviction: at that date the boys withheld the one and the school lacked the other. The school did not press the point; the Corps would now rely on volunteers. The Major retired the following summer and the boys never heard of him again.

The revolt against the CCF preceded the release of *If*. After the present narrative was over, having no games duties, I saw the film one Wednesday afternoon at the Rexy. The truanting boys downstairs in the stalls cheered Mick Travis and his chums on as they massacred the staff and prefects from the chapel roof. They were quieter when the staff regrouped and fought back. 'A bit far-fetched,' Dent, one of the history A-level group, remarked when the subject came up in class. Arnesen laughed, rose in his desk and made as if to rake the room with an army-issue Sterling submachine gun. He would of course have been on the side of the establishment. Whatever had happened in the previous months, the waters had closed once more over Blake's.

FIVE

Not even Dr (Captain) Carson's trump card had helped with recruiting for the CCF. He possessed a document signed by Hitler, acquired in his work as an interrogator following the German surrender in 1945. The single page was preserved like an unholy relic in a leather-bound folder which he would bring in from home to show selected boys. In my day I had been impressed and chilled by the jagged, mad but oddly precise inscription, but in 1968 perhaps Carson considered the dark magic to have worn off and the boys were not shown the exhibit, as being considered unworthy of its import. Although they might kick lumps off each other in the quad and on the rugby pitch, a majority found better things to do after school and at weekends than line up and be shouted at by Risman and 'that ponce Culshaw' as the boy corporal was universally known among his peers. The interchangeable nature of principle and convenience was thus established early and made clear.

Carson himself expressed no view on the boys' dissent, except to remark that the bible of the older boys now appeared to be *Private Eye*, and that cynicism was often used to justify ignorance. At the time I assumed that he recognized the inevitability of change, but now I suspect that he was doing as a priest was expected to do when deserted by his faith, by continuing to observe the forms and rituals of belief.

As I went up the rear steps to the library, I heard the company marching off under the arch that led on to the field. They began to sing the song of the Corps of Engineers as they moved away:

> You make fast, I make fast, make fast the dinghy
> Make fast the dinghy pontoon.

For we're marching on to Laffan's Plain,
To Laffan's Plain, to Laffan's Plain
Where they don't know mud from clay.

It was comic and poignant. The CCF would not be going anywhere near Laffan's Plain or Aldershot. These days money was tighter: they would count themselves lucky to end up in annual camp at Strensall with two blank rounds each. But I paused to listen to their voices fading beyond the arch and away over the darkened field. The melancholy diminuendo seemed somehow already historical.

The cadets had been building a raft that could ferry them out to the island in the lake. The lake, big enough to be exciting for military purposes, was a survival from the school grounds' previous mid-Victorian incarnation as a zoological garden, and had been artificially created by putting sluice gates in the creek that marked the western boundary of the school grounds and then piping water underground to replenish the lake. Around its mile-long shores there remained an unusual variety of plants and trees, fruits of the botanical labours of long-forgotten collectors. Among those of most interest to the boys was hemlock, which was said to be there for the use of disgraced masters. Recently there had also been an invasion of the sinister giant hogweed, whose hollow, woody stems, often growing to eight feet in height, had proved irresistible to Arnesen. He appeared in the Memorial Hall attempting to use one as a giant trumpet, not realizing that Maggie and I were there painting flats. She called out a warning but it was too late. Arnesen developed a rash and went about looking disfigured for a week or so, after which the ground staff set about burning the stuff out. It seemed to some like an omen. 'Change and decay in all around I see,' said Topliss, the music teacher, after a rehearsal of *Ruddigore*, gazing out from the Memorial Hall across the fields towards woods newly charged with menace from these cousins to the Triffid.

'Decay, certainly,' said Maggie Rowan. 'Dry rot beginning in the head.' Topliss, a mouse for whom every day was a struggle to survive and be allowed to give his life to Handel and Mozart, looked appalled but said nothing.

When the raft was at last complete the cadets would spend the weekend camped out in the woods, staging exercises, attacking and defending the island and in all likelihood developing bronchitis. For Renwick, the woodwork master, the building of the raft was a game played in deadly earnest, as though the Red Menace might manifest itself on a wooded island in the school lake. I remember that the project brought to mind an episode in *The Ministry of Fear*, where a British officer confined to a private asylum run by Nazi collaborators spends his days trying to defend an island in a pond single-handedly against unseen enemies.

Notwithstanding his madness, the officer's fundamental belief is correct. There is indeed an enemy within. Elsewhere in the same book, a well-to-do lady arrested following a séance at which secrets were passed to the Germans tells her interrogator, 'They don't hang women in this country,' to which he replies that she has no idea what they might do during wartime. When I first read the book as a sixth former, this struck me as merely an extravagant flourish. Events would prove otherwise.

A world within or behind the known world is something in which it is always tempting to believe. Much of the literature read by schoolboys depends on it, from the Hardy Boys to Sherlock Holmes, to Buchan and Erskine Childers. I read all that, and I went on seeking out similar material as an adult. There must always be a secret. It was an irresistibly exciting notion: such a thing would lend meaning to events which might otherwise remain merely their empty selves, like the long school days and the sobering prospect of equally mundane employment and responsibility to come. When I was in the sixth form, Carson had warned against conspiracy theories, directing us to the findings of the Warren Commission following the Kennedy assassination. The facts were tangled enough, he said, without letting the imagination loose. But fiction, I've come to think, appeals to our sense of necessity quite as powerfully as attested fact. In *The Ministry of Fear*, Greene's hero was over-age and recently released from prison. His involvement in the espionage plot ran wholly counter to his private preoccupations, but without realizing it he was enacting the classic thriller role of the man who knew – or was believed to know – too much. Carson was also very strict about the distinction between history and 'entertainment', a word he handled as though with tongs. What would he have made of the present, where it can seem that entertainment is the only form in which history is palatable? To illustrate his point, and to indicate the proximity of entertainment and propaganda, he arranged a showing of *Went the Day Well?*, which was written by Greene, in which German paratroopers take over an English village and are held off by the locals until help arrives. It remains a stirring and rather frightening film. Propaganda, said Carson: essential to morale and the conduct of the war, but propaganda, and, when the smoke cleared, to be firmly separated from fact.

A distinction is sometimes made between Greene's serious fiction and his 'entertainments'. *The Ministry of Fear* belongs among the latter, but it keeps company with Eric Ambler and some of the poems Auden had written a few years earlier as the world accelerated towards catastrophe and the cinema threatened to overtake literature. If *The Ministry of Fear* was an amusement, its disposition was sombre. Richard Hannay was honour-bright: Greene's hero was compromised by the necessities of love. But at least he had a story to be in. When sometimes I walked by the lake in the grounds at dusk and dawn the place seemed almost supernaturally representative of its kind and class, as though perfectly fictional, its existence sustained by the novelist's art – the art that for some unaccountable reason I had quite recently thought was to be mine.

The cadets' exercise at Blake's should have been undertaken in the summer, but in April the lake had been drained to clear some of the weed. It was not refilled until the end of August, by which time Renwick, ex-Royal Engineers, known as the Beast with Three Fingers after an unfortunate accident with a circular saw, was beside himself with fury at the delays to the construction of his beautiful raft. It was unthinkable for the project to suffer further delay: ergo, November or bust. The work was completed by the light of lamps that Renwick got a squad instructed by Sergeant Risman to rig up among the trees, run from a generator in the groundsmen's hut. Such an undertaking, with its slightly demented ingenuity, would be viewed as criminally dangerous nowadays, but the boys involved viewed it all as an adventure. 'The thing is, sir,' Arnesen had told me, 'it makes it all more real, if you see what I mean, at the same time as barmy. It's hard to explain. It's a story we can really be in.' Perhaps in some ways Arnesen was not such a fool.

Renwick had also recently constructed the Memorial Hall piano, much to the sorrow of Topliss, the one-man Music Department, who had been hoping for a Steinway from the allegedly substantial School Fund. Gammon was not keen on spending money from the fund. As far as he was concerned, the sole business of the fund was to grow larger. Since, as he pointed out, there was an urgent (though not in fact fulfilled) need to replace many of the more pitted and obscenely graffiti'd desks which had been there since the school was founded, other means must be found to pay for less essential items. Enter Renwick. He made the instrument in his own time, as a gift to the school, or perhaps as a way of undermining the Music Department, whose instrumental lessons often clashed with his own. Like the raft, the piano took rather longer to complete than originally planned. Smallbone suggested that this was because Renwick kept losing more fingers in its innards. It was said by the despairing Topliss that the raft and the piano could have been swapped with no loss of function or aesthetic effect. It was said that the tone-deaf Renwick himself, when the quip was reported to him, suspected that Topliss was right and as a result never forgave him.

Topliss was indisputably correct, but one day after school at the beginning of term when I was backstage painting in the Memorial Hall, Feldberg appeared with a pretty dark-haired girl in the green velour hat worn at St Clare's. They both sat at the piano, the girl removed her hat and they played a handful of duets, occasionally flinching with amusement when an irredeemably sour note issued from Renwick's spavined creation. Maggie was there too, and we listened to the performance without making ourselves known. When they had finished, the girl leaned over and kissed Feldberg on the cheek. He turned and smiled and placed a finger on her lips. She put her hat back on, they rose, gathered their things and slipped away again. They looked as if they had nothing to do with us.

I made a noise of sentimental approval. In defiance of the regulations, Maggie lit a cigarette.

'They're a clever pair, aren't they?' she said. 'Not seen her before.'

'I'm sure she's a nice girl,' I said.

'Of course she is,' said Maggie, turning back to the flat she was painting. 'They're all nice girls, up to a point.'

'They?'

'You know what I mean.'

SIX

The cadets' voices faded over the field. When I entered the library there were few lights on among the dark stacks. I saw Feldberg sitting behind the issue desk, reading. He glanced up and nodded. I did an hour's work, then looked out what I wanted and went back to the desk so that he could stamp the books.

'You're on night shift, then, Feldberg. Where's your oppo?' The place was open until seven.

'Off sick, I think, sir. Anyway, I get more time to read this way.'

'What is it this week?' He held up a copy of Trevor-Roper's *The Last Days of Hitler*.

'Good. Keep reading around, won't you?' Feldberg didn't need telling, of course. He gave me a slightly pained glance and uncovered another volume, Elie Wiesel's *Night*. Then he looked over my shoulder and his expression emptied and closed. Charles Rackham, another Old Blakean, who taught modern languages and was our only poet, was approaching from the stacks, making his characteristic motion of smoothing his hand across his lank black hair. He was still in uniform. I hadn't realized he was in the library. He must have come up by the rear staircase from the caretakers' storeroom. As far as I could remember, we had hardly exchanged a word since my arrival. I had never been taught by him as a pupil.

Rackham nodded to me and without looking at Feldberg held out a book for him to stamp. It was a biography of Pierre Laval, the collaborationist French prime minister. I had no idea we stocked such a thing. Who on earth had ordered it? Rackham himself, to spare the expense of buying his own copy? Feldberg rose slowly and took up the date stamp, then pressed it heavily into the inky pad, inspecting the results and repeating the process. Rackham looked at him and put the book down on the counter, at which Feldberg opened it, stamped it and slid it back to Rackham without once looking up. Rackham seemed as if he was about to speak in rebuke but thought better of it. He caught sight of what Feldberg was reading and gave his thin smile, then nodded once more at me and went out. Feldberg had coloured. He turned away and began packing his briefcase.

'There's no one about, sir. Mind if I knock off early?'

I wondered what to say. Dumb insolence was usually the preserve of the lower school, which made Feldberg's behaviour worse. On the other hand, Rackham had let the matter slide, hadn't he?

'This place is a mess, Feldberg,' I said. 'The returned stock needs moving on to the shelves. Don't let it build up behind the issue desk. Make sure the others do their share.'

'Yes, sir. I'll sort it out.' He understood what I was obliged to do. He waited patiently for it to be over.

'Well, think on, then. And yes, you may as well get off home.' He would probably be heading for the city library, which stayed open until eight p.m. in those days. 'Remember me to your father.' Samuel Feldberg ran the city's best bookshop, somewhere I had spent a good deal of time myself. He nodded and began to gather his things together.

I went back to the staffroom, hung up my gown and checked my pigeonhole. As I walked back across the quad and along the drive I wondered what I had just seen. It was not possible, surely, that Rackham had deliberately sought to insult or provoke Feldberg. That would be unforgivable. So – this is what I seem to have decided, forty-odd years ago – it could not actually have happened. Anyway, it was such a small, momentary thing. As I have indicated, casual anti-Semitism often surfaced in the boys' talk – though usually in the middle school rather than the sixth form – along with other kinds of racism and unceasing sexual obscenity. The masters would know better. In the city there were golf clubs which did not admit Jewish members, but that was not – and I cannot now remember what I thought it was not. There was a substantial Jewish population, established since the waves of late nineteenth-century immigration, active in business and the professions and local politics, playing an important part in the life of the place. People made off-colour remarks. They *said* things to each other. But it didn't signify. There'd been a war. People knew. Nothing could happen. The massacre had taken place nearly seven hundred years before.

And what had Rackham done? He'd borrowed a book from the library. He hadn't said anything. He had simply given his lipless smile and looked at me, as though I should know what was meant – as one Old Blakean to another. He did, I had noticed, provoke a certain reserve among his colleagues, and without quite knowing why, I saw that there was in the case of Carson a degree of watchfulness, or wary expectancy. I attributed this to Rackham's reputation for unpredictability. An enthusiasm for Laval, I now thought, would not commend him to Carson either.

Blake's was, as I may have indicated, philistine at heart, but the school admitted exceptions against which to measure its norms the more clearly. Rackham was a literary type, so he was allowed to be a bit odd. I suppose I was curious firstly because I knew Maggie. Rackham, who seemed younger than what must have been his age, as if he had been set aside to wait, had published a couple of collections of poems at the end of the 1940s and nowadays contributed essays and reviews to obscure literary journals. I'd come across the poems in the school library. I seemed to be their only borrower. They were the kind of Rilkean work whose vogue had long since passed, along with *The White Horseman* and Apocalypse and *Poetry London* – part of a lost world that seemed beyond resurrection. My own preferred poets were of the Movement generation, formal and unpretentious, at times – I now see – suffocatingly so.

Rackham should have held no interest, but his books – their physical pages, their poor-quality paper – somehow smelt of the war, which gave them a resonance beyond any verbal life they might have possessed. After coming across these works when I took on the library, I asked Tim Connolly, the Head of English, about him. Connolly brightened, cautiously, at the enquiry: here perhaps, he thought, was someone else who cared about the only poet Blake's had ever produced. Rackham, he explained, did not encourage enquiries about his work, any more than he sought friends on the staff. He had flirted with Mosley's British Union of Fascists – like a lot of people who saw the error of his ways, Connolly hastened to add. It was said that Rackham had substantial means, which presumably made his schoolteaching a hobby or a vocation. It seemed his life was elsewhere. Connolly made his investigations privately. He told me that Rackham had at some point in the 1950s become a Poundian. Since then he had apparently been working on a book-length poem, from which tiny provisional scrapings appeared at long intervals in severe and exclusive like-minded journals where Pound's economic theories, such as they were, seemed to be viewed with the same seriousness as his *Cantos*.

'Is the later stuff any good?' I asked Connolly.

'I've no idea,' he replied. 'It's very impressive and learned and modernist but half the time with the extracts I've read I've no idea what's going on. You need to be polyglot and a polymath to follow it.'

'Is it worth the effort?'

'Well, he's all we've got at Blake's, isn't he?' Connolly gave his wry grin. 'I'm assuming that since you haven't mentioned it, you aren't doing any writing yourself.'

'I'm sorry to say that's correct.'

'Ah, well. Anyway, apart from Carson's early monographs Rackham is about it for the literary tradition of the school.'

'What about General Allingham?' I asked.

Connolly gave his weary sigh. 'Yes, well, Allingham. The

military stuff's a bit technical. And as a writer he's not exactly Liddell Hart. As for the rest, well . . .' He shook his head. The General was, to say the least, an ambiguous figure, as perhaps Oswald Mosley must have seemed to Wykehamists, though of course they, unlike us, had a great many notable old boys to choose from. 'Anyway, as I say, Rackham's not very approachable where his writing's concerned,' Connolly went on. 'I've looked into all this without his help. Someone has to keep an eye on this aspect of school life.'

'So it's a matter of duty.'

'Like everything else, Maxwell.' Connolly gave his smile again. Perhaps it was a way of assuaging disappointment. 'That's what it comes down to. You know the score. We're all old boys here. The angel has to record everything.'

'Why do you stay?' I knew the answer to this. Connolly and his wife had four rapidly accumulated sons, all of whom would in turn be educated at Blake's at staff rates.

He laughed. 'Well, it's the company store. And I might ask: why have you come back? Funny how people do, though. When I finished National Service I meant to go into journalism. Just the way it goes, eh, Maxwell? Quick – run away before it's too late!' It would have been too complicated to explain that it was running away that had brought me back here.

As I came out into the square beyond the gates, Rackham's green VW Beetle went slowly past in the thickening darkness. He raised his hand in a wave, as though we were acquainted now, on the same side. I wondered what he thought he knew about me, and about what part of that was true.

SEVEN

After Rackham had driven off I returned to my flat on Fernbank Avenue, ate, washed, changed and, as if there were no alternative, went out and round the corner to the Narwhal. As usual I was meeting Smallbone but I was a bit early, so I bought a pint while scouting the main bar and then went through and sat on a stool in the empty back lounge with the framed boxing photographs covering the walls. I spread the local *Chronicle* out on the counter. Fish, rugby league and council corruption – the comforts of home. The newspaper's style persisted in hyphenating street names, as if this were the eighteenth century. The pub was in effect the out-of-hours centre of the universe. Its evening noise sounded agreeably muted in the lounge: quiet was always hard to acquire.

A movement drew my attention. Across in the little mirrored snug known as the Coffin Bar, a tall, astonishingly ugly man with pitted skin and the huge jaw and brow of a sufferer from acromegaly, wearing an army surplus parka the size of tent, listened impassively to a pale fat companion in a brown wide-brimmed soft hat. The tall man was Lurch, one of the groundsmen's assistants at Blake's, a troll-like figure in his forties who was feared by the younger boys for his habit of looming in the woods. I'd never heard him speak and he wasn't speaking now. I couldn't hear what the second man was saying, but he offered repeated decisive chopping gestures, as though demonstrating Occam's razor. From time to time he would pause and nod as if his sense of things had been confirmed, though his silent companion remained expressionless.

The shorter, fatter man was Claes, the proprietor of Vlaminck Books, the second-hand shop round the corner, just off the main road. He was usually glimpsed sitting in an armchair by a paraffin heater in an inner room of his premises, speaking on the phone, gesturing as now, his eyes widening as he nodded. There was a peculiar bland softness about Claes, as though his outline did not contain him securely. He made me think of canals and flooded landscapes. He was Belgian but had lived in the city a long time, apparently a refugee of some sort. He had acquired something of the accent but retained the stereophonic nasality of his fellow countrymen, as though used to breathing in tunnels half-underwater.

I had started going to Vlaminck's as a teenager. When after returning to the city I had visited the shop he was perfectly affable, sitting in his captain's chair at his desk with the paraffin heater on whatever the weather, surrounded by columns of books. He hardly seemed to move once he was installed on the premises. People handed him books and the money and he rang up the transactions on an ancient mechanical till before resuming his reading or his many long telephone calls, conducted in what I gathered was Flemish. He ate chocolates continually. He smelt slightly of chocolate, but with a hint of something more distasteful, as though overcooked, behind it.

Claes was completely indiscriminate as a bookseller. If it had a cover, he would sell it – a view diametrically opposed to that of Feldberg's father, who saw no point in making money out of material he despised or the unserious people who sought it. There were, I liked to think, not many customers like me who had a foot in both camps. At Vlaminck's, behind the steamy windows, sets of Dickens and Conrad cohabited with Frank Harris and *Fanny Hill*, textbooks of seamanship with *Health and Efficiency*, *Parade* and other men's magazines. I went there because I liked collecting early Penguins, on which he seemed to place little value. He would point out a new pile of rusty orange-and-white covers whenever he'd unearthed them in a house clearance, which was one of his several other businesses, in which he apparently employed

Lurch on a cash-in-hand basis. Away from his shop Claes and I did not speak or even acknowledge each other, a practice which seemed to suit both of us. It was somehow a form of courtesy, one which we continued to observe this evening.

For his own reading Claes seemed to go through phases – green Penguin Crime for a while, then military history in several languages, including General Allingham's book on tank warfare (much admired by Guderian, the Panzer commander), then an excursion towards Mickey Spillane and his English epigone Hank Janson, the covers of whose novels had offered scenes of intense depravity which had also been attractive to passing schoolboys such as myself a few years earlier when it was understood that Blake's did not approve of the shop (as though Blake's really advocated the use of any bookshop), which gave us another reason to go there. And there was a more serious side to Claes. One day I found him reading Spengler, then later a biography of Leon Degrelle, Mosley's Belgian analogue, of whom I had not heard at the time.

'But you are a teacher of history,' he said with a delighted smile. Not for the first time I noticed that his tongue seemed too large for his mouth. 'He is a major figure in my country's history.'

'Forgive my ignorance. He hasn't come up in my reading, I'm afraid. Belgian history appears to have been rather neglected in this country.' As far as I am aware this has remained the case. Apart from Hergé and Simenon, what do the English know of Belgium? 'Who was Degrelle?'

'Degrelle was a patriot and a hero, some of us think. Others would say the opposite. Poor Belgium.' He gave his wide, mad, hound-tongued smile again. 'She is unknown, ignored, divided, derided, created as a country of convenience and treated as a whore by the powers who brought her to a disfigured birth.' I wondered for a moment if Claes would climb on top of the heater to continue his oration. But he fell silent and nodded, his lips pursed.

'Blimey.'

'You think I am making a joke, Mr Maxwell. To the English no one except the Germans is really serious, perhaps because the Germans most resemble you. Your queen is a German. It is perhaps a joke even to speak of my country. Perhaps. We shall see. But now' – the smile was back – 'you surely cannot help but be curious about Leon Degrelle. See how we are all Europeans together now.'

'De Gaulle would disagree.'

'I do not speak of him. No.' He seemed about to issue a denunciation. Then his expression altered, and, if it were possible, softened. 'I regret, my friend, I cannot sell you this, my personal copy. But I am sure I can find one for you in a French translation, if you wish. I can find almost anything, if you should wish. Whatever is of interest. I have many links, here and in continental Europe. History, literature, art books, photography of all kinds, also meat products and carpets and also cultural and political organizations with whom you might find contact beneficial and even profitable. Catholic societies, for example.' I said I would bear all this in mind, paid for a couple of early Greenes and left him to the contemplation of history, a damp-seeming and unsung Napoleon there by the paraffin heater, sealed behind the steamy windows of the shop.

Leon Degrelle is probably no more familiar to English readers now than in those days. He was the leader of the prewar Belgian fascist party, the Rexists, seeking to mend the linguistic and cultural divisions present since the creation of the country in 1832. After early success, his electoral support fell away as his fascism became apparent. He served as an SS Volunteer in the Brigade Wallonie, one of several SS units made up of foreign nationals. Degrelle himself, who began as a private, gained a commission, and seems to have fought with distinction, if it can be called that, on the Russian front. He was condemned to death in absentia by the Belgian authorities after the war, but escaped the fate of some of his erstwhile colleagues. He spent the rest of his life living in unrepentant and comfortable exile in Spain, beyond the reach of retribution. Asked if he had any regrets, he said, 'Only that we lost.' Contrast Claes, marooned in the English provinces and running a seedy bookshop. Discuss.

A third person appeared at the bar. This was Shirley, a curvy blonde girl – never quite a woman – of my age, and thus much younger than her strange companions. She smiled and waved. For a time in the sixth form I'd gone out with her. She was one of those bright children who fell quietly back into the class they were supposed to be escaping through education. St Clare's was as far as she would go. She would never leave town, never complain. She was a brilliant seamstress. She made most of the costumes for the joint production of the Scottish play that Blake's and St Clare's had put on when we were in the sixth form.

When she finished school, all she wanted to do was read and smoke dope. Shirley was what would now be called an early adopter, a few years ahead of the fashion for drugs. In the blues clubs near the docks, where she and her girlfriends had ventured quite fearlessly, there was already a small, discreet trade from sailors returning from Durban and other African ports. Shirley's father had left when she was a child, and her mother seemed resigned to solitude and fortified wine. She made no attempt to control or even advise her daughter. Shirley and I would smoke and make love in her room at the top of the house, listening to music and talking about books.

'How do you know what to do, Stevie?' she asked once. We lay there hearing the television blaring from downstairs in competition with Shirley's prized Dusty Springfield LPs.

'How do you mean?'

'You're off to university. You've got a plan.'

'Or someone's drawn one up for me.'

'Yes, but you know where you're going. But how do you know it's the right way?'

'I suppose it feels right. I'm interested in doing it.'

'That's the difference.' She sat up and pulled an LP cover on to her lap and began to roll a joint. 'I haven't got that feeling. I don't know what's the right thing.'

Shirley should have been a librarian – that had been the school's plan, with which she had seemed in passive agreement – but somehow although she passed her A-levels she had ended up working in Claes's bookshop, for the time being at first and then indefinitely. She also made the occasional garment on request.

'You should get away from here. Everyone should, for a while, anyway,' I said. 'I can't wait.'

'I like it here. I'm at home. I know people. At St Clare's in the sixth form the teachers told us all to be ambitious. But I'm not, and anyway, what were they? They were only teachers. I just like reading and sewing and smoking dope and being in bed with you. I don't want you to go away. Because when you go this will be over.' And there she stayed, when most of her contemporaries had left town.

Like Claes, when business was slow, Shirley got on with her own vast and entirely indiscriminate reading. The last time we had spoken in the shop she was alternating between Georgette Heyer and Sven Hassel. Claes had recommended the latter, she said. I imagined that apart from Shirley, Hassel's readership was exclusively male. His gruesomely violent accounts of action on the Russian front were popular among the boys at Blake's, myself included at one point.

These were also, if you follow me, books that men could read without apology, like James Hadley Chase and Harold Robbins. Trawlermen, dockers, mechanics, feedstuff workers, taxi drivers and the rest were in those days often united by a common indulgence in the view of the Second World War from the other side. This was of a piece with the widespread admiration for Rommel, whose prowess some of them had seen at first hand in the Western Desert, but it also bled off into the fetishism of militaria. There were a lot of German helmets hanging half-proudly on the doors of sheds in the back yards of terraces, plus the odd decorative dagger discreetly kept in a drawer. The father of one of Shirley's friends was said to have a Luger buried in a box on the railway allotments behind Blake's.

I hadn't seen Shirley for a little while because I'd been avoiding Vlaminck's. The last time I'd called at the shop Claes was busy on the phone and indicated that I should look after myself until he'd finished his call. After a while he followed me into the back room where I was picking over a new consignment of rusty Penguins.

'That was the General himself,' he said, smiling and nodding as if I must already know.

'Keitel? Zhukov? You need to narrow it down, Claes.'

'The schoolboy humour, always, of course,' he said. 'I refer to General Allingham.'

'Does he want his house cleared?' Claes looked injured at this. 'Sorry.'

'I have the honour to be part of the committee arranging his campaign.'

It dawned on me then. 'You mean in the by-election?'

'I do. Great days, Maxwell, great days. A time of destiny.'

I was inclined simply to walk out of the shop, but instead I held out the books I had chosen. Claes took a moment to grasp what I meant. Then we went to the till. When the transaction was done, he said, 'The General is an Old Blakean, of course.'

'That's correct.'

'You should meet him, Maxwell.'

'I don't think he'd find me very interesting. We wouldn't have much in common.' Apart from Blake's, I thought. Claes was about to protest, but stopped, running his great tongue along his lower lip, then nodded.

'As you wish,' he said. 'You can always change your mind. A young man should be open to new ideas.'

'How d'you mean, *new*?'

Claes shook his head and made his way back to his chair and his reading. I had offended his sense of courtesy. So be it, I thought.

Claes and his chums were not simply egregious. In the stratum of the unskilled, the permanently unemployed and the unemployable, their concerns could find a hearing; a blend of socialism and racism had considerable appeal to some, to whom it must have looked like common sense. And there were others who'd sympathize, from the grey margins of respectability and disappointment and an urge to deny to others the life they seemed to have denied themselves, part of what Adorno called 'the dream of oppression of all by all'. Anyway, they would have their day. The by-election was approaching, following the death of the incumbent through ill health, and the British Patriot Party would be putting up a candidate, namely our very own General Allingham, lately returned from long exile in rural France to his family estate on the Plain of Axness.

Allingham was not just some wall-eyed estate agent. He was a name, one of ours, our very own Mosley. There was, of course, as 'everyone' knew in those days, and as everyone thought would remain true forever, no chance of him winning. But Allingham and his men would do their best to spread their poison. That would be their victory. I read these pages over now in the year when the region has elected a Euro MP from a neo-fascist party, as if that were normal. Forever is, as they say, a long time.

I couldn't see Shirley fitting into the BPP's particular underworld of opinion, though. Her politics, I thought, could scarcely be called politics: they seemed to extend no further than the vague sexual goodwill induced by the next joint and the one after. In Shirley's head it seemed to be always afternoon, the room blue with smoke. As for me, all I knew was what I did not believe in, though I continued to observe its forms, perhaps, despite the evidence up to that point, still thinking or hoping that I might be set on a different path, that of art, which I seem to have viewed as occupying a separate category from sewers and the balance of payments and all the other dailiness of the despised 'art of the possible'.

EIGHT

As far as I could tell, Shirley had never held a grudge about our lapsed romance. It was my fault it ended. By the end of the summer before I went up to Cambridge I'd been bored. I slept with one of her friends, who then saved me the trouble of telling Shirley myself. Shirley didn't seem surprised. While I was away at university she wrote me the occasional letter about what she was reading and listening to, hardly referring to our relationship. Whenever we ran into each other on my occasional visits home, she seemed happy to flirt in her slow-motion way, sometimes as if we were the vaguest of acquaintances, at others as if passion must soon overtake us. I retained a guilty fondness for her, and I was afraid of what might be in store for her, which I thought might be nothing much. Her position at Vlaminck's suggested that I was right. But it was not my business to save anyone, having failed to save myself, was it?

Men, so far as I knew, partly from Smallbone's observations, seemed to come and go in Shirley's life without commitment or on their part or resentment on hers. They were a mixture – layabouts from the local university, a trawlerman, at one point a failed priest-turned-librarian. She remained attractive in a half-aware way, always beautifully dressed and made up, as if the call might at any moment come to be somewhere else. Of course she would never really strike out on her own account, though I gathered she had moved out of her mother's to an address I hadn't bothered to discover. When I visited the shop she was happy to advise me on my purchases. At that time I was collecting all and any editions of Greene, Ambler and Geoffrey Household, as well as occasional rarer items, all of which she had read and remembered. She absorbed books as she smoked dope – in large quantities, content to go on doing so, rarely expressing any opinion beyond yes or no.

Now, from her position at the bar, she raised in my direction a glass of Babycham that had been poured the moment she arrived. The two men looked incuriously over at me for a moment. Claes raised his hat formally as if I were a stranger. I had never seen Shirley mixing socially with her employer. The combination seemed faintly monstrous. She smiled at me, then turned back as Claes resumed his monologue.

'Drinking alone?' asked Smallbone as he climbed breathlessly on to the stool next to mine. He smoked too much.

'If I'm left in peace to get on with it and have a read at the paper.'

'I'll have a brown mix,' he said. I caught Stan's attention. Smallbone lit a Regal and looked about him critically. He was getting fat, working in his mother's stamp shop, 'pro tem', as he put it, since completing his own history degree at the local university just as *les evenements* erupted in local form on the campus with the occupation of the Senate House in protest at the university's investments in South Africa. He made me feel like a monster of ambition. Smallbone's father had been a Labour councillor, in the teeth of his wife's *Daily Express*-minded antagonism. Perhaps seeing the advantages of a quiet life, Bone himself affected the *Telegraph* (which he claimed had the best racing coverage) but admired Anthony Crosland. At least, unlike me, he had politics of a sort. He seemed to have given up reading, though, in favour of following the horses and going to the dog track in the far-off east end of the city, as well as committing himself to an exhaustive and indiscriminate pursuit of the opposite sex. The day would come soon enough, he had explained, when he could not get his hole, so until then what was the point of wasting time on things of the mind?

'Oh aye. They're in, then,' he said, nodding towards the group in the snug.

'I can't work out what Shirley's doing with that lot,' I said. 'Socially, I mean.'

'Perhaps that's where she gets her dope. Or maybe she's become one of them.'

'I doubt it,' I said. 'She doesn't care about that sort of thing. Not as far as I know. She just thinks people should be nice to each other.'

Bone adopted an Ed Murrow voice. 'Democracy is under threat tonight, not from Hitler's bombs but an equally deadly source. For the Munich beer-hall read Greenland Street. The fascists, for which read the British Patriotic Party, are putting up a candidate in the by-election, using the democratic process in order to threaten democracy itself. Good night and good luck.'

'They'll lose their deposit,' I said.

'I dare say,' said Bone. 'But they're vicious bastards. And they've got Allingham standing, after all. Someone people are likely to have heard of. Another Old Blakean, of course. Not that Blake's advertise it.'

'No, but his books are all in the library. He sends them. Vegetarianism, indecisive battles, the Jewish plot. The last sort don't get put on display, of course. How serious are this BPP lot, really, compared with Allingham? It sounds like play-acting.'

'Depends how you define it. They *are* play-acting, but they seem to mean it anyway. That business last year with the petrol bomb thrown through the window at the hostel where the Nigerian medics stay – you were still away at the time – Claes's little band were meant to have done it.'

'This is according to your mother, I take it?'

'One thing my mother has got is sources. That's probably why she walks that way. Anyway, she probably agrees with Claes and his lot. She thinks the Nigerian medics are taking our boys' jobs. She's not very sophisticated in her analysis.'

'I suppose not. And the police did nothing.'

'Not enough evidence, apparently – not that they'd care

about a gang of coons.' I stared at him. 'I mean, that's how the police would look at it. You know what they're like. But it got in the paper, with a photograph of Claes and his goon squad, composed of Lurch and a few others in camouflage gear, stood round this old half-track they've got parked in a yard somewhere, preparing to go on manoeuvres on the Plain of Axness. They said they were unjustly blamed because they're English patriots. Which Claes isn't, of course. And where the hell did Lurch spring from?'

'East of the river, obviously. Your stamping ground.'

'Piss off,' said Bone amiably. 'I go there for anthropological reasons.'

The city was divided by a muddy trench, the Ouse. Dwellers in the east were known to be inbred lunatics. According to Smallbone, however, the web-footed women were strangely susceptible to his indefinable charms.

'How many of this lot are there?' I asked. 'I mean, running about in old lorries . . .'

'Who knows? Depends on the state of the moon, I should think.'

'But Shirley? I mean, she's—'

'A woman? No flies on you, are there? She is indeed. I'd give her one. It must be my turn one day.'

'She's a nice girl,' I said. 'You be nice about Shirley.'

'Of course she's a nice girl. All the better,' said Smallbone, rubbing his hands together. 'All the better for the Bone.'

'Shut up.'

'Now then, fair's fair. You had your go.'

But Smallbone would have to wait. Rackham had just entered the snug. Over his shoulder hung a camera case. He said nothing but looked at Shirley in his bloodlessly amused way. She finished her drink and left, taking his arm. Claes carried on talking.

'Now I've seen everything.' Smallbone groaned. 'That corpse Rackham. Is she fucking blind?' Rackham was, in fact, rather handsome in his saturnine way.

'De gustibus, I suppose. Rackham's not actually a paid up one of them, is he?' I asked, more nonchalantly than I felt. *Rackham?* But Shirley used to go out with *me*.

Smallbone shrugged. 'Well, hardly. Not with the teaching, surely.' In one of those unstated ways in which Blake's was so effective, it was understood that staff did not undertake public political activity or make their allegiances known, though for the most part, Blake's being Blake's, these were self-evident. Rackham had not precisely breached this protocol, any more than he had committed any overt offence in the library. He had simply come in to meet a girl at the pub. He was too old for her, I thought, by a couple of decades. But he didn't act or somehow look that way. Once again he was hard to place. Perhaps 'act' was the word: the cinema was full of leading men far older than their love interests.

'He must be a wrong 'un, though, Bone. Look at the company he keeps.'

'Yes, Maxwell, but look who's talking, eh? Perhaps Rackham's a fellow traveller, a dabbler, someone who gives them intellectual weight. Claes would like that. Rackham's a poet, you tell me. Or else they want to have a go on his boat so they can claim to have a navy.' Rackham was a keen sailor, active in the sailing club at Blake's. His impressive motor yacht *Lorelei* was moored in the creek.

'At the end of school today, when I was in the library, I think he meant to insult one of the sixth form, a Jewish boy, Feldberg,' I said.

'He's the bright one, yeah? Samuel Feldberg's lad.'

I described what had happened. It seemed to grow vaguer in the telling, though my disquiet hadn't gone away.

'Did the boy complain?' Bone asked, putting on his overcoat.

'No, he didn't.' I stood. Bone turned away, eager for the off, but I hesitated and he turned back. 'It was something and nothing. But I was there. I saw it. I told Feldberg off for being insolent in return.'

'Well, then.'

'Well, then, what?'

'Well, then, actually I dunno, Maxwell. Is it important? You said it was something and nothing. And the staff always have to back each other up. You know that. Let it go.'

'It wasn't quite nothing.'

'And now you seem to be feeling guilty. Not much use, though, is it?'

'I think I told Feldberg off because I didn't do anything about Rackham.'

'That's too subtle for me. But there's not much you can do now, is there?'

'Perhaps I could talk to Feldberg.'

'And say what? You'll just look like a pillock. Let it go, man. He's probably forgotten by now. Save it for another day. I'm just going for a quick recce of the bint situation.'

Smallbone, I suspected, would be intending to buy some contraceptives. The local chemist would probably have informed his mother if he'd tried it there. Given the implacable, grasping disposition of the rusted machine in the Gents he might be a little while. And if there were any women he knew in the bar, it would further extend the delay while he rehearsed a few introductory moves.

I ordered another half. The street door opened and Maggie Rowan came in.

NINE

Did we know each other in here?

Stan appeared as if through a trapdoor.

'For the lady, sir?' he said. Was the ghost of a sniff, a smirk? I turned to Maggie.

'I'll get this,' I said.

'Oh, well then, a gin and tonic, please, Stan,' Maggie said, as if all this were an accident.

'Large gin, Mrs Rowan?'

She nodded. 'And I'll have twenty Kensitas.' She put the money for the cigarettes on the counter. 'Getting ready for Christmas, Stan?'

'Have to ask the wife about that.'

'I haven't done a thing. I'm panicking. As usual. Dare say we'll survive.' She raised her glass. Stan nodded politely, handed over the change and went back into the bar. 'He doesn't like me.'

'He probably doesn't like unaccompanied women coming into the pub. He's of the old school.'

'Not our school, he's not.' She lit a cigarette. 'Why, what does he think I am? A tart off the street?'

I gathered she'd had one or two before coming out. She looked OK, vividly auburn and beautiful in a slightly old-fashioned way, a little like Kay Kendall in *Genevieve*. Her lipstick seemed too bright for the setting.

'I imagine he thinks you're the Headmaster's wife.'

'And does that mean I can't go out if I want to?'

I shrugged and lit her cigarette.

'Your brother was in just now.' I nodded across at the snug, where Claes and Lurch remained, now looking expressionlessly over. They had put down their drinks and seemed as though waiting. 'He came in to collect a girl. Has he got a date?'

'Do I look like his keeper?' she asked, unsmiling.

With slight surprise I realized that she never talked about Rackham. Not that there was any particular reason why she should. They seemed very different, and he was some years older.

'Those two seemed to know him.'

'I imagine he knows lots of people, just as you do,' she said. Now Claes rose to leave. Lurch held the glass-panelled door for him, and for a second there were two of Claes in view. He doffed his broad hat to Maggie, who did not appear to notice.

'Do you ever go on the *Lorelei*?' I asked.

'What? The boat? It's not his. I let him use it sometimes with the sailing club. I use it myself now and again.'

'I didn't know you were a sailor.'

'Well, there you are. Are you trying to annoy me, Stephen? Why are you talking about boats?'

'I'm just curious.'

She sighed and breathed out smoke. She was irresistible when being unreasonable, which was much of the time.

'The young lady in question was Shirley – you know, from Vlaminck's, the bookshop.'

'Bookshop? I don't think I know her. Shirley. Well, at least somebody's happy.' Maggie looked at me impatiently.

'She's very young. She's my age.'

'Must run in the family, then, cradle-snatching. Honestly, who cares? As long as she's old enough to vote, which according to you she is.'

'She's a friend of mine, actually.'

'A friend?' Maggie's tone made this sound like a dubious idea. 'Men don't have female "friends", do they?'

'I used to go out with her. Now we're friends.'

'Commendable.'

For some reason I had hoped to gain an advantage by

revealing this acquaintance, by placing myself at the centre of some imagined sphere of relations. Instead I seemed to be diminished, browbeaten by the older woman who had come here in search of me.

'Charles has odd tastes,' Maggie added. 'I mean, he's not a snob about that kind of thing.'

'What kind of thing?'

'Let's not dwell on it, shall we?'

I decided to cut my losses.

'I'm here with Smallbone. He'll be back in a minute. We're off into town.'

She finished her drink and lit another cigarette. 'Looking for mucky women.' Her attempt at the local vernacular was jarring and somehow hateful.

'I dare say Smallbone will be. I thought I might be spoken for myself, but it seems not, Mrs Rowan.'

Her expression softened a degree. 'I knew you'd be here. I mean, you usually are.' She paused. 'The thing is, Robert was supposed to be coming home this weekend, but now it turns out he won't be. So, anyway.'

'It's probably not wise. This doesn't count as discretion, does it?'

She bristled at this. I wondered if she might strike me.

'I know that, Stephen. You need hardly tell me. But there you are. I'll be at the flat.' She stubbed out her cigarette. 'Let yourself in. Up to you, of course.'

I wondered if I had just managed to exercise power, albeit of a low and perhaps contemptible order.

Stan Pitt appeared again, wiping a glass with a clean tea towel.

'How is Mr Rowan?' he asked. 'We used to see him now and again in here in the holidays.'

'Making progress, I think, Stan,' Maggie said. 'We're looking on the bright side.'

'That's good, Mrs Rowan. We look forward to welcoming him back.' Maggie gathered her things and left without looking at me. Stan went on polishing the glass. I wondered if it might simply disappear under his attentions.

'Stan, you know those two in the snug, Claes and his pal?' I asked.

'Aye. What about them?'

'Any trouble at all?'

Now he looked up. 'None at all so far, Mr Maxwell. All they do in here is drink and talk. Just like you and Mrs Rowan.'

'Don't usually see Mr Rackham in here.'

'That's not for me to say, Mr Maxwell.' He went through into the bar.

At last Smallbone reappeared.

'*I know what you're do-ing,*' he sang, with sweaty glee. 'Knocked you back, has she?'

'Be quiet, Bone.'

'Smallbone, like the night, has a thousand eyes. She looked keen, the lady who wasn't here.'

'You have a mind like a sewer.'

'Then at least I know where my interests lie.'

In due course Smallbone and I walked into town, drinking steadily, avoiding the agreed haunts of the boys as they avoided ours. Eventually we came to the Triton, an ancient and disreputable boozer near the pier. The lights on the far bank glinted distantly and there were ships leaving on the evening tide. There was a folk club in a back room of the pub, the kind of thing I could take or leave, while the front offered an explosive mixture of blue-suited trawlermen home for three days on the lash, local criminals and bohemians, and girls of uncertain provenance, whose charms tended, as the evening wore on, to provoke conflict between the fishermen and those they viewed as layabouts. It was not a wise place for the casual visitor. You could be stabbed for looking. And yet we went there: it was life, albeit occasionally fatal.

On the way back from the Gents I looked in through the door of the Singing Room. Some fisherman's jersey-clad fraud of a liberal studies lecturer from the Tech was doing 'The Irish Rover'. In a nearby street there stood a golden equestrian statue of William of Orange in Roman attire. Its gold was painted green the night before every twelfth of July. It was 1968, year of revolution, so this must have been ours.

Smallbone seemed to be in luck that night. When I returned he was sitting with a pair of ferociously backcombed twins in crocheted white minidresses. They were all drunk by now, and there seemed to be a move afoot to go on to the Club Lithuania, destination of many a journey to the end of the night, a frowsty knocking shop where violence was even more prevalent than in the Triton. I left Smallbone and his companions at the door of the club. It was guarded by two polite but terrifying Ghanaian bouncers, former merchant seamen who were rumoured to have sold the dismembered parts of an enemy for dogfood. They also discreetly supplied grass and uppers.

'Stamina,' said Smallbone. 'You lack stamina. Having a proper job makes you weak. You need to dabble more and waste time properly.' His companions roared with laughter and dragged him inside.

I began to walk back past the late bus queues in the centre of town, knowing that it would not be until I reached the Cenotaph that I would have to make a decision. It had grown foggy, and the bell of a lightship sounded faintly across the roofs, a reminder of the vast, agreeable cold of the estuary and the ocean a few miles downstream.

The Cenotaph loomed, the great slab in emulation of the Lutyens in Whitehall, remembering the mass slaughter of the local regiment on the Somme. Beyond this to one side stood the smaller monument to the Boer War, with its two stone soldiers, one crouching as though to reload, the other standing and taking aim across the marble slab from which they grew.

I stopped and lit a cigarette. Which way, then? To have become involved like this was dangerous, to put it mildly. To continue would surely guarantee disaster. There were, I told myself, no secrets in this place, not in the school, not in the city. But I already knew where I was going, didn't I?

There must have been pain, disappointment, tragedy and madness in the years covered in *A Firm Foundation*, Carson's first volume of school history. Yet beyond some benign comments on the demeanour of leading members of staff, usually couched in comparison with Roman generals (was Carson being satirical? 'Our rivals at the Grammar School must be destroyed,' etc.), it was not the kind of work to admit much personal detail or any but the mildest eccentricity. The school was a repertory theatre which never closed: the show should be reliable, efficient and traditional, and offer no disturbing surprises. Discretion was extraordinarily powerful. But there were limits, presumably, people sent away, gone in the night, no longer spoken of. I was in a fair way to join them if I carried on, and it wasn't even the end of the autumn term yet.

Beyond the new buildings on the edge of the town centre lay areas of merchant housing which had already gone to seed before the war, substantial terraces interspersed with bombsites that had joined up with back gardens run wild. The population was a mixture of the transient (students and the restless poor, the latter always flitting), the old, a few medical and dental practices, along with people who seemed immune to change and never moved out to the suburbs. Percival Street offered all these elements. It ended at the gate of a pedestrian railway crossing to a patch of allotments, from which another crossing led to the scrubland behind the grounds of Blake's. All in all, it was very handy.

I walked past the house down to the gate and leaned there looking into the fog. A goods train crawled past. The beer was wearing off. It wasn't too late to go home. I could risk crossing the foggy tracks and cut through Blake's and be in my own bed in ten minutes, reading *The End of the Affair*. It was time to put a stop to this business, but that had been true since the minute before it began. I looked up at the top floor of the end house. A light was showing. *Up to you*, Maggie had said.

TEN

At the end of the previous school year the garden party was held, culminating in the school summer play, a fund-raising event including dinner and champagne. Wives, girlfriends and female staff were enlisted to take part, sew, cook and so on (a different era, it is alleged). It was in some ways the highlight of the social calendar, along with the cricket match between the staff and the First Eleven. Having no other urgent occupation, and preparing to take up my post at Blake's in September, I was pressed by Connolly to help with scene-painting and fetching and carrying. He alluded to my earlier turn as Banquo as evidence of an addiction to grease-paint. Maggie Rowan, lust-object of most of the pupil population, taught art and was in charge of designing the set for the play.

Last summer it had been *A Midsummer Night's Dream*, so the Athenian woods sprang up on the stage of the Memorial Hall and the foolish mortals went through their immortal paces for the amusement of their supernatural betters. The production was, as always, well received. It signalled that summer was here in earnest. The Lord of Misrule momentarily got a foot in the door of Blake's: Titania, courtesy of St Clare's, was undoubtedly sexy. Feldberg and his girl, in evening dress, played the dud piano in the interval when drinks were served by sixth formers from both schools.

There was a party afterwards onstage for the cast and production team, and it would be fair to say that some of those present drank more than they would normally wish to be seen or known to do. The senior staff had long departed by the time the action wound down. Maggie took charge, ushered out the stragglers – the fairies and nobles and mechanicals bound for Connolly's house nearby – and said she would lock up. I found myself delegated to remain behind and help.

A little later I was tipsily carrying several bags of costumes and a bottle of wine past School House, where boarders lived, around the edge of the moonlit field, through the woods and over the railway line to the big attic flat on Percival Street. It must have been an enchantment: I was incapable of resisting.

Maggie kept the place as a studio, she explained, and for storage. It was convenient and quiet and, besides, there was no room for her to work at the Headmaster's House in the grounds, which is where I first imagined we were heading, and there were always interruptions, which made it such a nuisance that Robert had not felt able to break with tradition and live off-site, but there we were.

By this time we were going up the stairs of the tall end-terrace. Incredulous, I watched her slim, tanned legs flickering ahead in a skirt that would have been generally considered an inch too short for someone of her age in her position. I was doing it again. I watched myself doing it – climbing the stairs towards an irrevocable act, and at any of those thirty-odd steps I could have stopped and gone away, but I didn't. At heart perhaps I was already ruined and wanted to make sure by destroying the second chance I had been offered. It was a kind of punishment, I told myself, as Maggie dumped the bags of costumes and unzipped her skirt. It was punishment. I had only to wait and see.

When I woke, it was five a.m., still dark, the fog thicker at the window. My head ached with dehydration. Maggie was moving about in a blue kimono, a cigarette in her mouth, pouring brandy into two glasses.

'Not for me, thanks,' I said.

'You'll need it for the walk back,' she said, placing the glass on a tea-chest by the bed. 'By the look of you.'

'Class dismissed, is it?' I began to dress.

'When you come down to it, discretion is the only thing,' she said. She looked older now.

'I take it you're discreet, then.'

She nodded. Now she was staring consideringly at one of the paintings stacked along the wall. 'I certainly hope you are.'

'We shouldn't have done it, should we?'

'No, we shouldn't. Did you enjoy it?'

'Oh, aye.' I gave what I thought was a trawlerman's leer. 'You being the colonel's lady, as it were.'

'I've always had a lot of sympathy for Rosie O'Grady, myself.'

I'm not the first, am I? I thought. But I didn't mind. It was an adventure. It was everything I was supposed to be avoiding. It was important, like doom, like fate, like destiny and all those other things the likes of me did not possess. I joined her and looked at the painting. It was like a view of the school minus the buildings. It seemed slightly anachronistic, a Thirties or Forties romantic landscape, a daylight moon over a gold field beside a birchwood gathered at a pool, where the chalky moon was faintly reflected. Everything was slightly bleached, as if austerity had requisitioned the natural world too.

'It's good. A little reminiscent of Paul Nash,' I said, and bit my tongue.

'Do you think so?' she said tonelessly.

'I didn't mean it as a criticism.'

'No, I know.' She moved away. 'Of course not. You have a good eye. It's just one more turn of the key. No harm done. Anyway, finish your drink. I need to get on. Can you let yourself out?' She went through into the bathroom.

'Is that it, then?'

'I think so,' she said, coming back. 'Be careful crossing the railway.'

But that wasn't it.

I expected to have to do a stint of miserable hanging about, all the time knowing I'd had an extraordinary experience that I would never be permitted to repeat and could not entirely remember. Maggie was a much more authentic older woman than the don's wife, who had still been in her twenties and inclined to panic and send tearful letters and even turn up outside my room asking the bedder where I was. I imagined drinking a lot of beer, knocking about with Smallbone and trying to avoid the fatal mistake of telling him what had happened. But a couple of days later when I went in for a meeting with Carson about my timetable I found an envelope in my pigeonhole. At lunchtime, after the meeting, I strolled across the field and over the tracks again.

'Won't the people in the other flats notice these comings and goings?' I asked when she opened the front door.

'There's no one else living here. I have the whole place. I need it to work.' She was dressed for painting, in an old shirt and jeans, with her auburn hair tied back. When we got up to the attic, she indicated an upright chair by the large window. 'Just sit there. I want to draw you. And put this on.' She handed me a sleeveless pullover in muted autumnal colours. Even on a casual day like today she wore her dark, arterial lipstick. When she concentrated, her face became severe and remote. At the brow and the mouth and in the slant of the gaze, she had that slightly feral nobility you find among some Irish people. It was worth sitting still and being drawn, worth wearing the musty pullover, in order to be able to look at her properly. The bed lay unmade.

Eventually, she stopped, grimaced, closed her sketchbook and poured wine.

'Well?' I asked.

'There's nothing to show at the moment.'

'I'm sorry for what I said before. I did like the picture. I mean, I admired it.'

'I don't remember whatever it was you said. What picture was that?'

'The landscape with the moon and the pool.'

She shook her head. 'It doesn't ring any bells. Anyway, never mind. You can take the jersey off now. And can you put the kettle on? There's some milk left, I think.'

She lit a cigarette and stood looking out of the window across the tracks to the school. The weathercock glinted faintly above the stopped clock on the Main Hall tower. It was one of those flat white summer days typical of the city. A shunter moved slowly along the tracks below.

'Why do you teach?' I asked. 'It doesn't look as if you need the money. You could just concentrate on your own work.'

Maggie sniffed. 'What? Well, why does one do anything? It's what one does. It's something to do. It keeps the days ticking over, I suppose. The school finds it useful and it keeps me in touch with the school. No children of my own, of course. Not that I wanted them, though Robert did.'

I poured the tea and took it over.

'But you're obviously serious about painting.'

She made an impatient grimace. 'Oh, serious. Absolutely. And much good it does me.'

'Maggie, I'm not sure what's going on here.'

'I suppose it depends what you want, Stephen.'

'I want to go to bed with you again.'

'If that's all, then that's all right. A fuck is OK, isn't it?' Her use of the word shocked me a little, and she smiled at my surprise. 'Anything more would be out of the question, wouldn't it?' I didn't entirely follow this. 'But of course, anything at all is very risky. We're already being very stupid, or I am, leading a young man into temptation and so on. Especially one with your record.' I stared. 'Well, of course I know about that. I'm the Headmaster's wife – I know lots of things. People's susceptibilities and so on. But if that's what you want. If you're prepared to take the risk. Visit me here and I'll let you fuck me. All right?'

'What about the – your husband?'

'My husband is ill. Robert is ill.' She looked tired now. It was generally understood that the Head's ill health would keep him away for the foreseeable future. 'He's not at home. He's there sometimes, but not for long.'

'Will he recover?'

'They say we should be optimistic. But they have to say such things. Otherwise, who knows, I might end up as mad as he is.' This was the rumour, that the Head's illness was not leukaemia but something psychiatric instead or as well. No matter how discreet people were, no matter if no one said anything, rumour would find a way. 'What with one thing and another, I've had my moments.'

'I'm sorry.'

'It doesn't concern you, does it?'

'I'm just saying I sympathize.'

'With Robert because he's mad and you're fucking his wife? That's very sophisticated. Sounds like Graham Greene to me.'

'I didn't mean to upset you.'

'I'm not upset. I'm angry.'

'I'm sorry.'

'It's not you I'm angry with, for God's sake! It's – the whole thing, the circumstances, because there's nothing to be done but go on like this.'

I had already dealt, or failed to deal, with one troubled woman. Clearly I had not learned my lesson. Whatever was amiss with Maggie seemed only to increase her attraction. There was a richness to it which forbade boredom just as it prevented repose. I took her hand. She did not resist.

'It was a breakdown,' she said. 'More than one, actually. A series. Just got to get on with it. Life goes on, tempers the steel, Dunkirk spirit, all that rubbish. Don't you ever wish we could all just bloody shut up? Stop talking and just *do* something. Has the world ended and I've not noticed? It's bloody Purgatory like this. Come on, then. Come on. I haven't got all day.'

I had no reply.

PART TWO

ELEVEN

After Maggie had come to see me in the pub I ended up at Percival Street for the weekend. On Monday morning Maggie was nowhere to be seen. Why hadn't she woken me? I dressed quickly. If I went through the allotments and over the pedestrian railway crossing I should just be able to nip over the road to my flat for my briefcase and get back in time for assembly.

Boys were forbidden to enter or leave the grounds by this route because of the trains, and in the foggy morning I could see no one else about. A muffled siren sounded, out on the river. I waited while a coal train crawled interminably past in the direction of the docks, and then I hurried across the line and went into the woods. My shoes were instantly soaked.

The path brought me to the edge of the lake. The ground near the wooden jetty had been churned up by the boots of the cadets involved in the exercise. There was someone else there. I slowed, thinking of how I might explain myself. As I came closer I saw it was Arnesen. He was hanging around, looking into the water. I assumed he was having a cigarette before lessons. If Gammon found him he would be expelled.

'Arnesen. What are you doing?' He looked up but didn't reply. He held an unlit cigarette. 'You know the woods are out of bounds.' I wondered if I could turn a blind eye to the cigarette. I wished he would put it in his pocket. Then he let it fall into the water and I followed his gaze, wondering idly why the raft of lashed-together planks and oildrums turned slightly among the lilypads. I realized that it was unmoored. Had the boy done this?

'Have you been messing about with the raft? You'll get yourself expelled, and that's nothing compared to what Mr Renwick will do.'

'Renwick, sir?' said the boy. 'Sod Renwick.'

When the raft turned again, something else turned, caught half under it, and I realized I was looking at a pair of legs in uniform trousers.

'Arnesen? What's happened?' He looked round and shook his head. 'Who is that?' Again he didn't speak. 'Go and get Sergeant Risman. Now. You understand?' Slowly, as if moving underwater, he went off into the fog. I wondered if he'd return. I wished I could disappear myself. I went closer to the water's edge.

I should have left it alone and let someone else do the discovering, but I was unable to wait for Risman's arrival. I hauled on the rope, and the raft, twelve feet by eight or so, slid slowly towards me over the lilypads, bringing the khaki legs with it. I found myself unable to touch the body.

It seemed like an age, there with the corpse. I'd never seen one before. It lay patiently in the water. Behind the trees the trains went grinding past. It can only have been a few minutes before Risman arrived with Arnesen unwillingly in tow. The boy shook his head and refused to come closer than the edge of the woods. I went to meet Risman halfway.

'What is it, Mr Maxwell?' Risman said, striding over the leaves. 'I can't get any sense out of young Arnesen.'

'I think there's a body in the lake, Sergeant. I mean, there is a body.'

'Bloody hell. Are you sure. Is it one of ours? Is it a tramp? They get in here at night sometimes.'

'It's in CCF uniform.'

'Is it now? Better have a look, then,' Risman said. 'Arnesen, you stay there till I tell you.'

We went to the edge of the jetty. Risman bent down. I tried to gather my thoughts. The mooring rope had not been attached to its post but lay loosely on the planking. Hence the movement of the raft. Risman and I reached down and each took hold of one of the ankles. I was still not wholly prepared to believe that the figure could be dead. The body slid clear of the underside of the raft, face down, although I knew immediately from the back of the vast bald head that it was Carson. It was as if I'd always known it must be him, as if it should have been obvious that this was going to happen, since clearly it had happened.

'Bloody hell, Mr Maxwell,' said Risman. 'What in fuck's name's been going on here?' He shook his head as if to clear it, then hauled the body ashore and turned it over on its back. 'Captain Carson?' he said. 'You're not bloody all right, sir, are you? What the hell have you been doing?' He shouted to Arnesen: 'Go and fetch Mr Gammon right away.' The boy hesitated. 'Tell him it's urgent and to get an ambulance over here. Understand? Go on, Private, run like fuck or I'll cut your balls off, supposing you've got any. Understood?' The boy set off at an unsteady run back across the field into the fog.

Risman turned to me. 'Why was it me you sent for, Mr Maxwell?'

'I suppose I thought you would know what to do.'

He nodded. 'Did you now? Don't see there's much we can do. We can't move him from here ourselves, of course.' He paced slowly about. 'Let's hope there's no other smokers like Arnesen lurking about in this fog.' He knelt down again and peered into the water. 'What in the name of God happened to you, you daft old bugger?' he said quietly. 'What the hell were you up to, fannying about out here?'

I moved a little further off so as not to hear him. I walked backwards and forwards over the bed of leaves. My mouth was dry. The grey fog hung between the birches. It was as if I had never been there before.

Nothing happened for some time. The trees dripped and Risman remained crouched by the body at the water's edge. At last Gammon came hurrying out of the fog into the wood, his gown flapping behind him.

The ambulance got as close to the lake as possible but the body had still to be carried through the silver birches to the edge of the field. The driver and his mate moved slowly and carefully through the fog with the corpse wrapped in a red blanket on the stretcher. There was no rush now. The others in attendance were Sergeant Risman, myself and Gammon, plus a police constable. Arnesen was being dealt with by the nurse, Mrs Carew.

'We shouldn't be moving the body, should we?' I said to no one in particular.

'We can't leave him lying there in public,' said Gammon, as if this were obvious.

We came out of the woods ahead of the stretcher party and then stood to one side like a ragged honour guard as the body was stowed in the ambulance. Carson's uniform cap had been placed on his chest. The blanket dripped lake-water on to the floor of the vehicle. We watched in silence. I blinked in disbelief: we were all acting as though what had taken place was entirely possible. Risman offered around a packet of Park Drive, which Gammon disapprovingly declined.

'I've ordered that the field be placed out of bounds,' Gammon said, as though daring anyone to defy him. 'Assembly is cancelled and the boys have been sent to their form rooms.'

'Do the boys know yet, any of them?' I asked.

'Bound to, Mr Maxwell,' said Risman. 'Like a pack of dogs. They can smell death like they can smell women.'

Gammon looked as if he was about to admonish Risman, but the Sergeant sniffed the air and scowled into the fog, which showed no signs of thinning. The story went that he had killed five German soldiers single-handedly with a Wilkinson dagger. Where death was concerned he had seniority here. I think he was looking for someone to kill, as if this were a battlefield.

'Why was Carson here by himself?' I asked. 'The exercise would have been over by yesterday lunchtime, wouldn't it?'

'That's a matter for the authorities,' said Gammon. 'There's no room for speculation, Maxwell.'

'The man's dead,' I said.

'I'm well aware of that,' said Gammon. 'I'm telling you that we have to act in a responsible manner. For example by not adding to the rumours that will already be spreading. It's a crisis for the school.'

'It's a crisis for Carson too.'

'It does you of all people no credit to make light of Captain Carson's death,' said Gammon. 'There's no excuse for showing off, but I will ascribe it to shock. Go and calm down. Sergeant Risman, would you escort Mr Maxwell?'

Another figure appeared in the wood, a small, weaselly man with thinning hair. He wore an overlarge sheepskin overcoat and a pork-pie hat. He looked as if he should be standing under a bookie's blackboard at the races.

'Thank you for coming, Smales,' said Gammon.

'Should the body have been moved?' I asked.

'In the case of an accident,' said Smales, looking me up and down. 'And who are you, sir?'

'This is Maxwell. History. He found the body,' said Gammon.

'That's not exactly true,' I said, but I was beginning to feel dazed.

'Off you go, Maxwell,' said Gammon. 'I'm sure the inspector will need to talk to you later.' Smales nodded without looking at me. 'So make sure you're available. Risman, escort Mr Maxwell to your office and wait for us And we may want to talk to you as well.' It felt as if I were being placed under arrest, but no words came with which to point this out.

As we drew level with the ambulance, Smales was speaking to the driver through the window of the vehicle. The ambulance pulled away, leaving tracks on the frosty grass at the edge of the Spion Kop pitch. It vanished into the fog that deadened the noise of its passage.

'Come on, Mr Maxwell,' Risman said. 'You need a bracer first before they question you. We've got a few minutes.' We made our way to his cubby-hole at the back of the Main Hall stage. I sat by the one-bar electric fire while he poured two glasses of rum.

'Is that policeman one of ours?' I asked.

'Smales G., 1942–47, early leaver. Inspector Smales to you and me.' Risman nodded and sucked his horse-like teeth. 'Redcap in Malaya during National Service. Known to some of my muckers in the Regulars. Nasty little bastard.' Though Risman had a talent for insult befitting his former rank, he was not given to personal comments of this kind. He took his cigarettes out again and offered me one. This time I refused. I was starting to feel sick.

'You don't seem very shocked about the death, Sergeant,' I said. The rum was making me dizzy.

'I'm not much for seeming, Mr Maxwell,' said Risman, in a manner that invited no further enquiry. 'You have to deal with these things, somehow, in my experience. Happened a lot in wartime and things just had to be got on with. There's always something useful that needs doing.' He drained his glass and offered me a refill, which I declined.

'I heard you served with Captain Carson.'

'That's correct, sir. Good officer in his way. And it's because of him that I'm working here. He put in a word.' Then Risman changed tack. 'What I don't understand is why he was down at the lake at all. The exercise was finished by three o'clock yesterday afternoon and everyone would have been off the grounds by four p.m. when it was getting dark. I was last to go, had a look round as Mr Renwick and the Captain requested. They left me to it, so the Captain must have come back. I didn't find any waifs and strays to report, no forgotten bits of kit. The raft was secured at the shore side. I was reading the paper back at home with Mrs Risman by five.'

'I'm sure you were,' I said.

Risman looked at me sharply.

'What I'm saying is,' he went on doggedly, 'why did he come back? There was no need.'

I had no reply. Did it matter if Carson felt like going for an evening walk? The woods in darkness didn't seem the most practical place to choose, and he didn't live exactly nearby. Risman seemed to collect himself and stood up.

'Well, as I said, Mr Maxwell, we'd just better get on with it, hadn't we? Mr Smales will be needing to talk to you.'

'I've got lessons.'

'Then I'll go and tell them to read a bloody book, sir. And a word to the wise: just watch out, OK? This is messy, so you don't want to get tangled up in it. Do things by the Queen's Regulations, that's best.'

'Messy.'

'Well, people don't die here every day, do they? The school will want it sorted out quick smart.' The phone rang and he rose to answer it. He listened a moment and said, 'Right. I'll send him over now, Mr Gammon.'

TWELVE

I made my way to Gammon's office. There were no boys about. But I could feel the place waiting.

I sat in the anteroom, anxiously observed by the school secretary-cum-nurse, the motherly Mrs Carew. She had made me a cup of tea which I couldn't drink. She offered me a Phensic which I declined. I looked out at the empty field. The fog was slow to clear. The place felt stone cold.

This was like hospital in reverse, I thought: the terrible news followed by the waiting. At length I was admitted to what Gammon now clearly regarded as his rightful domain. He sat behind the desk, under a time-darkened portrait of the founder, 'a man of liberal piety, a believer in human fellowship and the transforming power of the word', as Carson put it in *A Firm Foundation*. I sat directly in front, with Smales standing over by the window so I had to half turn to speak to him. It was an arrangement familiar from my own pupil days, one effective in interrogation.

The room was warm but Smales had kept his increasingly loathsome car coat on, and now he played with a set of keys as though he might leave at any minute, so that quite against reason I wished him to remain. The two men seemed disappointed in me, disapproving. The fact that the Chief Constable was also an old boy passed uninvited across my mind. I wondered if Smales and Gammon thought I had brought the death about by discovering it. For some reason the idea had already occurred to me. I wished Carson were here to assist me through the questioning. But he was dead, and if that was possible then so was anything else.

'Why don't you tell us what you saw?' Smales said. I wondered if Gammon had any business to be there, and whether

I should have a companion of my own, but I wasn't prepared to risk asking the question.

I explained how I had happened upon Carson's body. Gammon turned an expressionless gaze on me when I told the policeman that, as I quite often did (which was, in a sense, true), I had been getting some fresh air before school began.

'A fresh-air fiend,' said Smales, as if this were somehow a dubious tendency in an institution obsessed with taking and enforcing frequent exercise on the merest pretext.

'Not particularly, Inspector. But it helps to clear the head and prepare for the day's work.'

'Overdid things at the weekend, did we? Head needed clearing, I imagine.'

'Not especially.'

'Fresh air didn't clear Captain Carson's, did it? Sad to say.' Smales continued to scrutinize me as an interloper in the peaceable but distrustful kingdom where he was the law.

'Do you mind if I smoke?' I asked.

'Yes, I do mind,' said Gammon. 'It encourages the likes of that fool Arnesen to do the same.'

'I don't think he needs any punishment after what's happened,' I said.

'Stick to the matter in hand,' said Gammon.

'You don't live on that side of the school, over by the lake, though, do you?' Smales asked after a pause. I assumed he had already checked this with Gammon. 'You're from the other side, on Fernbank. I mean, you have to take the trouble to go down to the woods for a stroll.'

'I like the woods, and the lake,' I said. I prevented myself from adding that that was what they were there for, for enjoyment.

'Do you now? Why would that be?'

'I find they calm me down. At any rate they did until this morning.'

'Meet anyone interesting? Down in the woods, on your constitutional, while you were calming down?' I shook my head. 'Not Captain Carson? You didn't meet him on one of these tranquil outings of yours?'

'I never see anyone one at all. Well, except the groundsmen now and again.' Smales nodded and sniffed, dismissing this.

'You don't seem to have brought a briefcase with you on this walk. I assume you use one for your work.'

'It's at home. I planned to nip back to my flat and collect it,' I said. 'It's not far.'

'It seems a complicated arrangement, though. Having to go to and from like that.'

'I suppose it does. It hadn't occurred to me.'

'Can't have, can it?'

I wondered for a couple of bowel-melting seconds if Smales was really about to accuse me of somehow being connected with whatever had happened to Carson. But he just nodded and went on looking. Gammon stared too, outraged at some incoherent level.

After a while, Smales said, 'I understand you're Captain Carson's man.'

'He was my senior colleague and my mentor. He taught me when I was a pupil. He had a hand in my appointment.'

'A hand in it, you say. And you were on good terms.'

'I think so.'

'Not sure?'

'Then, yes, we were on good terms.'

'Anything worrying him that you'd care to tell us about?'

'No, but I wasn't his confidant.' *All in good time*, Carson had said, seeming to say nothing except that life would take its course.

'You were just his man.'

'I don't like the way you say that, Inspector.'

'I dare say. Why did you touch the body?'

'I don't know. I thought I had to do something. You seemed to think it was all right before. I suppose there was a slim chance Captain Carson might still have been alive.'

'So you made sure he wasn't.'

'Sergeant Risman was there with me. He helped.'

'I see. So it was the two of you. Taking the initiative.'

The bell rang for change of lessons. The hall outside began to fill with voices. Eventually, Smales rose and turned to Gammon.

'There may be more questions. We'll have to see what the post-mortem says.'

'A tragic accident,' said Gammon.

'Very likely,' Smales said, looking at me again.

'Captain Carson was a great teacher,' I said, as if this would change things.

'Oh, I know,' said Smales. 'Mr Gammon and I were in the same class. We know all about Captain Carson, believe me.'

'Is that it, then? Are you finished with me?'

'For the moment, Mr Maxwell. We know where to find you now, anyway. Until then, try and stay out of the woods, eh?'

'Maxwell will continue to make himself available,' said Gammon. 'Do you wish to be excused teaching for the rest of the day, Maxwell?' he asked. His tone indicated his view of this possibility. And the idea of going back to the empty flat was intolerable. What would I do there but think?

'No, thank you, Second Master. I think it would be better to get on with things. That's what the Captain would have done.' I could see that Gammon didn't like me allying myself with the dead man's authority. 'I'll go and get my stuff from home and come back. I've got a free, then the upper sixth.'

'Very well.' Gammon turned away to talk to Smales.

When I returned from the flat I found Maggie alone in the staffroom. She recognized that something was amiss.

'Should I go away again?' she asked. 'Is something wrong? I've only just got in.'

I turned back to the room. 'Where were you this morning?' I asked. 'I woke up and you were gone.'

'None of your business,' she said, producing lipstick and

a compact from her bag. She opened the compact and began to apply the lipstick, though her appearance was already immaculate. 'Well, what's got Gammon so excited? Who's that horrid little man sneaking about with him?' When I didn't reply, she asked, more quietly, 'Does somebody know?'

'I think perhaps. But that's not it. Gammon's companion is an Inspector Smales.'

'What we get up to is hardly a matter for the police, is it?' she said. I found myself wanting to laugh.

'It's Carson.'

'What about him? What's he done?'

'He's dead.'

'What? What do you mean, dead? He can't be. Dear God. When was this?' She turned pale. She put down the lipstick and continued to look into the compact mirror.

'Not sure,' I said, looking at the tremor in my hands. 'Sometime yesterday night, I think.'

'So we're in the clear, at least.' I couldn't quite believe she'd said this. 'How did you find out?' she asked.

I sat down across from her. She resumed work with the lipstick, not meeting my gaze.

'I discovered his body,' I said. 'I mean, there was a boy there too, Arnesen, who'd found him first, then I came along. Carson was floating in the lake.' I wanted her to put her arms round me, but that was impossible – doubly so because just then the bell rang for the resumption of lessons following the mid-morning break. 'Why didn't you wake me?' I asked.

'We can't speak now,' she said. She gathered her bag and her folders of work, shaking her head, and went out.

I went back to the window. Below me the quad began to fill up with boys, all of them scenting the air. School had not been cancelled for the day. To Gammon that would have been a defeat. Better to control and contain. It was madness, but no one at Blake's would be surprised at this approach. If there were casualties then routine would absorb the fact and move on.

I watched how, as Maggie passed through the crowd, it turned its collective gaze on her, as if its many eyes and minds were those of a single animal. She seemed not to notice. I found myself aroused by the juxtaposition of the flesh and death. Which just left the Devil. I thought: well, gentlemen, I have seen what you will never see – Mrs Rowan naked but for her nail-varnish, lying on a bed and smoking a cigarette. Then I wondered how I could be thinking about that, given the situation. If I went now I could be in for what remained of a double period with the upper sixth. The prospect resembled madness, but there seemed to be no alternative.

THIRTEEN

Most of the group were talking in a subdued way when I arrived, standing looking out across the field towards the woods and the lake. Arnesen was missing, presumably closeted with Gammon and Smales. Feldberg was making notes on whatever he was reading. The boys looked at me. What could I tell them? Nothing, for the moment. I had no instructions on the matter. We turned to Gladstone and the Irish Question, though nobody's heart was in it. As the lesson neared its end Rackham came in without knocking. He approached my desk.

'I need to speak to the boys, Mr Maxwell.' I nodded. He turned to the group. 'I have in my hand an announcement from the Acting Headmaster.' He brandished a sheet of paper. 'Many of you will have heard that there has been an unfortunate incident. There will be a special assembly after lunch, when further information may be given. Until then the field, the woods and the lake are strictly out of bounds. You will co-operate willingly with the school and other authorities.'

Feldberg raised his hand. I shook my head but Rackham spotted him.

'Did I not make myself clear?' he asked.

Feldberg did not look at him. Instead he spoke to me.

'Does this mean there will be no more European history, sir?' I glanced at Rackham, who smiled sourly, as though at the wit of this.

'There may be a temporary interruption,' I said. Now the group looked at one another. The rumours had been confirmed. 'You may go to the library during that period.' The bell rang. Rackham had been about to speak again but thought better of it and stalked from the room, still looking at Feldberg while the boy packed his books away. Rackham seemed to have undergone an elevation in rank in the light of the crisis. I thought 'crisis', then I thought 'death'.

The classroom emptied. The noise in the Main Hall beyond seemed louder than usual, the silence that followed the last door-slam more complete. It was as if the clock had stopped. Then I imagined the hands of the great clock over the dais in the Main Hall stirring and beginning to run backwards.

I blinked. Carson was still dead. It was as if one of the walls of the world had gone missing. The word 'accident' presented itself for inspection, in the guise of the only reasonable conclusion, given the circumstances and the setting and taking all in all. But it was a lie, of course, or I would not be writing this; and Carson was wrong about conspiracies.

The post-lunch assembly was brief. There had been a tragic accident in which Captain Carson had died, said Gammon. There was almost no audible reaction from the boys. By that stage most of them must have known anyway, and rumours of how and why Carson had died would have begun to circulate. The story element would be coming to the fore, as a way of fending off what the event might mean. But Carson had been admired, particularly by the older boys, and there was an atmosphere of subdued shock. Everyone, Gammon went on, was to conduct themselves as usual and to co-operate as and when required by the police (here he indicated Smales, who sat among the senior masters) and the school authorities, who were investigating. The woods and the lake were to remain out of bounds until further notice. The production of *Ruddigore* was postponed. I saw Topliss blink at this. Evidently he had not been consulted. Further arrangements would be announced in due course. The less people talked about this episode, the better, especially outside the school. Everyone knew how much Captain Carson had cared about Blake's, and so on. For a second I thought Gammon was about to add that careless talk cost lives, but he dismissed the assembly with an instruction to treat the afternoon's lessons as normal.

I did my best. The boys were by turns listless and excitable. The fog returned by three o'clock over empty fields and woods. 'Blake's,' Carson had written in *A Firm Foundation*, 'inculcated a profound loyalty among its pupils, one whose influence remained active long after they had moved on into the adult world.' Carson gave no indication of whether this was a good or a bad thing.

At the end of school I looked for Maggie in the art room and backstage in the Memorial Hall, but she was nowhere to be found. I needed someone to talk to, not so much in order that I could put words to what I'd seen by the lake as to be in ordinary human contact. In which case, why choose Maggie? Sympathy was not what she offered. So when I went home I rang Smallbone. His mother answered suspiciously. She had, inevitably, already heard about Carson via her numerous contacts.

'You don't feel safe in your own bed,' she said. I had to put a handkerchief in my mouth to prevent myself laughing at the idea of anyone wanting to get into bed with her. 'And of course this doesn't help with your situation, you being the Captain's protégé,' she added, disliking the foreign word but seeming to brighten a little at the prospect of my getting what she had always, according to Smallbone, considered my comeuppance for 'my filthy exploits'. 'It will all come out in the wash, mind you, one way or another.'

'Have to wait and see,' I said, speaking her language.

'Yes, Stephen Maxwell, I dare say you will.' With this she handed the phone to Smallbone.

'To Carson,' Smallbone said, raising a first pint in the Narwhal. It was Monday evening and quiet. We could hear the clack of the old men's dominoes from the bar. Carson was still dead.

'To Carson.'

I explained what I knew, and described the conversation with Risman and the interview with Gammon and Smales. Smales, it turned out, was, like many people, known to Smallbone's mother. Smallbone's impression was that Smales was a vindictive little wanker and thus to be avoided.

'And the reason you were there in the woods is one it would be unwise to reveal,' said Smallbone. 'Cherchez la femme and what have you. You need to break it off. Perhaps literally.'

'Shut up. I know. It's difficult.'

'Follow Smallbone's Rules for Romance. Find 'em', fuck 'em and forget 'em.'

'I'm sure any girl's mother would be proud to have you as a son-in-law. And her father would take you in the yard and brain you with a coal hammer.'

'I'm not the miscreant in this case, am I? Be practical is what I mean. Anyway, you won't be marrying the lady in question, will you?'

'You can be very literal minded.' We drank.

'D'you think Smales believed you about what you were doing there?' Smallbone asked.

'I don't think he believed a single word I said, up to and including my name.'

'You've got to stick to the story now. Otherwise, nasty complications.'

'Actually, Bone, it's Carson I'm mainly thinking about.'

'I'm not in a position to advise or help him, am I?' said Smallbone, rising on his stool and leaning across the bar to summon the barmaid for a refill. He waited until we'd been served before continuing. 'OK. But it must have been an accident.'

'Smales wants to blame someone.'

'He's a copper. He won't like untidiness. The world is untidy. Therefore he blames the world, i.e. you. I imagine he'll get over it.'

'The thing is, Carson recently asked me to be his executor.'

'Yes, well, that is indeed a thing, Maxwell. But why you?'

'He didn't say. Well, he said there was no one else. I didn't feel able to refuse the request, given who was asking.'

'No, I see that. Does Smales know?'

'Not yet. It just never occurred to me to mention it, in the middle of the whole business. It never crossed my mind. I was having trouble thinking clearly.'

'Smales will be certainly interested when he does find out. Especially since you didn't tell him when you had chance. Nasty.'

'I'd have to be an idiot to become Carson's executor and then do away with him,' I hissed.

'Well, obviously, but bear in mind that for Smales the world probably consists of two kinds of people. The first kind consists solely of Smales. The second is all the criminals and idiots.' We drank in silence for a while. 'But why are you talking about Carson being done away with?'

'I'm not. I mean, that's what Smales would think. According to you.'

'Leave me out of it. I make a point of not thinking anything.'

'But it is a coincidence, isn't it?' I said. 'He asks me to be his executor. Then he dies.'

'Was he ill?'

'He said not.'

'Eh, well, I dunno. Could have been depressed. Could have slipped. Just have to wait and see. But tell Smales about being the executor.'

Suddenly I felt sick. I went through into the Gents and splashed water on my face. The coffin-sized urinals looked immovably solid, and the green, wave-patterned tiling around the sink seemed frivolous, as if the death of Carson had not been made known here or was being ignored. I wetted my face again and then leaned on the sink, uncertain whether my legs would keep me upright.

There was a bang as Lurch came through the door. He

didn't look at me, but went to the urinal and began to micturate copiously, staring downwards at his handiwork. I went back into the bar. Now I wanted to laugh. Birth, death, copulation. Why did no one mention urination?

Smallbone had ordered me a brandy.

'I liked Carson too, you know,' he said. 'In case you thought I wasn't bothered. He was the best teacher I ever had. He knew I wasn't up to much but he never let on. He encouraged me. There's no one else there like him now and they won't find anyone like him, and they won't want to. It's fucking awful.' He paused, nodding several times. 'So, can we leave it at that? I don't think talking in this way really helps. Unless you're a woman, in which case it can be a life's work.'

'Thank you, Bone. And by the way, you're a monster. Lucky the girl who gets a ring on your finger.'

'I'm a realist,' said Smallbone. 'I know myself to be idle and lustful.'

We toasted Carson and called it a night. It was cold. The fog had gone and the sky was sharp with stars. The edges of the empty pavements glinted with frost. Whatever happened, I would never escape this place. I would keep turning a corner to find these streets there before me, populated by the dead.

At the railway line we stood on the footbridge while a goods train clanked underneath towards the marshalling yard. We seemed to have been doing this forever, in my case as if some sign would be delivered. As kids we'd loved standing in the plume of steam and ash. But the steam trains had gone now. As we parted at the foot of the steps Smallbone said, 'Keep it simple, Maxwell. It's probably not Smales you really need to worry about. Gammon won't need much excuse to get rid of you.'

'I thank you for this encouragement.'

'My pleasure, comrade. Mind how you go. See you on Friday, I suppose. Unless you're in jail, ho ho.'

I was exhausted but unable to sleep. I wrote up my diary in an untidy hand, struggled to concentrate on a book, then switched off the lamp and sat looking across the road at Blake's. Beyond the woods the tower of the Main Hall rose, spotlit from the roof below, the flag flying at half-mast. As I watched, the lights were turned off, leaving the world 'to darkness and to me', as I repeated aloud before trying once more to get some sleep. Some things are coincidences, Carson had said more than once in class. No, I thought, not this one.

FOURTEEN

The Coroner, an old boy himself, ordered a post-mortem, which reported at the inquest held a week later that it seemed that Carson had drowned, probably after hitting his head on the raft. He had been in the water for somewhere between eight and twelve hours, so that whatever befell him had taken place on Sunday evening after the cadets' exercise was complete. No theory was advanced as to why Carson had been in the water in the first place, but the Coroner observed that the explanation might be that Carson had lost his way in the dark and slipped into the water. The death certificate was issued releasing Carson's body for burial. Under the circumstances there was little else the court could do. There was no reason to suppose that the death was anything but a tragic accident. The inquest was adjourned.

This was not the end of the matter as far as Smales was concerned. The fact that I was Carson's executor was, as predicted, of considerable interest to him when he found out. He asked why I had not mentioned it in our meeting following the discovery of the body. I replied that it had not occurred to me to do so. It had not seemed important. He didn't like that. What I could not explain to his satisfaction was that the role of executor had never seemed credible to me, since surely it entailed a duty I would never be required to fulfil, because Carson had not been going to die. Smales liked that even less and, in line with his general approach, clearly supposed I was lying for some reason, though what exactly these lies concerned was not something he was inclined to share with me, or even, such was the weaselly mania I sensed in him, with himself. As Smallbone had suggested, Smales probably viewed everyone else as a liar until persuaded otherwise. We spoke several more times. Once he appeared on the doorstep on a Saturday morning as I was leaving the flat.

'There's something about you I don't like,' he said, worrying away at his set of keys. The elderly lady who lived next door went past with her shopping bag, clearly curious about this caller.

'I didn't know this was personal,' I said.

'I mean, I know your background and I know about your adventures chasing after fanny down south, but I can't see why you're back here now.'

'That's just the way it worked out. The opportunity arose. I needed a job. A job was offered.'

'And Captain Carson. Why did he pick you?'

'I've wondered about that myself.'

'Have you now, Sonny Jim?'

'There was no particular reason that I can think of. There were good reasons *not* to offer me the post. I'm as much in the dark as you, Inspector.' Smales folded the keys into his hand and came closer.

'I tell you what, you half-clever little bastard. You're a wrong 'un. Sooner or later I'll have you, if not for this then for some other thing, because one thing you are is fucking trouble, and I won't have trouble here, not in this city and especially not at Blake's.'

'Perhaps I should leave. Would you like me to go and work somewhere else?'

'You stay where I can fucking see you, sunshine.'

'Inspector, I might make an official complaint about all this. You're harassing me.'

Smales laughed. 'Yeah? Go on, then. See where that gets you. Strapped to the fucking steam pipes at North Dock nick if I've got anything to do with it.'

At school a day or two later I received a letter from Bundrick and Teale in the afternoon post. Carson had left a will. I was its sole beneficiary. If I would make an appointment the details would be explained to me.

I stood in the staffroom for several minutes, incapable of thought, then found a seat at the table and re-read the solicitor's elaborately matter-of-fact letter. Why me? Carson had been unmarried, with no living relatives, but was there really nobody else? A fever of transferred loneliness gripped my mind. Poor Carson. Had he been so alone? I was no candidate at all. This was too much – his hopes of me were too great. His position had damaged his judgement. I would let him down. Surely he must have known that. I was already doing so. It was wrong. It was a mistake. I would have to explain to some authority that this was beyond my capacities. No such authority suggested itself.

At the school there was an air of discreet relief that the funeral could take place. Something practical could be done. A terrible accident, everyone agreed. It just went to show. Now the matter needed to be closed, for the good of Blake's, as Captain Carson himself would, of course, have wished. That was the general tone.

I contacted the funeral directors and made arrangements. In Carson's honour a half-holiday was declared for the funeral and an instruction was issued that all sixth formers and members of the cadets should attend the service at St Michael's, the nearby parish church.

The ceremony took place on a bright, cold Wednesday afternoon. The trees in the graveyard were bare. Black-suited sixth-form boys and cadets in full uniform obediently filled the rear pews of the church. Carson had been alone in the world, and it fell to the school to do him appropriate honour. The boys, I knew, were inclined to view him with a blend of awe, mockery and affection – the highest accolade they had to offer. I served as one of the pallbearers, with Gammon and Rackham, Sergeant Risman and a couple of the senior cadets.

There were only a handful of adults present who were not members of staff – a couple of academics from the History Department at the university, some elderly ladies, the odd military-looking type and others unidentifiable.

In his coffin Carson patiently endured the toneless nasality of Gammon, who reduced the Twenty-third Psalm to the status of an announcement cancelling house rugby fixtures because of measles. Later, Rackham delivered, to my surprise quite beautifully, an extract from Ecclesiastes, including 'Of the making of many books there is no end; and much study is a weariness to the flesh'. The vicar eulogized Carson's life of study and service and declared him a soldier, a scholar and a Christian gentleman, and we sang 'Onward Christian Soldiers'. For a moment I thought I would lose control. We carried the coffin out into the graveyard for its interment – one of the last on that crowded site. Carson had been a lifelong parishioner and had earned the privilege.

The funeral refreshments were served in the hotel across the road. A chilly, damp-smelling function room looking onto the park had been laid out with sandwiches and sherry. I served a couple of elderly ladies from Carson's evening courses at the university with drinks and sandwiches, exchanged pleasantries with the vicar, who had somewhere else he needed to be, and watched the staff and the history sixth form milling about. It was tempting to get completely plastered, but I seemed to be a representative of something, so I held off.

Again there was that air of relief. This is common on such occasions, but here it was as if, since Carson's death was assumed to be accidental, all was well and the school unharmed. The great man had been given a ceremonious send-off but clearly he was now to be thought of as having decisively left the premises. The truth of that was hardly disputable, but the underlying tone was of discreet haste, if not of any want of affection for the deceased. Things had to be got on with – a view Carson himself would have endorsed. I felt slightly disconnected from what had happened. It was like postponing a nightmare. Carson was dead. The word fell flat in my mind.

I saw Arnesen among a group of boys surrounding Maggie. I hadn't spoken to her since the day Carson's death had been discovered. She was making the boys laugh, and they looked round to see if this was a punishable offence, given the occasion, but the volume of the whole party was rising as the sherry went down. Feldberg stood to one side. Arnesen seemed to have recovered from the shock of the discovery.

'Are you all right, Arnesen?' I asked. He remembered what we were there for and looked slightly guilty.

'Thank you, sir.'

I moved him slightly aside from the others. Smales appeared in the doorway but I ignored him and he did not approach. He was talking to Gammon.

'There was something I wanted to ask you. I know you will have been asked before, but I'm curious.'

'Sir?' He became wary.

'What were you doing by the lake at that time of the morning?'

'Just having a smoke, sir. Do you have to report me?' I shook my head. He relaxed. 'After we found him, Dr Carson, in the lake, no one asked me anything about being there. They just – the detective and Mr Gammon – asked if I was all right. I was a bit surprised. I thought I'd be expelled. My dad would have done his nut.'

'Well, let's say no more about it.'

But Arnesen needed to complete the memory.

'Then my mother came and gave me a lift home. And we've hardly said anything about it since.'

'It's probably for the best.' Imagine saying that nowadays, during the permanent triumph of emotional incontinence. I nodded a dismissal, but before Arnesen could go Maggie came and joined us.

'I hope you're not belabouring poor Arnesen, Mr Maxwell,' she said, with a note of affable challenge. 'It's bad enough for him having to come along today, without you making it worse. I'm not sure it's really suitable for the boys.'

'It's all right, Mrs Rowan,' said Arnesen. 'We all wanted to come, to show our respect for the Captain.'

'Good boy. Your friends are still over there,' she said, and waited until he disappeared. 'When can we get out of here?'

'I have to stay, I'm afraid.'

'Christ. I feared as much.' She finished her drink, took another from the table and moved away to join a group of staff wives. They studied the expensive and faintly Parisian cut of her black suit, and clearly viewed her as an exotic and improper creature, but would never say so openly. I shuddered to think what their coffee mornings were like.

At a loss, I went to the window and looked out across the park in the direction of Carson's house, a large Victorian semi-detached that stood on the far side of the park pond, its dark frontage partly masked by the bare black chestnut trees. It was as if an element of the prospect, a dimension of the real, had been irreplaceably removed, and some part of my own feelings arrested with it. The house stood there like a prison, waiting for me to enter and be immured. That would be my duty. As I was testing this egotistical hypothesis to see if it might hurt, Feldberg approached.

'I wanted to offer my condolences, and those of my father, sir. I believe you and Captain Carson were friends as well as colleagues.'

'Thank you, Feldberg. That's very considerate of you. We shall all miss him a good deal.' The boy lingered. 'And don't worry. I know what Captain Carson had in mind for you. We're still on course for that, as he would have wished.' Feldberg nodded his thanks and I turned back to the window.

As Feldberg's reflection vanished from the dimming glass, Gammon appeared, accompanied by two others I did not recognize. Give me a minute, I thought, tempted to seem not to have noticed, but I turned to meet them.

Gammon, whose black suit showed a remarkable quantity of dandruff, given his complete baldness, was flanked on one side by someone I immediately knew to be a retired senior officer, a tall, severe, cadaverous man of sixty-odd, and on the other by a younger civilian whom I took to be a civil servant of some kind. He introduced them as Colonel Dennison and Mr Hamer, two Old Blakeans.

'Maxwell will be looking after History for the moment, and he of course knew Captain Carson. He will do all he can to assist you gentlemen, I'm sure.' Smales chose this moment to approach, but Gammon steered him away and left me with the two strangers in the bay window. It felt like being surrounded.

'Following on from my old friend James Carson, eh?' said the old soldier, taking my unsatisfactory measure. 'Knew him at school, and in Germany in 'forty-five, of course. Sound fellow. A good soldier and, so I've been told, a fine teacher.'

'It's true. He was an inspiring teacher.'

'Good, good. And you're the heir apparent.' The Colonel sipped his sherry and grimaced. The other man gazed out of the window.

'Well, not exactly, sir,' I replied. The Colonel looked through me and nodded as if confirming something to himself. 'I hope I shall do my best until a permanent appointment is made.'

'Of course you will. A challenge to rise to. A proving ground with live firing, one might say. Important that the CCF is maintained, of course. Never know when they'll be needed. Things are not all that handy on the Rhine at the moment. As I'm sure you know. The Czechoslovakia business, of course.'

'Not my field, Colonel, I'm afraid, the cadets. I look after the library.'

'Do you now? Of course. Well, Carson would certainly

have understood the imperatives. Saw a lot after Luneberg Heath.' The old soldier looked at his pale companion and nodded.

'Carson claimed to be something of a scholar, of course,' said Hamer, shifting his gaze from the park and examining me curiously as if uncertain what language I spoke. His eyes, like his hair, were very pale and he seemed not to blink. He gave off an air of sustained patience in the face of tedious provocation. He irritated me.

'Captain – Dr – Carson wrote a number of essays,' I said. 'And a couple of books when he was younger, about the Civil War in these parts. He had some reputation in the field.'

'Civil War, eh? Well, that's another worry, eh?' said the Colonel. 'Unions and so on.' I tried to look as if I was giving consideration to this view. He grimaced again, more fiercely. I wondered if he had gout.

'A productive life, then,' said Hamer. 'Hard work and routine. Never married?'

'I don't believe so, no,' I said, not following this line of enquiry.

'So there was nothing else, though – no novels, journals, that sort of thing.' These were surely different sorts of things, I thought, but did not point it out.

'Not that I'm aware of. Did he teach you?'

I became aware of Miss Ormond, librarian of the city's Philosophical Society, approaching and then turning aside again with a discreet shake of her head.

Hamer did not answer the question. 'As you say, the deceased had a reputation,' he said, looking at his watch. 'I just thought he might have done more.'

'Teaching made his life very busy. And fulfilled.'

'Amen to that,' said the Colonel, extending his hand. Hamer looked away.

'What's your interest?' I asked. 'Are you an academic? A publisher?'

'Jack of all trades, is Hamer,' said the Colonel. 'Time we

were gone. Anyway, good to pay our respects to an old comrade in arms.'

'You're our point of contact, then,' said Hamer. 'If anything arises.' He began to move away. 'If you come across anything, Gammon can put you in touch.'

'Keep it up, won't you, Maxwell? There's a good chap. Know we can rely on you, yes?' said the Colonel. The pair retired through the crowd. My gaze followed them until I noticed Maggie looking at me across the room, all the while speaking to her dowdy companions. I gave what I hoped was a distracted smile. The burden of the Colonel's expectations seemed both onerous and mysterious. As for Hamer, I couldn't place him at all. I looked for Miss Ormond, but she too had gone. I went out into the car park for a cigarette. Smales was leaning against his car. Now he came forward and produced a lighter. I thanked him and made to step away, but he came with me. I turned, wondering what he had in store now.

'Friends of yours?' he said. He nodded to indicate the Colonel, who was climbing stiffly into his Bentley. Hamer had stopped to look over at us. Now he got into the passenger seat.

'I've never seen them before, Mr Smales. I'm not even sure who they are.'

'You don't want to be, Mr Maxwell. You don't want them taking an interest.'

'I'm sorry?' The Colonel waved as the Bentley passed. Hamer looked straight ahead.

'Anything you do know, anything crops up, come to me. Give those two the go-by. Don't tell Gammon. Tell me.' He gave me a card with his number on it.

'Who are they? I don't understand.' He looked at me as if baffled by my obtuseness.

'Well, that's for the best. Take my word for it.' Smales went back to his car and drove off. I made my way back into the function room. The crowd was discreetly thinning. Before long it would be dark.

FIFTEEN

'I thought I should go mad myself,' Maggie said. She tried stretching out on the settee in my flat but then found she could not be still. She went round the room examining books and pictures. 'All those women after the funeral. It's as if they were the ones who were dead, never mind poor old Carson.'

'Poor old Carson?' I wanted to say that he did not provide the object for anyone's pity. But I could see Maggie was in a volatile state. Things could go either way – frost or fire, it was hard to anticipate. I felt exhausted and hollowed out, and to my amazement I wished she would leave me alone, so that I could lie on the bed and read and not think, until with luck I might eventually go to sleep. It had been a mistake to give in to her curiosity about my flat. She swallowed the last of her brandy and poured a second. I found myself wanting to ask about her brother.

'You know what I mean,' she said, with a touch of impatience. 'It's terrible, Carson's death, but that goes without saying, doesn't it? Can't be other than grim.' She went and looked out of the window. 'And of course he loomed large, a character. Not that it could save him when his number came up. There but for the grace of God.' She seemed half-distracted. I joined her where she stood. The woods opposite were almost invisible. I drew the curtains and she turned back to the room. 'Do want me to stay?' she asked.

'Of course I do. But it might be unwise.'

'And we don't want that.'

I shrugged, helpless. It was strange to be here, fully and formally clothed. She had kicked off her high heels. 'There's nobody downstairs, is there? No one will know.'

'Best to be cautious.'

'This is supposed to be an affair, isn't it? Reckless abandon. Or so I'd been led to believe.'

'You've changed your tune.'

'Well, maybe I have. That's my business. Aren't you going to take advantage? Death makes people randy, don't you find?'

'I haven't much experience to judge by.' I had meant to put aside the matter of Carson's will until tomorrow, when the funeral would be done and I was to visit the solicitors. 'I have something to do tomorrow. It's weighing rather heavily on my mind.'

'And do you want to tell me about it?'

'Not really.' But I couldn't help it. 'Carson's made me his heir.'

'Blimey.'

'Quite. Blimey.'

'How long have you known?'

'A little while.' I wanted to tell her my suspicions, but something made me hesitate.

'You've been playing that close to your chest.' She gave a conspiratorial grin.

'I don't know what to make of it.'

'Hay, I should think.' She poured more brandy into her glass. 'Anyway . . .'

'It just seems an odd coincidence.'

'What does?'

I didn't seem to have her full attention.

'Carson makes me his executor. Then he dies.'

She laughed. 'Well, at least he was prepared. Not everyone is.'

'What I mean is, well, I don't know, but it seems wrong.'

'It was sudden, Stephen, so that's hardly surprising. Like being struck by lightning.'

'But why was he there by the lake?' I asked.

Maggie shook her head. 'Was there some reason he shouldn't have been?'

'I don't know. I don't know why, but I feel as though there's something missing. Something I haven't grasped.'

'Perhaps you're trying to rewrite history, in order for it to make sense. That would be understandable.' She put her hand on mine.

'You're being unusually reasonable, Maggie.'

'Oh, well, serves me right for trying.'

'Sorry. As you can see, I'm in a tangle. A lot to take in.'

'Yes, I see that.'

'So it might not be the time for you to stay.'

She was drunker than I'd realized. Her expression was suddenly sharp with challenge.

'What? You think I'm in this get-up for nothing?'

I could simply have given in. She was as desirable as always. But I felt stubborn.

'I'm in mourning for a friend, let's not forget.'

'Are you now? That's very proper and commendable. Then what you need is a good fuck. Or at any rate I do.' Her tone was acid. Softening a little, she went on: 'Even Carson himself wasn't always utterly averse to pleasure, I understand.'

'What on earth does that mean?'

'Nothing. Nothing. Come with me.' She took my hand and led me out of the room and along the passageway to the door of the flat. She opened it and we went out on to the dark landing. 'Here. I want to do it here.'

It was late now and I was rather drunk myself, which must be why I decided to chance it. 'This is too much of a risk, for both of us,' I said. 'Isn't it?'

'Undeniably,' said Maggie. She had put on one of my shirts and was looking through my record collection.

'I may have a lot more work now,' I said. 'In the short term, at any rate. I won't have much time to spare.'

'I imagine so. You make me sound like a hobby.'

Isn't that what I am? I almost said it. I waited for her to

turn round, but she carried on looking through the box of records. 'What about the new chap?' Gammon had acquired someone to fill in for the rest of term and then until Easter, while I took on Carson's role. Gammon was by no means happy with this arrangement, but it was all that was practically possible at short notice.

'I haven't met him yet.'

'You must face the burden of command,' she said, smiling as at last she turned to face me. She was beautiful, I thought, but she was not a woman who should be here with me doing this. Her life ought to be elsewhere. It would be better for her to end our involvement now. There was her husband. But mainly there was me and my vanishing future. She would understand. She knew the score.

'"Command" sounds a bit strong,' I replied.

She shrugged and took a drink. 'Try it. You might enjoy it. It might be making of you, as the sainted Captain would say.'

'Maggie, in view of what's happened I think we need to call it a day.'

'Do you now?'

'Well, you say yourself it's too risky.'

'I do. It is. But now I don't think that matters.'

'I'm sorry, Maggie, but I can't agree.'

'For God's sake, Stephen. Relax. You sound like a bloody committee.'

'I'm just trying to be sensible for once. Before I make a complete mess of things again.'

'Well, don't strain yourself, Stephen. And it's a bit late for second thoughts. The deed is done.'

'I'm serious, Maggie.'

'And I don't want to stop now. As I hoped I'd just made clear.'

'Well, I'm sorry. Really. It's great, being with you. But this will be for the best. You can see that. It's not that I'm not fond of you. If things were different, then, yes, why not?' Was I really saying this drivel? 'But the situation's clear to both of us.'

'You're "fond of me" are you? You're not listening,' she said. She came towards me. I made to embrace her and she slapped me across the face. I sat down in shock on the settee. She leaned down and struck me again. Her eyes were bright with fury. The third time I caught hold of her arm.

'Maggie, stop this. It's crazy!'

'You're not listening,' she said. 'I told you I don't want to stop. I want to go on until I decide otherwise. I'm enjoying myself just as we are. So you just do as you're fucking told until further notice.' She climbed on top of me, straddling me, and took my chin in her hand. 'Now you're wondering whether you can afford to hit me. Whether you dare. Whether your conscience will permit it.'

'I don't want to hurt you, Maggie. I've no intention of hitting you.' She slapped me again. It was as if she actually wanted me to strike her. Such a thing had never occurred to me.

'Believe me, Stephen, it would make no difference if you did,' she said. 'I'll tell you when we've finished. Anyway, darling, you don't really want to stop. Think what you'd be missing.' She made to kiss me and I turned my head away. She let herself relax against me and nuzzled my neck. Whatever I thought, my body was taking Maggie's side of the argument. Her perfumed warmth was like a royal summons.

'You see,' she said. 'That's more like it.'

'Maggie, it's not possible. There's no future in it. It won't work.'

'Nothing works, Stephen. That's no reason to stop doing it. Don't make me tell Gammon that you made advances to me. He'd like that.'

'You're crazy.'

'Call it what you like. Anyway, stopping won't bring Carson back, will it?'

I woke early. The room still bore traces of Kensitas and Maggie's perfume. This was enough to cause fresh arousal, but while I washed and shaved and sorted out my briefcase

I wondered how I might extricate myself from this liaison as common sense and self-preservation dictated. I supposed desire would have to wear off first. Perhaps she would tire of me. For the time being I seemed to be her creature.

At school that day she completely ignored me, as though I had rejected her instead of eventually doing her bidding.

SIXTEEN

Among my post the next morning was a note from Miss Ormond asking me to call in at the Philosophical Society library at my earliest convenience. I felt a pang of guilt. My subscription must be in need of renewal. I hadn't been inside the place for months. Probably the funeral hadn't been the proper place to mention it. Anyway, she'd seen that I was occupied.

After school I walked into town, needing the fresh air despite the drizzle. I went first to the offices of Bundrick and Teale, in a discreet Georgian square at the centre of the legal district. This, I thought, was where the money lived.

Mr Bundrick, like a small and pink and silvery rabbit, a prewar Old Blakean wearing the Old Blakeans' vile green-and-maroon tie, received me in his office overlooking the dark square.

'This was completely unexpected,' I said.

'Yes?' said Mr Bundrick, taking off his glasses.

'I had no idea.'

'No, of course. Yet you are the executor, Mr Maxwell.'

'Captain Carson asked me to agree to that role a little while ago. I signed a document which you sent me.'

'Quite so. I have it here.' He put the glasses back on and opened the file in front of him. I needed someone competent to talk to about my unfitness for the task and the inheritance, but Mr Bundrick would not be lending a sympathetic ear. He would not be lending anything. He would send in his account in due course. I had the feeling he knew something about me to my disadvantage. Everyone else seemed to.

'The estate must now go to probate,' he said. 'Until that is settled there can be no transfer of property or funds, of course.' He paused.

'Of course.'

'And that might take some time.'

'Believe me, Mr Bundrick, I am in no hurry to acquire anything.' But I would say that, wouldn't I? 'I did not invite this role.' He did not look up.

'However, in order to proceed to probate, a valuation must be made.'

'What is there that requires valuation?'

'The house on Victoria Park and its contents. Books, mainly, it appears. Captain Carson, as you know, liked to think of himself as a scholar.' Bundrick gave a little smile. There was the philistine Blakean touch. 'As executor you may arrange for these matters to be dealt with. Or you may wish to instruct us to act in due course.'

'I'll deal with it.' I waited.

'Are there any questions, Mr Maxwell?' Mr Bundrick looked up at last. I wondered if I'd slept with his daughter and forgotten. Probably not, if she looked like him.

'No, it seems clear enough. I'll get Samuel Feldberg in to examine the library, and contact an estate agent.'

'Feldberg's. As you wish. For the house valuation, we would recommend this firm. We often have dealings.' Bundrick placed a card on the blotter between us. I took it. *Vlaminck Property Management. House Clearances*. 'No questions?'

'Am I missing something?'

'There is the other, ah, aspect of the estate.'

'Sorry, but I'm not sure what you're referring to.' Bundrick could not imagine anyone failing to enquire about this.

'There are savings and investments.'

'Well, thank you.' The struggle continued.

'I have laid out the figures for you.' He passed me a foolscap envelope and sat back. I placed it in my briefcase. He sat forward. Any kind of revenge would do me. 'You may wish to examine them.'

'I need hardly remind you that nothing can happen until the inquest is concluded,' I said, stealing his line. He blinked.

'If we can be of any further help.' He took a set of keys from a drawer and passed them over. 'You'll need access, though nothing can be removed at present.'

'I'll let you know if I need you. Did you know Captain Carson?'

'Our contacts were professional.' Bundrick had successfully absented himself from his own body. 'I was before his time at Blake's.'

Down in the hallway, observed by a curious office-girl, I examined the figures. Enough to live on. Plenty. Not enough to warrant murder, surely.

Five minutes later I entered the premises of the Philosophical Society, a fine but smoke-darkened Victorian Gothic building hidden away behind the railway station. Navigating the broad curve of the stone staircase to the main floor by underpowered lamplight, I remembered almost with physical pain how good it had been to come here as a sixth former and simply get on with some work. There never seemed to be time now.

The issue desk, partly masking the shadowy interior where scattered readers sat in islands of light, resembled a section of the bar at a gin-palace. It looked immutable, like a necessity in the world. Miss Ormond herself was manning the desk. She was an elegant dark-haired figure in her late forties. I had always found her combination of style and severity both intimidating and exciting. Summoning a junior colleague, apparently by telepathy, to take her place, she asked me to accompany her to the office. Tall stacks of books awaiting rebinding or repair covered a large table, beyond which lay the broad, lamp-lit calm of her desk and its pristine blotter. She directed me to a chair and closed the door.

She watched while I wrote a cheque for my subscription.

I knew the library was in difficulties, like all its kind, survivors of near-forgotten liberal enlightenment. I rose to go.

'There is something else I need to discuss with you, Mr Maxwell.' She had the faintest Scots accent.

I tried to remember if I had any overdue books and prepared to throw myself on her improbable mercy. She read my mind.

'It's not your borrowings I am concerned with this evening,' she said with a smile. 'May I offer you a sherry?' Baffled, I accepted. She indicated a chair and produced a bottle and glasses from a tall cupboard.

'To Captain Carson,' she said, raising her glass.

'Of course. To Captain Carson.' We drank. 'Did you know him well? I'm sorry not to have had chance to speak to you at the funeral.'

'I could see you were occupied. Yes, I did know James pretty well. And he was a very regular user of the library, a greatly valued committee member at one stage.'

'I've been struck by the affection with which so many people seem to have regarded him. As you may know, he was my teacher, my mentor. It was Captain Carson who brought me back to Blake's.'

She nodded and silence fell. Now I saw no way of proceeding. At last Miss Ormond put down her glass.

'James – Captain Carson – asked me to look after something for him, a package. This was a few months ago. He asked me to keep it in the safe here.' She indicated the small steel door set into the wall behind her. 'There were two items, a letter addressed to me, and another, more substantial envelope without an addressee.' She paused. 'I was only to open the letter in the event of his death. That seemed a little melodramatic, which was unlike him. But he said he felt as though his time was limited. Naturally I wondered if he was ill, though he seemed fit enough. But James was not a man one could simply ask about such matters. He would tell you what he wanted you to know. However – well, we know what happened, unfortunately, so I opened the letter intended for me. In it he instructed me to give you the unaddressed package.' She rose, opened the safe and took out a large manila envelope. She placed it on the table between us. 'So I think I have performed my duty, Stephen.'

'Thank you for letting me know about this.'

'You seem shocked, Stephen,' she said.

'May I confide in you?'

'If you wish.'

'Not long before his death Captain Carson asked me to be his executor. At his death I found that I was the inheritor of his estate. The policeman who investigated the Captain's death clearly feels I am a suspicious character.'

'That would be the delightful Inspector Smales?'

'Indeed. And now you pass on to me a communication of some kind, which for some reason the Captain felt it would be best to lodge here privately in case he died. So, yes, Miss Ormond, I am a bit shocked. Stunned. I wasn't expecting anything. Least of all the death. Everything else seems nonsensical, somehow.' Neither of us was sure how to go on from here. Eventually, I said, 'I had no idea that anyone could lodge material here for collection.' I felt obscurely as if I were somehow on trial.

'No, indeed,' said Miss Ormond. 'Well, strictly speaking, they can't now, not officially. It used to be relatively commonplace, of course, in the war, when people's addresses changed. We – the library – stayed open throughout, although some of the Board wanted to move the stock to York, from which bourn I daresay it would never have returned once our colleagues up there had laid hands on it. Librarians can be covetous, I find. We have a deep basement, quite adequate to our needs.'

Was Miss Ormond herself actually nervous? Her appearance betrayed nothing, though her gaze returned several times to the envelope. I put out a hand and picked it up. As she had said, it had no markings. I placed it in my briefcase and wondered what to do next.

'This is a bit odd, Miss Ormond.' I waited. She considered me a little longer.

'Another sherry?'

'By all means.' I sat back.

'James and I worked together at the end of the war,' she at last went on. 'I was a translator with the Intelligence Corps in Germany. It's all a long time ago.'

'Somehow at Blake's it doesn't seem like that.'

'No, well, there are a great many memories about the place, aren't there? To some people the war seems to have been the only thing that ever really happened. I admit I feel that way myself from time to time.' She paused, then went on. 'I think our shared wartime experience is the particular reason he entrusted the material to me, although of course I have no way of knowing what it consists of.'

'But you think this package is in some way connected to those days?'

'As I say, I have no way of knowing. And I would not enquire. But I can think of no other reason why he made such a secret of it.'

'What did he do? I know he was in Germany. What did you do?'

'I can't talk about that. I'm sure you understand. You should know,' she said, hurrying a little, as if I might interrupt or persist, 'that he thought very highly of you, Stephen. At one time he remarked that you were like a son he never had.'

No, I thought. Don't say that.

'That would be a great deal to try to live up to,' I said.

'But perhaps you *will* try?'

'I promise to do my best.'

'I said I can't talk about our wartime work, and I won't change my mind about that. But something happened to James in Germany. He was changed, somehow, never quite the same. A little distant in comparison with before.'

'Did you quarrel?'

'Goodness, no, nothing like that.'

'Something he saw or came across, you think. The concentration camps.'

'He saw Belsen, I know that. But this was a little later. The fighting was over and he was still himself, though clearly much troubled by what he had seen, and then one day he wasn't quite the same.'

'A delayed shock, perhaps?'

'Possibly.' But her tone showed she thought otherwise.

'And you think this material might be connected.'

'I couldn't say, obviously. But perhaps. I've always wondered what it was that happened.'

Miss Ormond took a couple of deep breaths and then sat back as if her role was complete. I fished the envelope out of my briefcase again and stared at its blank manila face. But Miss Ormond hadn't finished.

'I should tell you that someone came in and was asking about James this afternoon. About any effects he might have left here.'

'I see.'

'I'm afraid I didn't like him. He was official. Once you've met them you can spot them. He tried to browbeat one of the girls on the desk. She called me and I explained that we were unable to offer him assistance since he was not a member.'

'You make it sound a bit sinister.' She nodded. 'What was he called?' She took a cigarette from an open packet on the desk. I lit it and one of my own for myself.

'He said his name was Hamer. I saw him and that military-looking gentleman speaking to you at the funeral.'

'Oh, him and the Colonel.' I should have guessed. 'He was asking me about things that Carson had written, as it happens. Clearly he wasn't there as a mourner.' There was a pause, into which we both looked.

'People like us aren't murdered, are they, Mr Maxwell?' she said. 'Not as a general rule.'

'I hope not. Why?'

'And James's death was a terrible accident.'

I considered how much I could tell her, and decided on caution for the moment. 'That seems to be the conclusion. As far as I know, there's no evidence to the contrary. People, colleagues, boys, everyone respected Captain Carson. You saw the turnout for the funeral. He was fair-minded. He was generous with his time and his help – I can testify to that. The boys thought a lot of him, though by and large they wouldn't say so, of course. Why would anyone wish him harm?'

She nodded. 'Blake's likes to keep it in the family.'

'Do you think it could have been something else? Have you considered that it might have been suicide? It seems very unlikely, I know.'

'I can't imagine the conditions in which he would give in to such an impulse,' she said. 'But then people are alone, aren't they, in the end? Aren't we? James was very fond of quoting Conrad: "We live, as we dream, alone." I sometimes thought that it cheered him up to think so. He was a lonely man, I think, more so as time went on.' She took another sip of her sherry. 'Oh, I don't know what I think,' she said with quiet fierceness. 'This is peacetime, isn't it?'

'Not at Blake's, it isn't.'

She smiled and went on. 'One of the ways you can spot people like our visitor Mr Hamer is that there's a bit of suppressed melodrama about them. Something a bit obvious, once you've seen it.'

'In what way?'

'I remember some of the security types from the war. He was one of their tribe. He was perfectly anonymous, as if he'd studied what he should be like. He behaved as if you'd been wasting his time before he'd ever met you.'

'Was he by himself when he called?'

'Apparently. He didn't bring the Colonel. I sent him on his way. He wasn't happy, but there wasn't much he could do, so he mustered his manners and left.'

'Security?'

'I could be wrong, but I think so. To be avoided.'

'Well, perhaps that's the end of it.' I remembered Smales's change of approach in the car park at the funeral.

'Let's hope so,' Miss Ormond said. 'I'd better burn the note, anyway.'

'Really?'

'It was what James requested.' So I sat and witnessed her burning the letter in the metal waste-bin, then poking the ashes to dust with a ruler. I didn't mention that a library seemed an odd place to be setting things on fire. I put the envelope back in my briefcase.

'Would you infer from our friend Hamer's visit that some covert authority might also have an interest in the material?'

'Perhaps.'

'And that therefore it would be wiser not to enquire into the subject.' Miss Ormond nodded. 'Perhaps even to let you put it back in your safe and forget all about it?'

'That might be a sensible thing to do,' she conceded.

'And what would you do?' I asked.

'I don't know. The right thing, I hope.'

'Which might mean placing friendship before other claims to loyalty.'

'It might.' After a time, she said, 'You can hand me back the envelope if you wish. It can go back in the safe. No one need know.'

'I would know it was there, and I'd be bound to wonder. I think it's out of the box now. I'd better have a look at it. May I return it, if necessary?'

She nodded.

I rose to go. Miss Ormond put out a hand to detain me.

'Would you like me to open it here?' I asked.

'Best not. But will you allow me to refer to another matter?' Miss Ormond asked. 'It is connected, in a sense, I think, though I'm not sure how.'

'Of course.'

She considered for a few moments. 'I find it very difficult to say this, so I had better just spit it out. You should perhaps be careful of your acquaintanceships.'

'I'm sorry.' I found myself bristling. 'I don't follow.'

'Forgive me, Stephen, but I can see you know what I'm referring to.' She smiled, as though in sympathy.

'And is this general knowledge?'

'I think not; not at the moment. James was aware of it.'

'I see. He didn't mention it. And how are you involved?' I asked, aware of a harsher note in my voice.

'James thought highly of you. He was concerned. That is the extent of my interest. I am not trying to interfere, Stephen.'

'I think you can leave it with me,' I replied. 'Discretion will be best for everyone.'

She shook her head. 'Mine is not in question, I hope.'

'I'm sorry, Miss Ormond. The situation is complicated and difficult. I would rather not say any more.'

'Nor would I ask you to do so. You're not the first person to be in such a position. And the point is that in this instance you can't have the sister without the brother.'

'They don't seem to have much to do with each other,' I said.

'As far as you know.'

'Do you know better? I don't want to intrude, but I'm not sure what you're hinting at.'

'I sound like a gossip, Stephen. I hope I'm not. I hate gossip. I hope you feel that I'm speaking out of concern for you, as James would have wished. There is something I want to tell you, but if you would rather, I can stop.'

'I think you'd better go on.'

'I remember Charles Rackham from a long time ago. We were at university at the same time. In those days he was a historian, as was I. He seemed likely to be a star in his generation. But he had some rather foolish political involvements.'

'One of Mosley's lot?'

'Rather worse than that, I would say. He was with Joyce for a time after Joyce broke with Mosley.'

William Joyce, aka Lord Haw-Haw, hanged for treason in 1946. That was some heavyweight foolishness. 'You seem to have followed Rackham with some attention,' I said.

'It was hard not to. He tended to occupy centre stage even when he invited ostracism. Of course, he wasn't alone in his view of things. A great many apparently respectable people, some of them quite influential, rather approved of fascism back then. John Amery was hanged shortly after Joyce. His father was a cabinet minister. So was his brother. People tend to forget. Or they affect to do so when the times are unpropitious.'

'And Rackham's sister?'

'Maggie, yes. A great beauty. Still is. You know she was an art student during the war? When the Slade had moved to Oxford. Pretty good, I think. But dangerous too, in her own way.'

I bit my tongue.

'Maggie decided she liked the look of my young man, so she took him, and then discarded him.'

'I'm sorry.'

'Oh, it was all a long time ago. Love and war and all that. I recovered, as you do. I'm simply offering an illustration of a tendency that seems to have continued. A free spirit, some would call her.'

'I'm not under any illusions,' I said.

'I hope not. I can tell you know very little about her,' said Miss Ormond.

'She doesn't invite personal questions. She's impatient of all that.' I am using ignorance as defence, I thought. I'm shallow, shallow as the lid of a biscuit tin.

'Better for her to be a moving target, perhaps. And there's the husband, of course. Poor man. Him I don't know.'

'He's ill.'

'Yes. I wonder why she chose him. Time passing, perhaps.

We're none of us getting any younger, of course.' Miss Ormond gathered herself again. 'Maggie tried farming for some years after the war, like a lot of the old BUF people.'

'I don't think Maggie's political.'

'Possibly, possibly not. Not in any normal sense. But anyway, she was growing turnips somewhere in the Midlands for a time. Staffordshire, if I remember correctly. In contact with the soil and so on. Or rather, her boyfriends were. She wouldn't have actually dirtied her hands, not in that way. She was painting. She did have promise at that. And then she was out of sight for some time. I'd more or less forgotten her. Until she reappeared as Mrs Rowan, wife of the Headmaster.'

'You seem to know a great deal.'

'James kept an eye on her brother. He talked about him as a great talent gone to waste. Charles Rackham was one of James's protégés before the war, of course.'

'That's news to me.'

'Oh, you'd never have guessed. After the war they were simply colleagues, living on terms of professional civility.' She smiled. 'But as you know yourself, Blake's can accommodate all sorts of things. That's why people come back.'

'The Captain never mentioned it.'

'No need, I dare say. A long time ago, like all the rest of it. James encouraged Charles Rackham. Then it seems there was a parting of the ways, over politics. I didn't ask for details. Blake's and discretion, eh? We can be pretty discreet at St Clare's too.'

'Well, it's food for thought, Miss Ormond.'

'You need to do more than think, Stephen. You would be wiser to extricate yourself and leave Blake's as soon as possible. Wherever that woman follows there will be trouble sooner rather than later.'

'And what about the envelope you've given me?'

'I said it would be wise for you to leave. I didn't say it would be easy. I'm sorry not to be of more help.'

SEVENTEEN

A few moments later I looked out into the rainy evening street through the glass panel in the doors of the library. There was no one about. I considered returning the envelope to Miss Ormond and walking away, but I couldn't see myself getting past the end of the street before I had to come back. I went into the phone booth in the foyer and rang Smallbone. When he answered I could hear the television in the background and his mother asking who was calling at this time.

'I'm busy,' he said.

'Meet me in the Judge and Jury.'

'I suppose I might.' I heard him tell his mother he'd do the washing up later on. Then a door was closed at his end of the line.

'Half an hour. Bring a bag.'

'What is this?'

'You'll like it, Bone. Wait and see.'

I went to find Mr Jacks, the caretaker. He was seated in his smoke-filled storeroom under the stairs, reading the evening paper as if nothing had changed in half a century. I asked if he would mind letting me out by the rear entrance since my car was parked behind the building and the rain was worsening. Mr Jacks, whom I had known since prep school, observed affably that a bit of rain shouldn't bother a big lad like me. I agreed that it was a pathetic performance, that I didn't know I was born and that it was a disgrace that National Service had been abolished. In exchange for this age-old conversation I got what I wanted.

There was little traffic on this side of the library and the rain came down steadily. I stood in the doorway for a minute, thinking my precautions absurd, but equally feeling disinclined to abandon them. I made my way through one of the city's several areas of decayed gentility, through a small park and past the huge white elephant of the Theatre Royal, where a revival of *The Ghost Train* was being staged. I cut back southwards down the cobbled back lanes past the rear of the brewery and towards the smoke-encrusted law courts. As far as I could tell, no one followed.

The Judge and Jury was an ancient pub somehow crammed in between solicitors' offices. It was famous for not admitting women to the bar-room. Even on a wet weeknight it did a reasonable trade, with a mixture of lingering law clerks and beehived, miniskirted secretaries crammed into its many impossible dim brown spaces with their caricatures of dead lawyers and cases full of ancient papery-looking trout and pike. I'd just sat down in the smoke room when Smallbone arrived, shaking his umbrella and brandishing a shopping bag. He got himself a pint and came over.

'So what is it, then? Wanderlust? The lure of the sinful city. We never come in here. Typists, eh? They have nimble fingers. They can do it without looking, so I've heard.' As if by magic, two girls turned to scrutinize Smallbone. One whispered to the other.

'Now, then, ladies. You'll have to take turns,' he said. They roared with laughter and turned away.

'You'd be surprised how often it works,' he said.

'Shut up, Bone. I've got something I want to give you.'

'You're being creepy, comrade. What is this, *The Avengers*?'

'I just need you to hang on to it for me.'

'Is it a mucky book? Did you obtain it postally? Am I implicated in your filthy escapade?'

'I'm serious,' I said. 'I'm in a bit of an odd situation, I think.'

'And now you want to drag me into it with you. Mr Dillon, my leg hurts. Is this to do with Carson? If it is, I don't want to know. I told you to keep it simple.'

'I'll explain when I see you next. But now you've got to

finish your pint and get back in your van and go home.' I handed him the envelope. He looked at it doubtfully.

'It's not very impressive, is it? What are you going to do now?'

'I'm stopping for another.'

'This is barmy, Maxwell.'

'You may be right, Bone, but please just do it. I'll explain later.'

He swallowed his pint in one, bowed deeply to the ladies and left, shaking his head, with the envelope in his bag.

I waited a few minutes. Rather than retrace my steps, I used the other exit via a covered alleyway to bring me out near the marketplace. Cold was coming up the alleys off the river. I went and stood in the doorway of a fish shop. After a few minutes, a bus came. On the upper deck a drunk in a cowboy hat was singing Marty Robbins's 'Devil Woman' to a female companion who refused to look at him. I got off on the far side of Victoria Park and walked along a disused railway line until it joined the tracks near the Narwhal. There was no one much about. The rain had eased and the dark pavement shone in the streetlights. Back on Fernbank I approached the house along the far side of the street, in the darkness under the dripping trees where people parked their cars. The whole place was in darkness. I was the only resident. The ground floor and the attic were both to let. I wondered idly about buying the place if I could raise the deposit, which Carson's will seemed likely to enable me to do. You had to start somewhere. Would ownership mitigate the loneliness of occupation? But then all this might be academic. I might be gone at any moment into the wide blue yonder of the unemployable.

I stood in the hallway, listening for a moment before going upstairs. My flat seemed perfectly undisturbed, but I sat for a while in the dark, looking down into the rainy street, which likewise maintained its habitual uneventfulness. The fact that nothing was happening seemed to indicate that something might, without warning or reason. I took out Smales's card. He had warned me about Hamer and the Colonel. They were, he had implied, a worse kind of trouble than him. Perhaps, but that in itself hardly recommended him as a confidant, given his previous attitude. The only person who could advise me properly was dead. Loneliness overtook me again.

I drew the curtains and went to bed. I lay reading until the small hours. It was like living during an enormous pause.

PART THREE

EIGHTEEN

I had hoped, for the time being, to commit myself to a programme of intensive routine, so that boredom, celibacy and fear would be mitigated by the sense of a working life's ordinary tasks being completed: admin, teaching, preparation, marking, the odd staff meeting, overseeing detentions, refereeing a house rugby match made almost unplayable by fog – much to the boys' amusement. I contacted an estate agent and arranged for them to view Carson's house. Samuel Feldberg agreed to come and look at the books. I made no contact with Maggie. But my hopes were not to be fulfilled.

The atmosphere in the school had been marginally subdued by the funeral, but as we know boys are savage and in most cases resilient creatures. The interest of many of them was now absorbed by the prospect of the mock election. Usually this would have been Carson's project, part of the civic education he tried to maintain. Characteristically, he had made thorough preparations well in advance, and had briefed me about the assistance he would require me to provide. When I spoke to Gammon about the subject now, he made it clear that I was free to continue, that it would be a shame if the tradition were not maintained, but that no else could be spared to help me. I was thus placed in what became a familiar institutional position, being at once obliged to do something while made to feel a both a nuisance and an anticipated failure for doing so.

I called a meeting to identify prospective candidates. A notice was read out in assembly that interested parties were to gather in the History bookroom at lunchtime. When I arrived, a dozen or so sixth formers were waiting in the corridor outside, Feldberg among them. He was there to support the Labour candidate, an amiable classicist called Dent, whose communist father had beggared himself to get his son into Blake's. In the Conservative cause, Culshaw the boy corporal turned up in his cadet uniform.

'This isn't a khaki election, Culshaw,' I said. The others laughed but Culshaw did not understand the reference.

'I just think we need to show where we stand, sir,' he replied with dignity.

'Fair enough. Who's the Liberal?' There was no Liberal. 'Very well,' I said, 'under electoral law I nominate Staveley. Seconded?' Dent's men sniggered and raised their hands.

'But, sir, I'm a Conservative,' said the outraged Staveley.

'You'll hardly notice the difference,' I said.

The door opened and Rackham came in, accompanied by a boy called Steerman, a linguist taking Oxbridge entrance, a Rackham protégé, and by Arnesen. Both boys wore cadet uniform.

'Apologies for lateness, Mr Maxwell,' said Rackham.

'How can we help you, Mr Rackham?' I asked.

'I think we have another candidate wanting to enter the lists.' Steerman, sallow and bespectacled, wore a faint smirk. 'Cometh the hour and so on.'

'I see. Well, Steerman? Arnesen? Who are you meant to be? We've got the main parties. If you'd come a minute earlier one of you could have been the Liberal.'

'As far I'm concerned he's welcome to it,' said Staveley.

'The British Patriot Party, sir,' said Steerman. Rackham's timing had been deliberate. I could hardly oppose him in front of the boys.

'Fascists,' said Dent. 'Is that allowed?'

'That's a very harsh word,' said Rackham.

'But what are their policies?' Dent, his father's son, pursued. Steerman glanced at Rackham, as though for permission.

'Stop immigration. Repatriate immigrants. Seek immediate entry to Europe. Pursue a programme of national spiritual regeneration. And support Ulster against the Fenians. In other words, be patriots.'

'Enoch,' said Arnesen. 'He's got the right idea.'

'Fascism dressed up,' said Dent. 'We need immigrants.'

'No we don't,' said Culshaw. 'We'll do very well on our own.'

'You've never done anything on your own,' said Feldberg. 'That's the trouble. You always get someone else to do it for you, don't you?' Arnesen bristled at this. Rackham smiled. They were doing his work for him.

'What's it got to do with you?' sneered Culshaw.

'I'm a member of my party,' said Feldberg. 'I imagine your daddy looks after that for you.' Dent looked at his comrade with alarm. There was poison in the air now. It was not a rehearsal.

'That's enough, the pair of you,' I said. 'We're supposed to be learning about democracy.'

'Perhaps we are,' said Rackham, blandly.

'You can't let Steerman stand, Mr Maxwell,' said Dent, which was exactly what I was thinking.

'To exclude him would be undemocratic,' said Rackham. 'In any case, the senior staff have raised no objection.' Dent opened his mouth and thought better of it. He looked at me as if I might intervene. He knew his cause was lost. I doubted whether the senior staff were even aware of the matter, but I was not sufficiently sure to call Rackham's bluff.

'Leave it with me, gentlemen,' I said. 'I'll inform you of developments. Dates for the hustings and so on.' I opened the door and indicated that the boys should leave. Rackham nodded at the still-smirking Steerman, and remained, leaning on a radiator.

'Well,' he said. 'Well, now.'

'I don't know what to say.'

'Well, quite.'

'You put the boy up to this?' I asked.

'He's eager for experience.'

'I bet he is. And what about Gammon?'

Rackham shook his head and laughed.

'It's a bit late now to go running to him, isn't it? And really, when you think about it, and think about Blake's, would Gammon find the BPP's views so very eccentric? Anyway, it's your show. You're the anointed successor to Captain Carson.' He smiled as though he was untouchable.

'What do you get out of this, Rackham?'

'What? I also serve, of course. Like you. We all have our parts to play here.'

'You're not like me.' I wanted to shove his amused look down his throat. 'I could go to Gammon now.'

'And if you did, and if Gammon took your side, the story would be all over the school in five minutes. And if there's one thing we as a staff do' – he was quoting Gammon now, imitating that faintly effeminate West Yorkshire accent – 'it is to maintain a united front. Look around you, Maxwell. All across the city the schools are in uproar and chaos because they've gone comprehensive. The university's a nest of Trotskyists and worse. People can't cope. Blake's has to set an example, be a beacon. Otherwise the centre cannot hold. Steerman is speaking for a great many people. Even the dockers agree with Enoch Powell. Perhaps the red-brown convergence is upon us. It's very stimulating for the boys.' Rackham nodded as if agreeing with himself. His eyes were bright with amused energy.

'You're being very irresponsible,' I said.

Rackham laughed at this. 'Really? Well, so be it.' He made his way to the door, then turned and said. 'If you're in doubt, ask yourself what Carson would have done. How would the Goethe of the bookroom have responded?'

'You're betraying him, though, aren't you? Using Steerman as a puppet for some reason. Why? What did Carson ever do to you?'

'Betrayal? That's a very complicated idea. And, as I indicated during the meeting, the mock election needs to reflect the politics of the world beyond Blake's. Or else what does it mean? A democratic charade.' It was as if a brilliant, spiteful child, unaltered and renouncing none of its claims, had, accompanied Rackham into adulthood.

'What are you doing with Shirley?' I asked.

'Whatever it might be, it's none of your business. Anyway, I should think you've got your hands full as it is. Things could become very difficult for you here if you're not careful. Don't rock the boat.'

With that, Rackham was gone. Carson would not have allowed the situation to arise in the first place, I thought. But supposing it had? Posthumous advice was not forthcoming. The distempered bookroom looked grubby and tired in his absence. I must get it tidied up and have it redecorated, always supposing I survived at Blake's past the end of term.

A moment or two later the bell rang and the corridor filled with noise. I opened the door. There was a crowd of boys outside. Those at the front stepped back as I appeared. They'd been examining a piece of cartridge paper pinned to the door. There was a careful poster paint image of three chevrons – black, red, black – and the phrase: BPP: SOON. What was I supposed to do? Tear it down? The boys stared, expectantly. I told them to get to their lessons. Then, when they had gone, I tore it down. By the end of school half a dozen more had been posted.

NINETEEN

On Friday evening, relieved to escape the noise of battle, I went to the Narwhal as usual. The place was unusually quiet. I sat reading the paper over a pint. The real by-election was approaching and the paper's editorial line seemed to be that it was a matter of local pride that the government's tiny parliamentary majority made this an event of national importance, one comparable to the refusal of the city to admit the King during the Civil War. The fact the city had done this, I thought sourly, would be largely unknown to the *Chronicle* readership – and likely to remain so, since they were more interested in prices at the fish dock, in rugby league and items for sale under five pounds. With such unworthy thoughts I sought to deflect my sour anger from myself. Allingham's candidacy was barely mentioned.

Claes and Lurch appeared over in the Coffin Bar, followed by a handful of nondescript acolytes. Claes resumed his monologue and unfolded a poster. More in hope than in expectation he showed it to Stan, who held it up critically. There was a murky portrait photograph of General Allingham in uniform and the BPP slogan: 'SOON'. Stan shook his head and handed it back. He wandered through to where I sat.

'We don't put up political posters of any kind,' he said. He lit a Woodbine. 'I hear you're having an election of your own up the road, Mr Maxwell.'

'I'm afraid we are, Stan.'

'Is that a good idea? An election now?'

'It's meant to be educational, to give the boys an experience of being citizens.'

'If you say so. And you've got the BPP standing? The General's lot?' He nodded back at Claes and his sullen entourage.

'Not me personally, but yes.'

'You do know what they are?'

'I think so, Stan.'

He considered me for a minute. 'I was there, you know, in 1945,' he said. When they opened that camp. You know the one. We had to bury them in pits.'

'Yes, I've seen the films.'

'Films don't smell.'

'I'm not sure I follow.'

'Oh, aye, I'm sure you do. Not something to play at, Mr Maxwell. Sure you want them standing in your mock election?'

'It's not up to me, Stan.'

'That's the trouble, isn't it? The question of responsibility.'

'What I've got is responsibility without power,' I said. 'It would be easier if it was the other way on.'

He nodded and finished his cigarette. 'Well, we'd all like that. Good job we can't have it.'

Lurch was silently holding up his empty pint glass. The model of impassive courtesy, Stan went through and served him.

Shirley appeared. Claes bought her a Snowball, his own preferred drink. She smiled across the space between us and her companions glanced at me without acknowledgement. There was no sign of Rackham this evening. In any case, as he had so recently informed me, his spare time activities could be no concern of mine.

After a while Smallbone turned up. He ordered a brown ale.

'So, then, Chief, what's it about?' he asked. 'Is there anything I should know, about this mysterious package? I took it to Binns but they've got rid of the X-ray machine in the shoe department. Why wasn't I told? We live among barbarians.'

'Do you mind talking a bit more quietly? I hope you're keeping the item under lock and key.'

'It's in the safe with the Belgian rarities.'

'Very apt. Take it to the cafe in the arcade tomorrow lunchtime. And don't say any more about it now.'

'OK,' he said, doubtfully. 'You're serious about this business, aren't you?'

'I think so.'

'What's in the envelope?'

'I don't know and if I did I couldn't tell you.'

'Remember what I said. And I don't want any trouble either.'

'I'm trying to avoid it myself, Bone, believe it or not.'

He finished his drink. 'D'you want to go down the town, then?' he said. 'There's bound to be some spare lying about, hoping against hope that two eligible gentlemen of means will turn up to lead them into bad ways.'

'Not tonight.' I couldn't help laughing. 'I'm knackered and there's too much to do.'

'Well. I'll just have to have your portion as well, then.' Bone nodded, finished his drink and went off in pursuit of fleshly pleasures, rubbing his hands in a Sid James manner. I admired his staying power and his undented optimism. As he left by the street door, Shirley came in from the bar.

'Got a light, mister?' she asked.

'For you, Shirley, always. You look nice.'

She smiled and did a twirl and climbed on to the stool next to me. She was stoned and finding it all terribly amusing. Beneath the dark fur coat I remembered her finding at a jumble sale years before she was wearing a stylish, rather short red halter-neck dress, as though she'd been expecting to go on somewhere else this evening. I caught Stan's eye and he brought her a fresh Snowball and a pint for me.

'That's very thoughtful, Stephen. They do say you're a gentleman. But I never see you except now and again in the shop, so I can't confirm it for myself. You never come round like you used to.'

'You're not at your mother's any more, are you?' I asked.

'I don't know where you live now. Anyway, you don't seem lonely. With your pals over there, I mean.'

'Are you jealous, Stevie? Jealous of Mr Rackham?'

'Cripplingly.' I smiled. 'I just don't know what to do with myself.'

'He's a gentleman too, of course.'

'Yes, I'm afraid he is.'

'Then you could fight a duel. If you're that keen on me. I could watch from a high tower and let me hair down for the victor to climb up.' She shook her head. 'But you're not that keen, are you? It's OK, though.'

'Where is the gentlemanly Mr Rackham tonight?'

'Dunno.' She shrugged. 'We don't live in each other's pockets.' This was Shirley's version of being at someone's beck and call, immured in the moated grange of her books and her sewing until someone got in touch. It had been the same when she was going out with me. People would always take advantage of her.

'Like that, is it?' I said.

She rolled her eyes. 'Well, you know what to do if you want things to change,' she said. 'You could show me a bit of initiative.'

'We're past all that, aren't we?'

'Speak for yourself.' I doubted if she would remember this untypical vehemence tomorrow. We sat in silence for a bit. She finished her drink too quickly. 'I was sorry about your friend,' she said.

'I beg your pardon?'

'Captain Carson. I was sad to hear what happened to him.'

'What did happen?'

'Eh? How d'you mean? Are you taking the piss? He died. It was very sad.'

'Yes, it was. It was a shock.'

'Accident. Misadventure. It makes you think.'

I did not reply.

'I mean,' she went on, 'it could happen to any of us. You. Me.'

'Best not to waste time, then, any of us.'

'That's what I meant before. No one's going to die wishing they'd had more celibacy.'

'I imagine celibacy has its points.'

'Oh, you're hopeless, Stevie.'

'You're not alone in thinking that.' We sat in silence for a while.

'Of course you were a bit special to Captain Carson,' she said.

'He taught me a lot.'

'So now I suppose – don't get me wrong – it's sort of dead men's shoes for you.'

'That's one way of putting it.'

'Now I've gone and hurt you. I never meant to.'

'No, no.'

'You were always a sensitive boy underneath. My mam used to say that. Sorry – I'm just a bit out of it. Can you get us another drink? Brandy and Babycham.'

I did as she asked. Next door Claes and Lurch were leaving. They didn't look over at us. Shirley made as if to call out to them but changed her mind. She leaned against me and kissed my ear. I moved her gently away.

'What have you been taking, Shirley?'

'Too many googoos, that's for sure. Something for the weekend, eh?'

'You'll do yourself a mischief.'

'Aye, I know. Or somebody will. I'm reading *Opium and the Romantic Imagination*. It's dead good. Have you read it? You should. There's imaginary prisons and all sorts. Have you tried opium? They say it comes in off the boats sometimes down the east docks, but it's scarce. I've never seen it. Rarer than rubies.'

'No, I haven't tried it. And you don't want to be taking stuff like that. You know what it leads to.'

'OK, sir.' She grinned. 'Try anything, me. I mean, I prefer reading but you need a break sometimes.'

'Your friends have gone, Shirley. You shouldn't be in here on your own.'

'I'm not on me own, though, am I? You're keeping me company like a proper schoolteacher gentleman.'

'I ought to get off home. I've got a lot on.'

'You can come back to mine if you want. I've got some nice draw and some Mandies.'

'Best not, Shirley.'

'It's Friday bloody night, Stevie. You've got to have some fun. You're a long time in the coffin, as me mam likes to say. She should know. Her house is like one.' Shirley's attention kept drifting.

'Since Captain Carson died there's been a lot to do,' I said, 'looking after History, with a temporary replacement to deal with too.'

'Big boy now.'

'It's about time. Don't you agree?'

'Taking over from Der Führer.' She gave a heavy smoker's cackle.

'That's not funny.'

'Yeah, sorry, Stevie. Something your friend Mr Rackham said. Daft.' She lit a cigarette. 'I'm just a bit ratty cos you don't fancy me any more.'

'But you've got a boyfriend, haven't you?'

'Might have. Suppose.'

'Well, I obviously don't want to tread on his toes.'

She smirked and shrugged, and stroked the back of my hand with a finger. 'Did Captain Carson leave you anything?' she asked.

'What?'

'You know. Carson. I thought he might have left you a toucan of his esteem.' She burst out laughing. 'A little bird told me.'

'Which little bird was that?'

'I forget. There's always loads of people coming in and out of the shop.'

'Loads of fascists.'

'Well, yeah, there's them. And there's the wankers.'

'So was this little bird a fascist or a wanker?'

'Hard to tell, Stephen. They all look the same after a bit.'

So, I thought, Maggie had let the information slip. I wasn't surprised. She seemed to have run out of discretion lately. It wouldn't mean anything to her.

'So what did he leave you?' she asked.

'The odd book. A few thousand books in fact.'

'Stands to reason.' Her attention wandered again. 'Nothing wrong with books. The bright book of life and that. We could take them off your hands. Claes could, I mean.'

'I'm not sure your wankers would find them of interest.'

'You never know. People are into all sorts.'

'Thanks for the thought. Anyway, I've got Feldberg's coming to do the valuation.'

'Oh, I see.' She grinned. 'Feldberg's, eh? Too good for the likes of us, then. Doesn't stop you coming into Claes's shop and poking about. Slumming, are we?'

'I don't like you working at Vlaminck's, Shirley. It's a dead end.'

'It suits me, Stephen. Better than some office. Or the fish dock. Or the fucking Elastoplast factory. It's a bookshop – it's perfect. For the time being.' I wondered if she had any other idea of time in mind, for instance the time when she would no longer be young. She nudged me and said in a fruity whisper, 'I wouldn't mind being a kept woman, though. In a flat, in me negligee and nylons, smoking French tabs and drinking Pernod. Silk sheets. View of the park. What would you think about that? Probably not on your wages, eh? Patched elbows and mince for dinner.' I couldn't help but laugh. She grew serious again. 'Anyway, it's none of your business really what I do or who does it to me. You can't have it both ways. At least Charles has got a few bob.'

'They're not good people,' I said. 'Claes and his chums.'

She shrugged. 'You don't know them.'

I didn't want to criticize Rackham to her directly. It was a matter of self-interest. 'I think some of them are fascists,' I said.

'Some of your boys at Blake's probably say the same about you.'

'I'm serious, Shirley.'

'Course you're serious. You're a man, aren't you? I'm just some daft bint off the estate.'

'I didn't mean it like that.'

'But you should talk to Claes. He's dead interesting when he gets going about Europe and the Holy Roman Empire.'

'They'll drag you down,' I said.

'Where from, exactly? Mount Olympus? Look at me. What am I?' She blinked, suddenly tearful as the drink and the drugs met up. Stan appeared, towel and glass in hand, and shook his head. The other bar was doing a roaring trade now.

TWENTY

'Come on, Shirley. Let's get you home,' I said. I helped her climb off the stool. For a moment her balance on her stilettos was uncertain. It felt as if she must have lost weight. I guided her to the door. When we got outside there was frost in the air. She hung on to my arm.

'My mam said you were a gentleman. Lovely manners and nice hands.'

'And what does your mam think of Mr Rackham?'

'He hasn't been round for his tea yet.'

'You do surprise me. He'll need to be spiritually prepared.'

'He's a poet, you know. So he's dead spiritual.'

We crossed the main road and entered the maze of terraces along the curve of the railway. Within a hundred yards we could have been back in the 1950s, cutting through empty cobbled tenfoots, skirting bombsites and dim corner shops. After a few minutes we came to the edge of a slum area. Shirley stopped outside a shut-down pub on a corner. 'This is it. I'm upstairs.'

'Shirley, for God's sake, you can't live here.'

'Why not? We can't all live on Fernbank or in Vicky Park. I get it rent free. Claes owns the place.'

'In exchange for what?' I asked. She shrugged and searched her bag for her keys. She dropped them and I picked them up. I opened the door for her and made to hand the keys back.

'Are you coming in? Go on.'

'All right.' I wasn't sure she'd manage the stairs. 'You'd better show me round now I'm here.' Shirley switched on the light to show a bare staircase and walls painted an ancient brown, as if poverty had arrived at its true colour. There was something frightening in the bareness. From the landing I glimpsed two rooms piled with overflow stock from Claes's shop – great stacks of pulp novels, as though boredom and waiting had assumed physical form. The stock had found its way on to the landing passage, neat stacks of *War Picture Library* and *Commando Comics* alongside American men's magazines waiting to go back into grimy circulation, giving off their sweet headachy smell. We went up another staircase to the attic. Shirley unlocked the door.

'So this is the nerve centre,' she said, switching on a lamp. The place was a bedsit with a sloping ceiling and a dormer window. Off to the side were a tiny kitchen and bathroom. It smelled of patchouli and tobacco and the damp that the city kept in wait for the unwary and the poor. One wall was taken up with books, carefully ordered – the home of a librarian manqué. A table took up the space at the window. On it stood Shirley's familiar electric sewing machine. There was an armchair and a double bed. It all looked like somewhere someone had ended up, though she'd made cheerful curtains and put up posters of Billie Holiday and Eartha Kitt.

'Oh, Shirley,' I said, 'this won't do.'

'I'm a bohemian, me,' she said. 'I live for art. Only I don't do art.' She put the fur coat on a hanger behind the door. The coat fell down and I replaced it.

'You could still go to college. There's still time.'

'Well, I could. But I don't think I will. Or after, maybe. I dunno. Have to think about it. Music, let's have some music.' She fiddled with an old Dansette and Juliette Gréco started singing 'Autumn Leaves'.

'Don't leave it too long.'

'That's what me mam says. Only not about college. About getting married. Having kids. Settling down, being normal. Well, I'm not normal, am I? Anyone can see that.'

'Most people do get married eventually, I suppose. You never know. Don't you want kids?'

'I dunno. Have to see. Me mam had her eye on you. She thinks you should have been the one. Cos of your nice hands.'

She cackled and it turned into a cough. I sat in the narrow armchair.

'That would have been a very bad idea. I would have made you unhappy. You know that. Anyway, I don't think marriage is for me.'

'I'm just telling you what she said, Stevie. I know the score.'

'Well, it's always good to see you, and now I know where you are, but I'd better get going soon, really.'

'Have a fookin drink, man.'

'Best not.'

'Just the one. Can't let a lady drink alone. Be a gentleman.'

'I'm trying to, Shirley.'

'It shows,' she said with sudden bitterness.

'Go on, then. Just the one.' She went into the kitchen and came back with a bottle of port and a couple of tumblers. She poured the drinks, then lay across the high bed, facing me, and started rolling a joint. The activity seemed to give her a temporary focus.

'You'll be sick,' I said. She shrugged and completed her work with minute care. Even the joints she made had a feminine elegance. They could have been sold commercially. We sipped at the vile port. She lit the joint and began coughing again.

'You say Claes owns this place?' I asked.

'He's got several other houses. Some over in the east as well.' As if the east of the city were another continent, an ocean rather than a bus ride away. She offered me the joint. I shook my head. 'It's good draw, Stevie. Shame to miss it. Where was I? Well, there's some properties that he rents for flats and bedsits, some he uses for storage. He's got an old stables as well with a big yard. You'd never know it was there, but it's only round the corner from this place.'

'And Claes, with his property empire in every corner of our city, is your benefactor. He's doing this' – I gestured at the room – 'out of the goodness of his heart.' I pictured Claes's pale, unlined, ageless face, where he sat enthroned among his trash, or standing beside his superannuated armoured car. 'Aren't you a lucky girl?'

'He's all right. You don't know him. At least he's helped me. More than I can say for some people.'

'Or you could stand on your own feet. Get a proper job.'

'What, like you? Yeah, yeah. Heard it all before.'

'He's a fascist. I know that,' I said.

'Why d'you keep saying that? What does it mean?'

'What do you think it means, Shirley? Come off it. You've heard of Hitler.'

'History is written by the victors,' she said.

'Is that what Claes says?'

'It's more complicated than – than, you know.'

'Than what?' I didn't know whether to shout at her or laugh.

'Not everything's the way it seems. Who's in control? That's what you have to ask. Behind the scenes.'

'Enlighten me, Shirley.'

'Why don't you ask your Mr Feldberg?'

'What on earth are you talking about?' I was shouting now.

'Those who have eyes to see will see.'

'Stop it, Shirley. Where's all this rubbish come from? You're an intelligent girl.'

'Am I?' She snorted. 'Right. If you say so, Mister Head of History. Thank you.'

'Why are you doing this?'

'Don't want to argue about it now, Stevie. As I said, it's complicated. Anyway, look. Have some of this draw.'

'No, you're all right. I'd best be getting off.'

'Look, we don't want to fall out, do we? Don't go yet.'

She got up and poured more drink. I sipped again at the sweet, grubby-tasting port.

'Old women drink this stuff,' I said.

'Got to think ahead. A girl can't go on drinking Babycham forever.'

'I mean it. I'm worried about you, Shirley.'

'No need.' Her voice blurred again. She stubbed out the joint, set about rolling another, then gave up and lay on her side. 'No need. Anyway, what you gonna do, save me?'

'What about Rackham?' I asked.

'Dark horse, that one.' She sniggered.

'Don't tell him I've been here.'

'No, I don't want to make him jealous. He can be very masterful.' She nodded and grinned.

'So you are together.'

'Suppose so, on and off. He's busy.'

'I bet he is. He's too old, as well.'

'I have to disagree with you there, Stevie. He's full of fookin beans, I can assure you of that.'

'And what do him and Claes get up to?'

'Grand strategy.'

'No, seriously.'

'They are serious. They play war games. They've got this attic in one of the other houses laid out like High Command. And they stage war games. They're re-fighting the Battle of Kursk at the moment to make sure the Germans win.'

'And that's it?'

She shrugged.

'Have to ask them, if you're interested.'

I got up to leave.

'I was a good fuck, wasn't I, Stevie?' I nodded, ashamed for the pair of us in that room. 'Then why won't you fuck me now? Cause you can, you know.' She reached out and took my hand.

'You don't know what you're saying, Shirley. You need to get some sleep.'

'I just need a hug, Stevie. Give us a hug.' She was tearful again.

I sat down on the bed and put my arms round her. She felt very hot, like a cross child.

'I know you're right,' she said, 'but I just seem to be stuck. There's something wrong with me.'

'You just need a change. You need to get away from here.'

'But where would I go?'

'Anywhere.'

'That's what I'm afraid of. Come with us?'

I shook my head. 'You know I can't do that, Shirley.'

She was fading now.

'Oh, well. Put us to bed, then,' she muttered. 'I feel all shivery.' She raised her arms and I pulled her dress over her head. 'Just like old times, eh, Stevie, you having your way with me. Only you're not. What d'you think of me underwear?'

'It looks expensive.'

'It is.'

I removed her shoes and pulled off her tights.

'Ooh, Sir Jasper,' she slurred.

I moved her under the eiderdown and into the recovery position, then waited uncertainly in case she woke again and was disoriented. The music had stopped. The damp stood in the air. I went to the window.

After a while, with no clear object in view, I began to search the room. The books were a jumble of literature, pulp and vaguely alternative works of the sort that were popular at the time, including Aleister Crowley's novel *Moonchild*, and the works of Eliphas Levi. There was also something purporting to be a grimoire. In the dressing table was an array of new expensive underwear and in a sandalwood box were some cannabis and an empty syringe but nothing to put in it. I thought about waking Shirley to confront her, but she was already deeply asleep.

At the back of the wardrobe I found a shoebox, one I recognized, in which Shirley had kept her photographs. She'd talked about finding time to put them in an album. There was an album there, but it remained empty. In the photographs, there they were, Shirley and two witches from *Macbeth* – raven-haired Nicky and red-headed Jo, long gone to university and beyond. It was barely five years ago but it seemed remotely historical, the three of them in costume looking naughty and schoolgirlish, and then dressed up in their finery at the cast party, wineglasses in their hands, among the crowd of admiring boys. And there I was, with Shirley at the seaside, in the park, in someone's forgotten kitchen at another party, then the pair of us at the seaside with Shirley looking chilly in a bikini, then squeezed together in the white light of the station photo booth, a bit the worse for drink, but happy.

And there was one I didn't remember being taken, of myself and Maggie Rowan at the cast party from *A Midsummer Night's Dream*. Shirley had not been present that evening last summer. But Rackham had. And from the photograph you could tell by our expressions that something was in the offing. There was also an envelope. It contained half a dozen photos – Shirley in her expensive underwear, then naked, then with two men whose faces were not shown. All of these pictures in the one box, as though all of them formed a record of ordinary life.

Shirley needed saving, but I wasn't sure I was the man to do it. I became a little afraid. Something was already happening. I turned off the lamp and went to draw the curtains. Outside the frosty rooftops stretched, and the gaps where the bombs had fallen in the heaviest raids outside London. Twenty years and more had still not seen the place rebuilt: it seemed to have given up waiting. The stars glinted. I heard the cough of an engine and looked down. A dark van was pulling away on the other side of the street. It had not been there when we arrived.

When I returned to my flat at about two a.m., the place seemed oddly chilly. I found the bathroom window half-raised. Someone had climbed in from the outhouse roof. I looked around and combed through the contents of my desk, but found nothing taken, nor any other evidence of intrusion or disturbance, from which I concluded that I was intended to know that there had been a visit.

It was, properly speaking, a matter for the police, but that would mean Smales and I decided against it. Had Shirley been following instructions? And if so, what was she getting in exchange? She must be in a worse state than I thought. If Carson was prepared to depend on me, then he must have been very much alone. I knew how he felt. Conspire or die: that seemed to be the lesson. So I would conspire, or try to.

TWENTY-ONE

The next morning was bright and cold. I sat in the kitchen drinking coffee. I hoped Shirley was OK and I wanted to go round and shout at her. The phone rang. I ignored it but it didn't stop.

It was Maggie. 'I'm thinking of taking the boat down to Carr's Point,' she said. 'We could take a picnic. I might do some sketches.' This was the first time I had been invited aboard *Lorelei*. It was hard to refuse, though doing something in public together was a risk. Perhaps she was testing me.

'It's a bit chilly for the seaside,' I said.

'You can keep your clothes on.'

'And anyway, I'm afraid I have a prior engagement. I'm sorry.'

'So what are you up to? Don't be secretive.'

'I've arranged to have Carson's books valued by Feldberg's. Got to be done. Sorry.'

'Well, I'll come and help. I've always wanted to see round that place.' She was not in a mood to be denied another wish.

'I'm not sure that would be proper. I'm there as the executor. The legal process isn't finished yet.'

'Stephen, who's to know? Honestly! What are you hiding? Have you got a floozy hidden away there?'

'I'll see you there at Victoria Park at eleven, then.'

When I arrived Maggie's green Triumph Herald was parked outside. She got out of the car and came over. She was dressed in painting gear.

'It'll be dusty, I imagine,' she said.

I let us into the wide, dark hall with its chilly black-and-maroon floor tiles. The house smelt of emptiness and something the world had done with. I had only visited the place a couple of times, in connection with work.

'The study's on the first floor,' I said. We went up. I opened the curtains but the day had clouded over now. I switched on the desk lamp.

'So this is the famous Carson lair,' Maggie said. 'This is where he'd lean like Caesar over the map. And here we have Herodotus over the fireplace giving birth to history single-handed. I think that one's Gibbon. Who's that one?'

'Macaulay, I think.'

'God, it's like a classroom without the boys. It's morbid. Didn't the old beggar live, at all?'

'He was a historian.'

'You mean he was a history teacher. I repeat my question.'

A familiar folder lay on the desk. I opened it.

'What's that you've got?' I showed her. 'Oh, that. The legendary item.' She opened a window and lit a cigarette, then leaned back on the ledge. 'You know it's fake.'

'I don't know that, actually. What makes you think so?'

'Something my brother said. Old Carson and his Führer fetish, as he put it.'

'Maggie, please. This is Carson's house. And it's difficult for me.'

'Well, I'm sorry, Stephen. I'll try to be more humble around the shrine. I just find all this Hitler stuff a bit morbid. I mean, it's ages since all that business with the war. It was enough of a pain at the time. Why would anyone want to dwell on it?'

Perhaps you should ask your brother, I thought.

'You're just being mischievous,' I said. 'If you're bored, don't feel you have to stay. I can manage.'

'What? Look, I'll just go and have a wander round,' said Maggie. She went out and up the next flight of stairs. I heard her moving restlessly about. Short of a row, how could I have stopped her?

The doorbell rang. Samuel Feldberg stood in the porch in his dark heavy overcoat and hat.

He offered his condolences, then added, 'Some people seem permanent, like fixed stars. I think your Captain Carson was of that order. But what can we do?'

'I imagine he would tell us to look at the books,' I suggested. Feldberg nodded at this. I led the way upstairs.

'Much of the material here will be familiar to me, since the Captain was a regular customer over many years,' he said, pausing to look at a print on the landing. Maggie's footsteps stopped overhead. I guessed she was looking down the stairwell.

Mr Feldberg took a notebook from his briefcase and laid his coat on the daybed. 'As it happens,' he said, 'Captain Carson kept a catalogue of his library.'

'That sounds entirely in character.'

'And as it also happens, he sent me a copy of it some months ago with a view to having a valuation made, but for some reason he didn't follow the matter up. I assumed he'd changed his mind or that his attention was taken up with work. So the best thing I can do now is examine the material. Perhaps you might leave me here for a little while, if you like. To be here is a sort of leavetaking for me. He and I talked a good deal over the years about books and history and David's education. Would that be all right?'

'I'll be around if you need anything,' I said.

I went up to the next floor.

'I'm in here,' said Maggie. She was in the box room at the front, overlooking the park. 'Your little man's here, is he?'

'Mr Feldberg.'

'That's the one.' She perched on the low window sill. 'Funny how we keep meeting in rooms like this, like a pair of hole-and-corner merchants.'

'Is that how you think of it?' I asked.

'Sometimes. What will you do with this place?'

'I haven't had chance to think about it. It's not all settled yet, anyway. It's not really mine.'

'The position's wonderful. I must say I could do with a view like this.'

'Buy it, then,' I said.

She laughed. 'It would depend what one had in mind for the longer term. Before anything else, it needs thoroughly cleaning and then redecorating. And most of those dreary pictures will have to go. But someone should live in it properly. It would be a shame to let it go to flats and those sort of people.'

'I'm those sort of people,' I said.

She rolled her eyes. 'You know what I mean.'

'I wouldn't be so sure.'

'You got out of the wrong side of bed, didn't you?'

'As a matter of fact, yes, Maggie. And as I say, I've not had chance to think about the house.'

'Well, there's certainly room for a tribe of miniature Maxwells.'

'In that case I'd have to find the girl first, wouldn't I?'

'There is that. Early days, Stephen. I wouldn't go rushing in.'

She lit a cigarette. I was going to object but her gaze warned me off. She opened the window. Faint traffic noise drifted up, and children's voices from the playground. The grass was with thick with leaves under the black-branched chestnut trees. A few couples strolled around the pond with prams. I couldn't imagine owning that view.

'It smells of old man in this place,' she said. 'The caged male beast.'

'I hadn't noticed that.'

'Of course not. You're just a younger specimen, after all. Give it time, eh? Anyway, Carson clearly didn't do much with it apart from occupy it, after a fashion. The bedroom's like a mausoleum.'

'What would you expect?' But the house did feel to me as

if no woman had ever lived in it. It was simply a space to occupy. You would not call it home. I wanted to be out of there. If I did inherit it I would not live in it. Let the flat-dwellers, 'those sort of people', have it, in the teeth of Maggie's snobbery.

Maggie grew more impatient. She stubbed out her half-smoked cigarette, threw it down into the garden and closed the window. 'Is your chap all right?' she asked. 'He won't have gone off with anything, will he?'

'For God's sake. He's the father of one of our boys.'

'Well, that's something, I suppose. You've got to be careful with them, though.' It was as if she wasn't saying these things, as if suddenly she'd shown me a place where they were self-evident and required no repetition. I turned away, unable to find a reply. I wondered why she'd bothered to turn up. What had she been expecting?

We stood there in silence until I heard Feldberg calling from downstairs.

'We'd have been better off taking the boat,' she said. 'It's deadly dull here.'

'You didn't have to come.'

'I thought I might help. But obviously not.'

Help do what? I thought.

'I certainly don't want to be in the way.'

'You're not,' I said, without conviction.

We went grimly downstairs. If Feldberg was surprised to see Maggie he didn't show it.

'This is Mr Feldberg,' I said. 'Father of David.' Maggie nodded as though not properly taking him in. 'Mrs Rowan has offered to help.'

'It's quite a job, this big old place,' said Feldberg.

'I'm sure you'll manage your end – Mr Feldberg, was it? – and find your way around. Nevertheless, I seem to be surplus to requirements. Nothing for me here. Do excuse me.' She went off downstairs. From the window I watched her drive away.

Feldberg produced his notebook and showed me a figure.

'It's a good collection,' he said, 'to fellow specialists. It would be a pity to have to break it up. Someone might make an offer for the whole thing. The university, perhaps. It would be too big and too particular for the school.'

I was finding it hard to concentrate.

'So what do I owe you, Mr Feldberg?' I asked.

'All I would ask is that you let me take the collection in due course and handle it for you. Except the Hitler item.' He smiled. 'Why not let your friend Vlaminck deal with that, eh?'

'I wouldn't call him a friend.'

'I should hope not, Stephen. And the Headmaster's wife, is she a friend?'

'A colleague. I've been helping with painting a stage set, so she returned the favour.'

'Of course.'

'I am very grateful for your assistance.'

'It is my pleasure.'

TWENTY-TWO

There was a cafe at the entrance to the Victoria arcade, popular with students and other layabouts, as well as workers from the fruit and vegetable market. I had arranged to meet Smallbone here early the following Saturday morning. He arrived in bad humour, hungover, looming among the steam and cigarette smoke. Hazel the waitress approached. I waited for him to go into the routine. I knew that Hazel was thirty, divorced and rather athletic.

'Bacon sandwich, please, darling,' said Smallbone, brightening a little.

'Right you are,' said Hazel, wielding her biro. 'Anything else, my lover?'

'And a tea.'

'Haven't seen you for a while,' said Hazel.

'Busy, you know how it is,' said Smallbone.

'Aye, busy with all them mucky women.'

'I've always got a soft spot for you, Hazel.'

'Soft spot's no use to me, is it? I'll have to mek me own arrangements, Maurice.'

Smallbone inclined his head in a gesture of concession. He hated people using his first name, understandably. Hazel swayed off into the fog.

'A hellcat,' he said. 'You've no idea. The problem is, her brother's a docker, built like a brick shithouse. Very protective of his sister's virtue, which he seems to think still exists. He said he'd chop me cock off if I went near her again.'

'Yes, but what a way to go.'

We considered this until Hazel returned with his sandwich and a cup of pale grey tea. She sniffed as though her suspicions had been confirmed, then went away again.

'I take it you're aware that these are unlicensed premises,' Bone said, finishing his bacon sandwich in two bites.

'Have a bun.'

'You cannot deflect me with buns,' he said. 'I do have other things to do besides carting your dirty books around.'

'It's really not a dirty book, Bone. I'm sorry to disappoint you.'

'How do you know until you open it?'

'Have you got it?' I asked.

'Have I got what? Syphilis?'

'The envelope.'

He passed it over.

'Thanks, Bone.'

'Is that it? Am I dismissed? Dwell I but in the suburbs of your good pleasure?'

'For the moment. I'll be in touch.'

'Can't I have a look? After all, I've been minding it for you. Go on, guvnor.'

'I'll have to see. I'll let you know.' I leaned closer. 'Look, it could be serious. I think it has to do with Captain Carson's death.'

'Bloody long suicide note, given how thick it is.'

'I don't think that's what it is, Bone.'

'I don't like the sound of that. You should pass it to the police.'

'I'm not sure that would solve anything.'

'No. Look, comrade,' he said, with an anxious smile, 'you don't know what you're doing, do you? And therefore neither do I.'

'I may have a better idea when I've had a look at the stuff.'

Smallbone shook his head. 'You could have dropped me in it and me none the wiser. Why can't you stick to sex like a normal pervert? From now on don't keep me in the fucking dark. If I end up at North Dock nick I at least need something I can confess to.'

'All right. Drink your tea and piss off. I'll see you in the Narwhal later on.'

From the pier I watched the ferry manoeuvre its way to its moorings. It was quite full, mainly with headscarved women who had come across for the shopping the city afforded. As they advanced up the ramp a few ancient men with bicycles could be seen in the crowd, which soon dispersed in near-silence.

Apart from a girl from the art college carrying a large portfolio, I was the only passenger boarding for the return trip. To begin with I went to the upper deck, but the wind was too cold and there was rain in it, so I retired to the bar, which was shuttered at this time of day. The big old paddle-steamer laboured back across the river. I wondered if, as often happened in those days, we would get stuck on a sandbank, but after twenty minutes or so we docked at Dutch Houses.

I considered going straight back again but made myself walk into the village. Dutch Houses, it seemed to me, was only in the most technical sense a place at all. A handful of tall, incongruously distinctive red-brick houses in the Dutch style lingered by the shore, as if still hoping against hope that the port expected to flourish here in the late eighteenth century might suddenly be manifested. But everyone knew that there was room for only one city on the river, and that was the one I had come from. Such inhabitants as lived in the few terraced streets of workmen's houses and the postwar prefabs were occupied mostly, if at all, in the agricultural hinterland which drizzle and mist obscured from view.

It had been a rite of passage in the sixth form to come here on the ferry and get drunk in the Vermuyden Inn, named for the great Dutch hydraulic engineer, much celebrated on this side of the river. As I approached, the side door was opened and I slipped inside.

In the bar a fire had been lit. I ordered a pint from the landlord's beautiful and bored daughter and took a seat near the hearth, at a table topped with red Formica. She went back to listlessly reading a copy of *Honey*. I renewed my acquaintance with half a dozen mediocre paintings, in the Dutch style, featureless rural settings enlivened by occasional drains and the odd cow. If I were seeking a place of exile I might have chosen Dutch Houses. I drank my pint slowly, procrastinating. So, then. This was neutral ground. The barmaid was called away into the interior of the pub, and I took out the envelope.

It contained two items. First was a typed copy of a version of Horace's Ode i.4, 'Solvitur acris hiems' by Louis MacNeice, then somewhat out of fashion and not long dead. The version dated from the 1930s. I read it over, several times lingering on the concluding lines:

> . . . and O my dear
> The little sum of life forbids the ravelling of lengthy
> Hopes. Night and the fabled dead are near
>
> And the narrow house of nothing, past whose lintel
> You will meet no wine like this, no boy to admire
> Like Lycidas, who today makes all young men a furnace
> And whom tomorrow girls will find a fire.

Was there a Lycidas for Carson, then? Surely not. But then why not?

I turned to the other item.

Carson had small, neat handwriting of the kind that used to be taught in the prep school at Blake's, a lesson a week on Friday afternoons, when the master would carefully rule a stave of lines on the board and set out the florid alphabet with its reversed capital F and the impossible Q. There seemed to be no crossings-out.

He began with a letter addressed to me.

TWENTY-THREE

15th June 1968

Dear Stephen,

I know that you must come to despise the man who writes these words and performed these acts, but I hope you will try to understand who he was and why he behaved as he did. More than that, I hope you will see the necessity of preventing them from having terrible consequences in the here and now. You will quite reasonably ask why this responsibility should fall on you. I am a lonely man with few friends. It may surprise you to learn that I count you among them. I would quite understand if you felt unable to act in this matter, but, unless I am an even worse judge of character than I take myself to be, I suspect that you will do so.

I shall of course be dead when you read these pages.

James Carson

Next came more handwritten pages, which seemed to have been neatly removed from a larger journal.

Tuesday 19th June 1945

Sergeant Risman reported to me in the Company office at Spa on the morning of Monday 18th June. At dawn he and his squad had intercepted three men trying to join a train carrying released Allied POWs when it halted on its way back to Antwerp. It seemed he had brought me some deserters to examine. I observed that this was more a concern for the Military Police than for us. He replied that he thought I might like to have a look at them for myself.

He explained that one of them claimed to be an officer and was clearly a gentleman. We went over to the glasshouse, where the three men were being held in solitary confinement. I recognized two of them from reports. The first of these was Private George Carr of the Royal Engineers, described as having been recruited for the Britisches Freikorps whilst a prisoner of war following capture during the Cretan debacle in 1941. The second was Harold Crossley, a deckhand on a merchant ship sunk off Ireland in 1943. The third man was known to me personally but neither he nor I gave any indication of this at first meeting.

Carr and Crossley were sad cases. Carr, the older man, from Tyneside, where the BUF presence was strong, had been a boxer. He had some history as an enforcer with Mosley's lot. When war broke out he was mindful of Mosley's instructions to BUF members to serve the Crown loyally in the conflict with Germany; but by the time the attempt was made to recruit him in a holding cage in Italy he was demoralized and far less interested in Hitler or politics than in better rations and conditions. He had never expected to see action on the German side and insisted that had this seemed likely he would have refused to fire on his own people, though he gave me to understand that he would not have objected to shooting Russians, had the opportunity arisen. I advised him that he should be glad that opportunity had passed him by, since the Russians numbered millions and would have had little interest in who he was and why he was there. He said he supposed he would hang. I did not feel able to disabuse him of this prospect.

Crossley was a grotesquely overgrown youth who seemed to be of limited intelligence. After a period among the British prisoners on the German tanker Altmark, *he ended up in the Merchant Navy prison camp near Bremen, from which he was recruited. Thereafter he had first followed Carr's lead, he said. I was inclined to believe this. He seemed baffled by his circumstances and asked if he would be sent home now, since his family would be worried. I was unable to offer reassurance to this pitiable boy.*

At this point Carson had attached a later note, dated June 1968:

In the event both men were returned to England, tried and condemned to death. Their sentences were commuted to life imprisonment. What later became of Carr is unknown to me. For reasons which may become apparent, I followed Crossley's career with interest.

The original text resumed:

The pair claimed to know little of their companion, other than that he seemed to be an officer and that he had led their attempted escape to England. When they were challenged by Risman and his men, their companion had turned them in and might have got away with it if Risman had not instinctively felt he was a 'wrong 'un'.

I told Sergeant Risman that as an officer the third prisoner might be in possession of material of particular sensitivity and that therefore I would speak with him in his cell alone.

When I arrived, Charles Rackham was lying on his bunk. Trying to show as little reaction as possible, I sat down opposite and produced my notebook. He greeted me fondly, as though nothing unusual had happened. He described our encounter as an unexpected pleasure and asked if I was not in turn glad to see him, and referred to my notebook, suggesting that it would be a good idea to record his 'table talk'. When I asked what he had done to find himself imprisoned, he laughed and said it would take less time to set out what he had not done, since he had not been idle.

When I warned him that he would be viewed as, at the very least, a deserter, he said he did not think so. When I said that the likelihood was he would be tried as a traitor, he said, 'Well that won't happen, will it?' He seemed amused by the whole situation. When I asked why he was so confident of saving his neck, he replied that he thought I knew the answer to that question and we must together make sure we did the right thing. When I indicated that my own freedom of action was limited, he said that in fact I had only one choice.

I told him that I refused to be blackmailed. He asked how I could prevent him. He wished me no harm but would expose me if I sought to obstruct him or prevent his safe return to Britain. He added that I had known what he was like when I first took him to bed, and that part of the attraction for someone as self-controlled as myself had been to lay hands on a bit of evil. I was not the only one so tempted; he had bigger fish to fry, and once back at home he would be looked after. I objected that I could arrange for him to be shot while attempting to escape. That sort of thing had been known to happen. He replied that I would not do this because when it came to it I would not in the end be able to, and that we should dispense with the melodrama and deal with the practicalities of the situation.

Struggling to master my anger and shame, I returned to the office and summoned Risman, instructing him that Carr and Crossley were to be forwarded to Britain for debriefing and trial. I would need to speak to the third prisoner again. Until instructed otherwise, Risman was to deny all knowledge of this prisoner's presence.

The next passage was typed on paper yellowed with age.

Transcription of Recorded Interrogation of
Charles Rackham by James Carson,
Wednesday 20th June 1945

R: What equipment are you using? You're obviously going to be recording this, aren't you? German recording equipment is much better on the whole. What I shall tell you is true, James. It has all been a great adventure.

C: You have taken the side of the murderers.

R: Well, possibly, possibly. But do you want me to tell you about it so you can have it for posterity? Not that you'll be able to do anything with it.

C: Why should I believe you?

Here again Carson had attached a later note:

This was an unprofessional question. It was like being mad, holding this conversation in this setting, given our history. This smirking creature – for that is what he seemed to have become – had been my pupil, a protégé, a lover. Rackham seemed wholly unperturbed, as if viewing the situation externally for the purposes of amusement.

The interrogation resumed:

R: In practical terms it makes no difference whether you believe me or not. But as I have tried to indicate, you have no choice in the matter.

C: Then you had better get on with it.

R: Before the outbreak of war I was, as you know, active on the livelier fringes of the British fascist movement. As a result I made several visits to Germany in which I established contact with officials of the Nazi regime. These facts were clearly known to the authorities at home, who were also aware of my liaison with [here the name had been left out] a member of the aristocracy known to favour appeasement. It became evident that not only were such hopes entertained by more than a few political figures, businessmen, civil servants and diplomats (this after all was hardly a secret at the time), but also, as is less widely appreciated, that there were those in both groups prepared to work in a clandestine way to secure the end sought by ——. They did so both while the conflict was approaching and then after war was declared.

C: They were prepared to commit treason?

R: 'Why, if it prosper, none dare call it treason.'

C: But it has not prospered, has it?

R: Well, not yet. Are you going to keep interrupting? When I joined the army in autumn 1939, my card was marked by two gentlemen from the relevant department. They gave me to understand that I might be of use to them. The alternative was jail. It was clear that this was no idle threat. Having settled that, they explained that at some future moment of crisis I might receive instructions from a senior source concerning arrangements with the German Foreign Ministry. That day might never come, but I was to be ready and to obey without question.

C: A senior source?

R: That's what I said. They named ——, you may not be surprised to hear. During the Fall of France in May 1940 my unit was involved in a rearguard action near Audenarde. I received telephoned instructions from a staff officer that I was to surrender at the earliest opportunity and make myself known to the enemy officer commanding. I was also told that once I was a prisoner of the Germans I would be contacted with further instructions. I followed these orders. Several months went by. I was imprisoned with other officers at a camp in the vicinity of Kassel. I reconciled myself to boredom. Then orders came – the source was not made known – to join a planned escape. The escape party would be allowed to get out of the camp and disperse as planned before being rounded up. I would be captured and disappear.

The plan succeeded. I was moved to Berlin. After this I was given employment of two kinds. Firstly I wrote propaganda material for broadcast to Britain, as well as doing some translation work. Secondly, later on, I was used to recruit disaffected prisoners of war for the British Free Corps. During this period my initial contact contrived to resume communication and I supplied information about my activities. After a time it was no longer in fact clear to me which side I was working for, or, indeed, whether there were sides in this tragic and unnecessary conflict, or what my eventual role might be. Certainly, strong bonds of mutual interest should have led us to make common case against the Jewish Bolshevik threat.

C: Don't editorialize, Charles. Just let me have the facts.

R: The Free Corps recruited very poorly compared with the SS Nordland and Charlemagne and Walloon units, and never saw action. As the war came to its close my contact fell silent. My work for the Germans came to an end and it was clear I would be abandoned to cut my own devices. I could understand this, given the larger situation. I would need to fend for myself. I had no intention of being taken by the Russians when they got to Berlin. So I did my duty as an officer of the Queen and sought to return to my unit.

C: Who was your contact on our side?

R: —— [Name omitted].

C: Why should I or anyone else believe you?

R: [laughing] I am a brother officer.

C: You're on the books as a traitor.

R: It's a little like that passage in *Ashenden* where he's told that if he succeeds he'll get no credit and that if he gets into trouble he'll get no help.

C: Ashenden's loyalties were not in question.

R: Neither are mine, I assure you. We can leave this a stalemate, James, but if you move against me you will leave me no choice. Just get me on a boat and I'll deal with the rest of it back at home. Exercise discretion. We know you can do that, don't we? The war's over. The soldiers can go back in their box for now.

C: Supposing I can get you on a boat, the likelihood is that you'll be picked up as soon as you land.

R: Don't worry. I'll put in a good word for you.

C: For God's sake leave me out of it.

R: As you wish. That wasn't so difficult, was it?

And now Rackham's handwriting resumed.

15th June 1968, continued

At the time of this encounter with Rackham I was seeing Claire Ormond, who was over working as a translation clerk. I was in fact about to ask her to marry me, and I'm pretty sure she sensed this and would have accepted my proposal. I considered confiding in her – no, I longed to confide in her – but although I believed in her absolute discretion, the knowledge, which was verboten from every perspective, would have been a cruel imposition. Claire was at least as principled as I might have liked to imagine myself to be had Rackham not turned up in the glasshouse that day. But if I were to live with her I could not bear to have secrets – which in turn demonstrated to me that I should never have considered marrying her in the first place. So I broke things off with Claire. She behaved with a dignity of which I was clearly quite incapable. She has been a lifelong friend. But I had loved Charles Rackham, and desired him beyond reason, and the memory has remained, composed on the one hand of guilt and regret, and on the other the sense that I was never so alive as during that damning folly. Enough. And I was saving my skin. Had I passed on the names he mentioned, I am pretty sure the axe would have fallen on me. So I was a coward as well as a fool.

I need you to have a fuller picture of the world, Stephen, and the temperaments, from which these events arose. Charles Rackham was a gifted pupil, the son of a landed family for whom local loyalty meant that their sons would be sent to Blake's. He came into the sixth form in 1935 with a reputation for great if erratic brilliance in classics and the humanities, clearly bound for Oxbridge.

Rackham's hold on me, as he keenly appreciated, was not created simply by the fact of our involvement. Such things are not uncommon; men have borne the subsequent exposure somehow. No, the important element was the shame I would feel at having betrayed my own profession. To some – perhaps to you; I am unsure – such a sense of things must seem antiquated, and even perhaps absurd in the seriousness with which it regards the fall from grace. To that I can only reply that this is how I was made – conscientious to a fault but not wholly able to follow the dictates of that conscience. Rackham knew that I would kill myself if he exposed me. At times, now especially, I wish I had done so anyway. In retrospect, I see that I was the one seduced, though I seemed to make all the moves. When I asked him in the cell why he threatened me, he looked at me as if the question were meaningless. 'Put it down to experience, love,' he said. 'That's what I've done, anyway.' You will understand if I reveal no further details of this brief liaison. For me it was a coup de foudre, from which I have never properly recovered.

We had our share of youthful communists in the 1930s. It was to be expected. Some of them showed the courage of their convictions. One former pupil, a boy called Arram, from another landed family on the Plain of Axness, joined the International Brigade and died of wounds. His family arranged for a privately published book of his poems, which I very much doubt if anyone read but themselves. We have a copy in the case of pupils' publications.

Rackham went in the other direction.

Mosley and his men did not spring fully formed into existence. As you will know, there were precedents, albeit of a feeble and eccentric kind, among vegetarians, spiritualists and in our neck of the woods, for some reason, dentists. But of course there were also embittered ex-servicemen hoping for someone to speak for them when MacDonald's spineless Labour government failed to do so. Certainly the BUF found a vein of support among the unemployed dockers and sailors, with a convenient scapegoat in the local Jewish community. Fascism was more exciting and theatrical altogether than the grim priesthood of the Marxists, and it offered more opportunities for action, for parades and brawls. As is well known, much of Mosley's public support, and almost all of its middle- and upper-class element, withdrew in distaste after 1934. Which is not to say that parts of that support did not continue in the background. The true facts about fascist sympathies in Britain in the years leading up to the war have yet to emerge. Were I not a historian I would predict that what emerges will be at once startling in detail and not in the least surprising in general.

Rackham was in some ways too eccentric even for the BUF. He would rather have been a one-man party, the permanent vanguard of deranged anti-Semitic extremism. Yet while he could be brutal in word and, I imagine, in action, he was also a remarkably intelligent and charming young man. It seemed to many that his political involvement was simply a phase which he would outgrow when he went off to university. The famous charm certainly assisted in his exculpation over an attack on a well-known Jewish baker in the old town. A couple of his working-class comrades served time in prison, while Rackham never saw the inside of a courtroom.

After he left school for Oxford I lost track of him, or perhaps he relaxed the attention he paid to me. I made no enquiries. When Regulation 18b was enacted, placing Mosley and a number of his supporters in prison for part of the war, I would not have been surprised to discover that Rackham was among them. Nor was I surprised when I found his name on the watch list of deserters and traitors we sought to apprehend at the war's end. The surprise was that he turned up in that cell. But, as he liked to remark, he always tried to give good value.

When I resumed my teaching duties at Blake's, you may imagine my surprise at finding Rackham there too, as a teacher of modern languages. Yet it took only a moment for my surprise to dissolve; Rackham had been right, of course he had: his way back to respectability would be smoothed. He had gone back and completed his degree. A quiet life awaited him, writing and teaching, supposing he could bear such confinement. He did not say so, but I inferred that he was still acting under instruction: wait until called upon. I assume that it was through Rackham's influence that when Crossley was eventually paroled he joined the ground staff at Blake's. Crossley never acknowledged our previous acquaintance. He became Lurch, the wordless assistant groundkeeper and comic bogeyman to the school. For myself, I arranged that Risman become the school porter. He had seen Rackham at Spa. It was not necessary to explain the situation to him. He would be there by day, and if necessary in the watches of the night. We all adapted to these strange circumstances, forming a balance of unexerted powers, engaged in a sort of phoney war it was sometimes possible to forget was going on. Blake's was a strange place in itself in any case. We fitted in – I as the permissible element of academic seriousness, Rackham as the aesthete. And there was proper work for me to do, teaching, and by doing that I attempted, inadequately and in the end hopelessly, to make reparations for my failures of character.

Like many another returning soldier on the staff, Rackham said little of his wartime experiences, and his silence was treated with respect as a sign of decent reticence and maturity of attitude. It was the conventional way. It was known – as is the way of these things – that he had been a prisoner of war, and this added another layer of slightly awesome humility to his reputation. He had in any case moved on and was publishing his poems in the fag-end of the Apocalypse movement. They were bad poems in my estimation, but this seemed to matter less than that they showed Rackham as serious, a discreet asset to the school, the more effective because unboasted.

And twenty years went by, and in some mysterious way Rackham did not grow older as we did. He retained a youthful appearance and an air of imminent distinction, as if perpetually almost ready to be the coming man.

I have as little to do with him as is professionally possible; the setting of the school still enables a slightly anachronistic formality, as might exist between men from the same regiment who would only encounter each other in the Mess. He is, I understand, a charismatic if sometimes capriciously cruel teacher, extensively knowledgeable in European literature, art and music. The boys are both drawn to him and a little afraid, I suspect, for there is always the promise of the unexpected. But he behaved himself, I think, for a long time. It was in his interests to do so. His own sister is the wife of the most recent Headmaster and has also become a member of staff. Charles Rackham is in a sense part of the Blake's family. As you can see, although I have avoided him I must have been taken a keener interest than I realized, watching and listening when I scarcely knew I was doing so. Why have I not simply left? Because Blake's is also my home. It is all I have. And because, at some level, I have been waiting.

Rackham has no ambitions in the school, it seems, nor any wish to move elsewhere. And his literary activities have never gained recognition beyond the small circle of the likeminded, all of whom ostensibly shun worldly fame on the grounds that those who might bestow it are unworthy to do so. It is the realm of the self-declared giants, too great for the world that in turn finds them invisible and inaudible. Rackham and his poetic kind are not well enough known to be thought of as obscure. When a well-known poet living locally came to speak the sixth form last year Rackham's was a conspicuous absence.

I think he is bored. Time has passed. No threat to him has emerged and neither has the long-postponed call to duty come. His misdeeds seem to have been forgotten. Perhaps, like some drunkards, he supposed himself cured by a period of abstemiousness.

At any rate the disease has reasserted itself. It is a disease, surely, the anti-Semitism, the paradoxical love of order and violence, the thousand-year ideology whose one true aim is fiery extinction. People have begun to say that communism and fascism are two sides of the one coin, but I cannot believe that. Communism is predicated on a future as fascism is not. It has its own economics, as fascism does not. Fascism is a death-cult, much more an event than an idea. It would have been better if, like Henry Williamson and some others of Mosley's men, Rackham had taken up farming, but there seems not to have been anything in him of the love of the soil and the seasons and the implacable endless demonstrable proof of something – what, exactly? – offered by farming life. Corduroys and physical labour were not for Rackham, it seems, although I think his protector could certainly boast of rural property.

What seems to have stimulated Rackham to involve himself once more in the right-wing political fringe is partly the exploits of Colin Jordan with his crackpot National Socialist Movement, recently renamed the British Movement. Rackham, I suspect, considers himself to be a more elegant, sophisticated 'political soldier' than the demented thug Jordan clearly is. And Rackham has always been tempted to make a splash – a feature of his temperament which will always in the end separate him from the upper-class appeasers and their children, in whose sphere he would otherwise naturally move, but to which he remained connected by ties of sentiment rather than politics, and perhaps – I would not be surprised – by his power to blackmail.

And now? Now I simply know that Rackham is at work again, spreading the poison, seeking a destructive opportunity. I see in him that familiar combination of the parochial and the grandiose that will seek to affect larger events while gorging itself on a local crime. Our lives, it seems to me, were a long time ago – in another country, as they say. I have kept up few connections with those days. But what of Rackham? Who keeps a protective eye on him? And what are they protecting? Him? Themselves? The general good? I feel too old to puzzle it out again. I want to be left alone to read my books and simply disappear. But he will taunt me with his deranged schemes. He will require me to be in attendance. His target, as you may have already inferred, is David Feldberg. I do not know how far Rackham is prepared to go. But Feldberg must be protected somehow. I am asking you to do that.

You should be aware that Rackham may suspect that a record of our encounter in 1945 still exists. Rackham is, on any serious assessment, a failure, like his fellow traitors. It is failure that makes them dangerous.

I put the papers back in the envelope, and the envelope in the inside pocket of my coat, left the Vermuyden Inn and walked back to await the ferry. The day remained cold, with drizzle closing down the horizons. There was no one else at the ferry landing. A green bus arrived empty and left empty.

So, after the war ended, while William Joyce and John Amery were hanged for treason, the one illegally and the other because he was also to hand, it seems that Rackham must, as he claimed to Carson, have had a protector, perhaps more than one. Assuming this to be so, whoever it was ensured his safe passage back into the civilian world. Was it a sense of honour and obligation that made them do so? To save one who had served a cause?

Possibly, but in the reckoning after the conflict there were graver betrayals than that of a single compromised agent: the fate of the Cossack officers, for example, arranged at the Yalta Conference. Rackham was interesting and strange, but the powers – for they must have been powers – had no expedient reason to treat Rackham well. Either he retained a potential usefulness (hard to imagine with Germany defeated) or he possessed some advantage which made them decide to spare him. Rackham had a hold on someone more significant than Carson.

Yet again, though, that might merely have hastened his end. So perhaps it must be that someone *cared* about Rackham, and wished him to be spared. And if so, suppose this affection had not lapsed in the meantime, but endured, balanced perhaps by Rackham's continued power to threaten and expose? If this were so, then Rackham's protector must be someone of such status as could make their wishes exceptions to the rule of law.

The ferry docked and I went aboard. The bar was open now. One of our other sixth-form amusements was to board at lunchtime and simply stay on board drinking as the boat went back and forth. It was very tempting to do so again. I ordered a vodka and went to stare out at the estuary. Ships were leaving on the tide now. I watched a freighter fade into the distance until it was merely a ghost in the eye. I blinked and it had disappeared.

I realized I was angry. Rackham was insane or evil or both, but what did it say of Carson that he had visited this on me? Was this the price of my being forgiven and readmitted? Anger was followed by shame, then a blend of both. Then came the thought that, while I had no doubt Carson was telling the truth about Rackham, the document did not constitute evidence – as Carson himself would have been the first to remind me.

We came inshore, and the vessel shuddered as it turned to berth. I went down on deck. It was bitterly cold. The gangway was lowered and I walked ashore. But if the document was not evidence, then why should anyone be interested in getting hold of it? Why would they even suppose it existed? Carson would have added, with a look of disappointment at my slowness on the uptake, that whoever the interested parties were, they could not be certain that it did not exist, nor that, if it did exist, it was *not* evidence, nor that Carson had not risked naming Rackham's high-born protector.

The pubs would not be open for some time. I wished we were more European.

TWENTY-FOUR

Feldberg's Antiquarian Books occupied surprisingly large, not to say labyrinthine premises in the Victoria Arcade near the Law Courts. This was the city's attempt to emulate the Galeries Lafayette. Feldberg's lay in the deep interior between a religious supplies shop and a joke emporium with a side-line in pornography. The idea was presumably that you graduated from porn to antiquarianism and then sought the consolations of the church. So far my progress had stalled at Feldberg's.

Usually, Samuel Feldberg was seated in his emplacement of books, working by the light of what must have been one of the earliest anglepoise lamps ever manufactured, and surrounded by a Marmite-coloured gloom designed to keep the frivolous from penetrating the shop. His years of labour and applied discouragement had produced an enviable quality of immersed silence that any teacher would have given much to reproduce in the classroom. Although the shop seemed to be thriving, the Feldbergs had never made the conventional move to the suburbs. 'This is the city,' Mr Feldberg had once told me, 'here, within the old walls. My father got off the boat at the bottom of the nearest street. Why would I want to be outside the city? We're not all from the shtetl.'

But this afternoon when I went into the shop he was not there. Instead, David Feldberg sat at the huge desk. When he looked up from his work, for a second he seemed annoyed at the interruption. This was his turf. He rose and came forward.

'Can I help you, sir?'

'I was hoping to see your father.'

'Was he expecting you?'

'No, but I said I might look in.'

'He should be back before long. Can I do anything, sir?'

'No, but I'll wait, if that's all right.'

'Then please have a seat. Would you like some tea?'

'You carry on with your work. Forget about me.' The boy smiled at this remote possibility. I wandered along the shelves. There were copies of a couple of Rackham's early volumes. I wondered about buying them.

Soon David appeared from the back room with a tea-tray. Somebody hates you, David, I thought. Someone has selected you as an object of hatred, a pretext, a representative. I could not imagine how to begin to tell him. The shop door opened and his father came in. I rose and went over.

'Mr Maxwell, have you been here long?'

'A few minutes.'

'I am sorry. I went to see an old lady, near the park, as it happens, who is uncertain whether to dispose of her late husband's books. Nothing was decided. We meet quite regularly to go over the matter. But she phoned and seemed rather urgent, as if the undertaker was coming up the path, so it was a courtesy. David, have you looked after our guest?' The boy indicated the tray and began to gather his books and papers together. The shop door opened again and the girl from St Clare's came in.

'Introduction, David,' said Mr Feldberg.

'This is Rachel, sir. We're on our way to the pictures.'

'I've seen you about the school, Rachel. It's nice to meet you at last. Are you a historian like David?'

'Actually I'm hoping to read medicine.'

'Her parents are very proud of her, of course,' said Mr Feldberg. 'Another doctor in the family. Soon they will have a complete set.'

Rachel blushed at this. Now that I saw her properly, her dark, vivid prettiness was apparent.

'What is the film this week?' Mr Feldberg asked.

'*Rosemary's Baby*,' said Rachel, still blushing. David shook his head at his father's teasing.

'Does your mother know, Rachel? Is this film suitable?' Feldberg asked, arch and mischievous.

'Dad, stop,' said David. 'You're embarrassing her.'

Mr Feldberg burst out laughing. 'And a young lady must never be embarrassed? Of course. How could I have forgotten? Go and enjoy yourselves David, make sure you see Rachel to the bus afterwards.'

'She seems a nice girl,' I said, when the pair had left.

'Certainly,' said Mr Feldberg, pouring tea. 'From a nice family. Both doctors. For some reason they choose to live out in the wilds, right on the edge of a golf course where her father is not permitted to play. I'm sure it makes sense to them. Sit, please. So, are there further items you wanted to me to examine?'

'Not at the minute.' What could I tell him? Why was I here, if not for that? Mr Feldberg considered me for a moment, as if wondering the same thing. But I did not say what I had come to say.

'Well,' he said, after a slightly baffled pause, 'since you have been kind enough to come in person, perhaps you won't mind if I ask your opinion. I know I should leave it until parents' evening, but why waste an opportunity?'

'Please. If I can be of help.'

'How is my son progressing, in your view?'

'He's extremely able and hard working.'

'You have a reservation about him.'

'No. It's nothing, really. David's an excellent student. That hasn't changed. If there's a problem it's that he has no peers in his classes.'

'Is he arrogant?'

'No, no. He's bored.'

'I'll speak to him, then,' said Mr Feldberg.

'But what will you say? He's done nothing wrong. The situation is not of his making.'

'If he is bored he should take pains to conceal it.'

'Is that really necessary?'

'It's wise, Stephen. For some people his presence itself will be a provocation.'

'Do you think so?'

Feldberg nodded and smiled. 'You know how things are. A degree of caution, circumspection – these are not the same as cowardice.' We drank our tea. 'You know he has become interested in politics now? He joined the youth organization of the Labour Party. Of course, I'm pleased by this, but I have told him not to let it interfere with his work. At his age, though, he has too much energy. School, music, politics – and the girl, of course. I would borrow some if I could.'

'He has become involved in the mock election.'

'Now that's something he has not mentioned. It doesn't comes as a surprise, though.'

'He's helping run the Labour campaign. He can be quite fierce.'

'Oh, yes? Fierce, you say?' Mr Feldberg smiled and nodded.

'He says what he thinks.'

'But fiercely?'

'There was an argument at the candidates' meeting. He made his position clear.'

'This is like pulling teeth, Stephen. Tell me.'

'He had a row with the BPP candidate.'

'The BPP are being allowed to stand?'

'It reflects the actual by-election if they are.' This sounded even worse spoken aloud.

'What use is such a reflection? Is this your idea?'

'Actually, I'm organizing the mock election. I inherited the job from Captain Carson. But my powers are limited. Others have more of a say.'

'This too is a reflection. Think of Weimar. Well.' He drank some tea and looked out into the arcade.

'The mock election's not the real thing, though,' I said. This was so obvious as scarcely to be true.

Mr Feldberg shook his head. 'The ideas and passions and hatreds are real enough, I would imagine. David is serious and some of the others will be doing something more than playing the game.' He poured some more tea. 'Of course, Stephen, don't imagine for a minute that I think it was your idea to admit the BPP to this election. Which of your colleagues argues the case for them?'

'I suppose that would be Charles Rackham.'

'Is that so? He is not someone I've met, though we have some of his work in stock here, along with all the other poetry books that regrettably nobody buys.' He gave a short laugh. 'And what is his motive, your friend Rackham?'

This was the reason I was there, wasn't it? But what could I tell Mr Feldberg? That according to a handwritten journal passed to me by a dead man Rackham's motive was to destroy his son? I could not yet imagine a world in which such a statement could be made with a semblance of sanity.

'He's not my friend,' I said. 'My acquaintance with him is professional. I can only speak for myself. I'm trying to ensure that the election process is conducted in the proper fashion, as Captain Carson would have done.'

'No doubt you are. Well, I will talk to David. He needs to remain calm and learn from the situation. And it will pass, and the fascists will not win, and then he can turn his attention back fully to his studies.'

'He is not neglecting his studies.'

'But you know what I mean. Let him attend to the future. When my friends and I were demobbed at the end of the war and came home we found Mosley's people back on the streets of London and other cities, this one included, spreading their poison again. So we took action. And from time to time since then it's been necessary to do the same thing. I don't want my son to have to do as we did. So I tell myself this will pass.'

I wondered how I could decently take my leave.

'And you,' Mr Feldberg asked, smiling, 'have you found yourself a wife yet?'

'Not quite, I'm afraid. Not so far.'

'Then do so. What happened to that pretty girl, the one

who made the costumes, that you used to go about with before you went to university? Sharon, was that her name?'

'Shirley. She's still here. She works in Vlaminck's bookshop.'

'If you want to call it that. What a waste. She was a clever girl, I thought. Certainly a reader. And now she works for Vlaminck? Let me tell you: nothing good comes out of that place, or Vlaminck's stupid mouth. It seems as if everywhere I turn his kind appear. They are parasites. Anyway, there'll other girls. A man needs a family – you will surely come to feel that sooner or later. It's no good to be alone, believe me: Anna died when David was six: every day since then has seemed very long. But I have David, and perhaps he has Rachel, and in turn you will find someone.' Feldberg laughed. 'Forgive me. The matchmaker! I'm too presuming. I'm sure Mrs Rowan is more than able to advise you on the way to win a fair lady? And – yes, now – am I right in thinking she is Mr Rackham's sister?'

I smiled and said nothing. Mr Feldberg rose.

'Now,' he said, 'forgive me. I must do some work. Come again, please. You are always welcome. Keep me informed, Stephen. I rely on you to guide David, like Captain Carson before you.'

You shouldn't do that, I thought, and took my leave.

TWENTY-FIVE

I went down the arcade and came out near Holy Trinity. The marketplace was deserted in the darkening later afternoon. There was frost in the air and a bonfirey smell that seemed charged with a sourceless nostalgia. The pubs closed at three in the afternoon then, but faint music drifted from one of them: someone was pleading with Ruby not to take her love to town.

I walked slowly round the church. It was still smoke-blackened and Dickensian in those days, with its madly elaborate exterior and its somehow uncomfortable tower that looked as if it had been arrested short of its full height. This evening there was nobody home, it seemed. I felt a brief fever of renewed loneliness at leaving the idea of the secure and affectionate family group that Feldberg's shop seemed to promise.

I sat for a while on a bench in the flagstoned churchyard among the pollarded plane trees. The church was neither high nor low. Inside, I knew, it was cold and smelled of stone and dust and the passage of time. Towards the end of the twelfth century, before there was a church on this site, the city had seen a pogrom against its small Jewish community. Following the massacre at York in 1190, Richard I had forbidden the persecution of the Jews, but no sooner had he departed for the Third Crusade than there was a rash of further incidents, which then continued sporadically until the expulsion of the Jews from England a century later. I knew about the massacre. Any educated person living in the city was bound to. But the event was historically so remote that it was possible to suppose it had never happened. I was a hundred yards from Mr Feldberg's shop.

And I had the envelope, and nowhere to keep it safe. I couldn't ask Bone again, or Miss Ormond, still less Mr Feldberg.

As I walked back through the city the streets were beginning to fill up again as people set out for Saturday night. Groups of girls went arm in arm, done up to the nines, taunting the groups of boys across the street, who responded with good-humoured profanity and invitations. That was the ordinary world, behind its invisible glass.

Without quite knowing why, I decided to walk via the school, though it was a slightly longer route. I went in at the side gate and past School House. Lights burned in the prep room, where I had spent the boring Saturday evenings of my boyhood. I went on through the woods at the eastern edge of the field between the railway sidings and the lake. A signal blinked on a gantry over the tracks.

The raft, which had not been used since Carson's death, was moored once more at the bank of the lake. On the island I could make out the CCF's climbing nets among the trees. At the gate to the railway crossing I paused and listened. A coal train came slowly up, heading for the docks. After that there was nothing but the night noise of the city coming and going.

I went over the crossing towards the lights of Maggie's studio. Over here, I decided, it should be a quite different place from the school side. It should be personal, a matter of pleasure and irresponsible happiness, somewhere that appeared to have escaped the clock, a little enclave of Bohemia, in which foreign policy had no interest. Clearly, I told myself, despite her attitude to Mr Feldberg, Maggie had little to do with her brother; she knew no more of his wartime experiences than anyone at the school except Carson, who was dead. And me. And anyway, I was going to Percival Street now to break things off between us, wasn't I? Another possibility occurred to me.

I let myself in and made my way upstairs. Gradually I made out the music playing in Maggie's studio. It was Annie

Ross singing 'Some People'. I remembered I was supposed to meet Smallbone in the Narwhal. No doubt he would forgive me if there was a skirt involved.

'I thought you weren't talking,' Maggie said, when I arrived in the studio. She poured two glasses of wine from an open bottle. A fire burned in the grate.

Without knowing I was about to, I said: 'I forgive you.'

'Do you now? If you say so.' She was almost demure, by her standards.

'Well, you were a bit brusque the other day,' I said. I was weak.

'So sensitive! Then I'm sorry.'

'I'm not talking about me, Maggie. I mean Mr Feldberg,' I said.

She shook her head.

'Oh, I know I must have seemed very ill-mannered. Did he mind very much?'

'He didn't mention it.'

'Well, then. No harm done. Shouldn't think he noticed, in fact. Are you going to sit down?'

I joined her on the settee. 'But why did you rush off?' I asked. 'You'd seemed so keen to be there.'

'To be honest, the place gave me the creeps. As I said, it stank of old age.'

'I suppose it does a bit.'

'And then I was cross about missing the chance to take the boat out. Oh, it was just one of my moods.'

Do it, I thought. In the name of reason, and to save your miserable hide, do it. Get out. But Maggie was beautiful in an autumnal way, her beauty on the edge of inevitable dissolution. It seemed to be the pathos that provoked the desire. She looked at me with amusement, her eyes narrowing in the smoke of her cigarette. I'm sure she knew what I was thinking.

'Shall we take up where we left off, then, Stephen?'

Later we ate bread and cheese at the kitchen table. I told myself that this was simply a postponement and that in due course the right moment would present itself. Or perhaps she'd take the initiative and drop me. That would be easier. It would look better, too. Meanwhile the envelope went on burning a hole in the inside pocket of my coat.

I wondered how to raise the subject of Charles Rackham. In the end the wine had loosened my tongue, so I said, 'Do you ever think it's a bit odd that you and your brother have so little to do with each other and yet work in the same place day after day?'

She thought for a few moments.

'I suppose it might look odd. But then there are married people who have less contact than Charles and I do. For unavoidable reasons, as you know, I don't see much of Robert, for instance.' She paused and stared into space. I tried to remember if she had ever mentioned visiting him. 'So I suppose it's all relative. Anyway, it all seems normal to us now.' Given Maggie's unguarded mood, I thought I would risk further enquiries.

'Normal?'

'I mean I'm used to it. It's been like that as long as I can remember. We were never great ones for birthdays and all that. Just not made that way. He knows where I am if he needs me and vice versa. But it never comes up. And actually, he wasn't very keen on Robert. The feeling was mutual.' She sharpened the coal of her cigarette on the rim of the ashtray. 'Does it all sound a bit strange? I can't tell. They say you can get used to anything. Why?'

'I'm sorry. Do you mind talking about it?'

'I suppose not, but I don't think there's much to say. And really it's not what you and I are here for, is it?'

'But it's curious. There must be a story. Were you ever close?'

'I thought it was women who behaved the way you are behaving. As children, yes, I suppose we were close. But people grow up and they change, don't they? For a long time, during the war, I didn't see him, of course. He was a prisoner.'

'Do you like his writing?'

'I think I do, rather. Not that I know much about it. He's neglected, of course. Like all the best poets.' She laughed. 'I mean, he must be one of the best, obviously. Otherwise he wouldn't be doing it, would he?'

'I suppose he is neglected. Certainly not a follower of fashion. Tim Connolly tries to keep us up to date with his work.'

'That drip? Does he really? I shouldn't think he understands a word, except perhaps at a pinch "and" and "the". Dreary little man with his ghastly washed-out wife and their little tribe. Who does he think they are? The Quiverfuls?'

We drank silently for a while.

'I don't suppose you ever finished that picture of me?' I said.

'I did, more or less, I suppose. God, now I suppose you want to see it, do you? Vanity, Stephen – beware of it. Remember, you might not like it. I don't think I really captured your naive beauty. It's just a picture.'

'The pitiless gaze of the icy heart. I was worried about that.'

'That's the one. I can see you've done your homework. Come on, then.' She led me upstairs to the attic she used as a storeroom. It was piled with years of work. 'Careful,' she said, as she switched on the light. 'Some of the boards are loose. I'm the only one who ever comes in here, so it never seems worth getting anything done about it. You're one of the first, you lucky boy.' I seemed to be spending a lot of time in women's attics.

She retrieved the canvas from a stack resting against the fireplace. The picture was about two feet by two, a half-portrait.

I propped the picture on the mantelpiece. I was shown seated in the light from the north window of the studio, my gaze directed slightly downwards. Maggie herself could be seen at her easel in a mirror that she had invented for the purpose of the picture. I was wearing the sleeveless pullover with its muted colours and old-fashioned horizontal pattern. The whole thing – like the landscape I'd commented on before – was finely done yet slightly anachronistic, as though painted before the war. I looked pale and somehow powerless, as though undergoing questioning I would not be able to satisfy.

'So,' she said. 'Shall we go back to not talking?'

'No, no, it's very good, Maggie. Very strong. It's just a bit eerie to find oneself represented. Laid bare.'

'You're fully clothed.'

'You know what I mean. I don't cut a very impressive figure, I suppose.'

'If you say so. No, you'll do. Anyway, it's not meant to be a Sargent, otherwise you'd be wearing a ballgown. Of course, if you buy it, you can burn it, like Clemmie with the Churchill portrait. I think that was quite a stylish thing to do, actually. Showed who was boss.'

I looked again at the young man marooned in the picture, at the brisk contrast with the image of the painter at work – that dark, slightly disturbing line of her brow, the green eyes looking straight through to a vanishing point. It was clever work, but I didn't like it. It seemed like a pretext.

'I don't suppose I could afford it.' I made a sad face.

'Better wait till your birthday, then. If you're good, we'll see.'

'What other people have you done?'

'Oh, all kinds really, over the years. Can't remember offhand.' She looked through another stack and then stopped, seeming bored with it, all her sharp energy gone in a moment. 'Why don't you have a look? If you want to. I'm going to get a drink. Don't forget to turn the light off when you come down.'

I searched through the stack by the fireplace. There were a couple of pictures of her husband seated at a kitchen table. One showed him reading; one had him looking at his hands with a book face down to one side. He was being absorbed into the dark ground of the picture, as though into an anglicized Bonnard, without the benefit of Mediterranean light.

With a jolt I discovered that there were also several paintings of Rackham, two of them with Maggie occupying the same position as in my portrait. One showed Rackham in uniform, seated by a window in autumnal sunlight. There was an unmistakeable satirical swagger about him – as though to indicate that he could carry off the look as well as any Guards officer but that the role did not define or contain him.

Next to her signature was the date: 1945. Rackham had been happy to wear the uniform in peacetime, to sit for a portrait as though everything was perfectly normal. Perhaps it *was* normal. Perhaps there had been mitigation that Carson never knew about.

Next was a half-portrait dated 1950 with the same set-up as the picture of me. Rackham looked up from under the family brow, his black hair half in his eyes, his expression one of complacent assurance and challenge. He wore no shirt under the pullover, but there was a red bandana round his neck. Maggie's facility was remarkable: here he might have been painted by John Minton. Behind this was a brown and bloody impersonation of Sickert, with a naked figure who, going by his black hair, could well have been Rackham, reclining on a disordered bed in the sour, impoverished light from an unseen window. No date this time. Another, dated earlier this year, showed him seated in suit and gown, his black hair unchanging in the cold spring light, his expression unreadable. How occasional could the contact between brother and sister be, to produce this body of work?

There was also a reclining nude after Manet's 'Olympia', with Rackham in the role of the African attendant. This was a good deal more recent, because the model for Olympia was quite clearly Shirley and the setting was Maggie's own bedroom, the high brass bedstead spread with white covers. Shirley was wearing her red stilettos. I remembered her shoe box of pictures – society portraits of a place where I would never belong, whose inhabitants I knew but scarcely recognized.

I went back downstairs to the kitchen. Maggie was at the table, going through a back copy of *Vogue* with a pair of scissors, cigarette in mouth, blinking against the smoke.

'I've opened another bottle. Since it's the weekend. Find what you were looking for?' she asked. I poured myself a glass and sat down opposite her.

'There are several portraits of Charles.'

'The old days. Long ago and far away.' She lied without hesitation, while knowing I must have seen the most recent picture.

'It was a surprise to see Shirley. I didn't know she did modelling.'

'Who?'

'Shirley. The girl in the homage to "Olympia".'

'Oh, her, yes, Olympia. Shirley? Is that what's she's called? Quite a natural. She models at the art school sometimes. I used to teach the odd session there and I was looking for someone suitable for that project. She came recommended. I'd forgotten you knew her. Of course, Shirley. She was good in a sleepy sort of way. Didn't mind taking her things off. Good at lying there. Didn't seem to know what was going on half the time.'

'Well, let's face it, who does?' I said.

Maggie smiled without looking up.

'Do you really never exhibit?'

'Not so far.' She lit another cigarette and carried on cutting things out.

'But you're serious about your work, so shouldn't you?'

She shook her head.

'It's because I'm serious that I don't exhibit.'

'I don't follow.'

'Just use your eyes,' she said.

'The work is very accomplished.'

'Yes. Isn't it? I've got nothing to add but the desire to add something.' I found that it was cruelly important to me that she should say this aloud. She put down the scissors and poured another glass of wine. 'But it's something to do in between all the rest of it.'

'The pictures of your brother are striking.'

'Well, he is. He was.'

'And you don't see much of him.'

'As I said. No, I don't. Why?'

'I don't know, really. It just struck me.'

'He has his own life to lead.'

'But you still paint him sometimes. That must take a while.'

'Sometimes, yes.'

'You seem very different from one another.'

'Perhaps. But again, why are you interested? Has he said something?'

'No. It's not that. Well, in fact he's said a lot, most of it about the mock election.'

'Oh, that. Isn't it a nuisance? I should think you've more than enough to do without taking that on.'

'Carson used to organize it,' I said. 'I inherited the task.'

'Oh well, if it's ancestor-worship.'

'Your brother and I disagree about the election,' I said. 'He sponsored the BPP candidate.'

'Did he now? Well, Charles can be a bit mischievous when he wants to.' She laughed. 'He gets bored, you see. But I don't really want to talk about him any more.'

'Can't I be interested in your life?'

'Charles is not my life. And no, you can't, not really. What we have is here, at times like this. This is it. This has to be enough. Christ. Why are people so sentimental? It's just – it's something to do, isn't it? Anyway, it's getting late. Are you staying?'

Later, when I was sure that she was asleep, I went back up to the storeroom and placed the envelope in the space beneath a loosened floorboard. It seemed suspiciously like taking the initiative, but I had no idea what the next move should be.

I awoke before her. As I dressed, I looked at her face in repose. It was cruel, somehow, and as if never-sleeping. I turned to go and she called out, a word or a name I couldn't catch.

TWENTY-SIX

Bonfire Night came and went. On Wednesday morning the city smelled of the aftermath, with spent rockets lying in the street and poking out of hedges, and vast, ashy, red-eyed circles smouldering on bombsites. Some idiot had fired a marine flare which had fallen on a greenhouse in the allotments behind the school. The morning paper called for tighter regulation of this danger to life and property.

Wednesday afternoon was given over to sport. Sporadic cries could be heard from the House rugby matches. I was in the library deciding which items among the older fiction stock could safely be transported to the storeroom and then forgotten about until someone braver had the temerity to dispose of them. Claes would have hoovered them up, I thought, though the idea of him on the school premises seemed unnatural. Marryatt and Henty, I supposed, had better stay. Percy F. Westerman could go, and I would risk removing Sapper. Q? Who had ever read Q in the first place? The Buchan material could be thinned out. *The Riddle of the Sands* could stay, though it had not been borrowed since a new edition had been bought five years previously. *The Four Feathers* had better stay. *Jock of the Transvaal* could go. I found this task calming.

Feldberg, who was excused games on medical grounds, perhaps having the disease of preferring reading to blundering about in the clinging mud and fog of the rugby fields, was assisting me, wheeling the laden trolley to the storeroom, where the books would await some kind of further organization – by my successor, at this rate. Inevitably as we worked our way along the stacks we both ended up reading passages from some of the books, while maintaining a desultory discussion.

'Anthony Hope, sir.'

'Keep it.'

'Meredith.'

'Storeroom.'

'Ouida.'

'How did that get in here? Storeroom.'

Feldberg made a note and added the book to the trolley.

'Are you happy at Blake's, Feldberg?'

He became wary. 'I'm not sure I understand, sir.'

'I didn't mean it to be a difficult question. I mean, do you like it here?' This was going wrong already.

'It enables me to study what I wish,' he said. 'Captain Carson was very encouraging.'

'And you miss him.'

He nodded, uncomfortably.

'Well, we'll have to do our best.' Another nod. My enquiries seemed to have stalled. I had merely exposed my own perceived inadequacy in comparison with Carson. I was myself a symptom of decline. Feldberg would be glad to see the back of the place, which would in turn choose not to remember him.

'Is there something else, sir?'

I felt I must press on, however crass the effect. There might not be another chance to talk.

'Do you feel at home? Do you feel you belong?'

'Does it matter?' he replied with a faint edge of irritation.

'I think so. It's important to belong.'

'But you can't choose it, can you? A person cannot belong by himself, if you see what I mean. Of his own volition.'

'And that's how you feel.'

'It's the way things are,' he said, patiently. 'The school is a means to an end.'

'I don't think Captain Carson would approve of that view of the matter.'

'But he might understand.'

I seemed unable to direct the conversation.

'To be honest, sir, I'm not really interested in belonging here. I just want to get to the A-levels and Cambridge entrance. The others can have the place in perpetuity and become Old Blakeans and all that, if that's what they want. I suppose that's another reason I don't belong. Not Old Blakean material.'

I stifled a grin and went blundering on. 'Are you being bullied or mistreated?'

'Sir?' He seemed shocked.

'You would tell me, I hope.'

'If the other boys were doing that, no, obviously I wouldn't tell you. Any more than they would in the same position. That's just how the place works. Anyway, the sixth form is different from the lower school. More gentlemanly perhaps. Less fisticuffs, generally speaking.' He gave a cold smile. 'After all, the founder wanted to educate the boys to be Christian gentlemen.'

'And other than the boys, how do you find it? Do the staff treat you properly?'

Again the cold smile. 'No comment, sir. This is not the place where such matters are settled.'

I didn't follow this last point. He took up his list again and I looked out of the window, at a loss.

'And the mock election?'

'I expect we will lose, given the political complexion of the electorate.' Feldberg kept a straight face while saying this.

'But there has not been any trouble?'

He considered this.

'People make a lot of noise. It remains to be seen if they will actually do anything more than that.' He turned back to the books. 'What about *Sorrell and Son*, sir?'

Below in the masters' car park the Bentley arrived with elderly grace in a space under the vast copper-beech tree. The Colonel got out of the driver's side. His passenger was Hamer. Gammon appeared and greeted the pair, ushering the Colonel towards the Main Hall. Hamer looked up, saw me and came towards the library. It was not yet three o'clock, but already the afternoon was darkening.

'Sir? *Sorrell and Son*?'

'Put it on the trolley, Feldberg. Take that load through to the storeroom and then you can go and do some of your own work in the carrels.'

If Feldberg was surprised at this abrupt change of activity he did not show it. Time to read was always welcome.

I went to the librarian's office and sat down, pretending to examine some publishers' catalogues. There might be nothing in the visit. The Colonel could be here in some benign military capacity. But that would not necessarily account for his companion.

'Hard at work?' asked Hamer, appearing in the doorway.

'As you see. The place has to keep ticking over.'

'Of the making of many books there is no end. Or should that be "marking"?'

'Can I help you, Mr Hamer?'

'Well, I hope so, Maxwell. Let's go for a walk, shall we? I need to talk to you.'

I was going to plead work, but his look stopped me.

The grounds were already sunk in murk when we set out. We went into the woods at the back of the science prefab, by what I thought of as the widdershins route, within sight of the fence and the houses of Fernbank Avenue beyond. Lights showed in a few of the porches. Hamer picked his way fastidiously along the gritty, rutted path, umbrella at half-rest. In the gloom he looked so pale as to be almost albino.

'I love the old place,' he said, gesturing widely with the umbrella. 'It was the making of me.'

'I suppose a lot of people would say the same.'

There was a silence.

'The thing is, Maxwell,' he eventually said, 'what you have to ask yourself, is whether this, here, Blake's, is where it all begins or where it ends.'

'Sounds a bit metaphysical.'

'If you like. But in practical terms?'

'I do know that I like my job.'

'Of course you do. And it's just as well.'

'I don't follow.' I stopped.

Hamer went on a few paces, then half-turned. 'It was all a bit of a mess, frankly. Lucky to get out with a whole skin. You won't be the last, I dare say. But whether you've learned anything? Hard to say.'

I stopped walking. 'What are you talking about, Hamer?' He looked steadily at me now. 'What has that to do with anything?'

'Mrs Crane, wasn't it? Wife of a don.'

We stepped aside as a group of runners stumbled past, followed at an effortless lope by the black-clad, white-haired Matthews, before I spotted the perpetual Senior Service cupped in his hand.

'Afternoon, gentlemen,' he said as he passed. Hamer raised his umbrella.

'So, Maxwell, you were saying.'

'No, Mr Hamer, you were the one doing the saying.'

He rested the tip of his umbrella on my shoulder for a moment, smiling his colourless smile, then walked on. We turned left and followed the wooded path that ran above the bank of the creek. The tide was high. *Lorelei* was leaving its mooring, Rackham stood on deck, but I couldn't see who was in the cabin. Rackham glanced across indifferently as we passed. I nodded. Hamer raised his umbrella. The boat moved steadily away under the railway bridge and out of sight.

'Sea fever, eh?' said Hamer. 'Are you a nautical type, Maxwell?' he asked.

'No. Please get to the point.'

He nodded. 'Not the kind of adventure that interests you, eh? You prefer a different sort of manly pursuits, I dare say. More of an indoor chap, eh?'

A train crawled over the bridge. I wondered how long Hamer was going to keep this up.

'She had a breakdown, I believe. Pills and gin. Such a pretty woman, and so *young*. Where is she now, d'you know? Of course not. Somewhere quiet and private in the rural depths. Lost the baby, of course, though Crane would have taken it on as his own. It was a tragic situation.' He shook his head.

'I'm well aware of that,' I said. 'I can't see what business any of it is of yours.'

'No, I understand you would feel that.' He nodded, as if considering a reasonable proposition, then moved on. We entered the further woodland by the railway line. 'And somehow you crawled more or less uninjured from the wreckage.'

Stragglers approached, gasping but quickening their pace when they saw us. Some way behind us in the gloom old Matthews, having lapped them, had stopped and was barking encouragement. I could imagine him running on the spot as he did so, nursing his cigarette.

'And Captain Carson took pity on you. Captain Carson could see something in you that no one else could see – not Mr Gammon, for example. Gammon was always blind to your virtues, even before your Cambridge performance. He thought you were a waster and a skirt chaser. Some would say he had a point. But you were Captain Carson's protégé. Not the first – he was always a great encourager, always, since first he came here as a master. It was part of his gift, part of his nature. People, even dim, dry people like Gammon, deferred to his, shall we say, charismatic authority.'

'He was a good man. He was kind.'

'Yes? I wonder what he saw in you as time went on. When you were a boy your promise would have been obvious. So he encouraged it, steered you, shaped you – took you in hand, as they say. And off you went, exhibition in the bag, off to his old college and then off again, down the road to ruin and catastrophe and tears before and after and for all I know during bedtime. Kaput. Gone in the night with a Third, a wrong 'un, expunged, as far as possible, from the record.'

I felt a sense of horror there in the wood. What Hamer said was true, but it was not his truth to tell.

'Have you finished? I have work to do,' I said.

'Not yet. As I say, I wonder what redeeming element Carson thought he could detect in you after your disgrace. What could he see in his fallen boy that made him so protective? So determined to overcome your detractors. I mean, he must have been well aware of your record. Aware of your stupidity and lack of self-control, aware of the waste of promise. If you were such a reckless skirt-chaser, what else might you not be, given the right circumstances? Perhaps he believed he could convert you.'

'I'm going to go back to the library now,' I said.

'No, you're not, Maxwell. We will finish our walk. This is the only time you will be told. This is your only opportunity. Walk away now and you will be packing your bags – and that will only be the beginning of it. Gabbitas and Thring will be unable to save you, Maxwell. You will be lucky if Binns will take you on to sell school uniforms. No, you'll be lucky if you're left in charge of a Salvation Army khazi. I hope that's clear. And apart from anything else, there is Blake's to think of.'

The path led briefly out to the edge of the trees before winding into the gloom again. Two mud-blackened, exhausted rugby teams clashed under a cloud of steam over a ten-yard stretch of the Spion Kop pitch. The air was blueish now, as if an army had been smoking heavily.

'Play up Old House!' shouted Hamer.

I was obliged to respond. 'Come on Flags!'

A penalty was awarded. The opposition retreated to the try-line while the full back balanced the ball on the mud. The whistle blew. He ran up to take the kick. The ball hit the crossbar. Both teams jeered amiably and the referee called no-side. The players trailed dankly off to the pavilion, stooped like old men in the cold. We walked on, past the pavilion and once more into the trees.

'As I say, I love this place,' said Hamer. 'Do you remember Keyworth, used to be Head of Classics?'

'Before my time. As I'm sure you know.'

'Or McPhail, the chemist?'

'Ditto.'

'Hard bastards in a hard school. But we loved them and it.'

'I can imagine.'

'We knew where we were.'

'Could anyone doubt it?'

'You don't play sport?' asked Hamer.

'Not nowadays. I prefer a book.'

'Books, of course. But – a great leveller, sport. Reminds us who we are, what we're part of.'

'Do you really believe that?'

'I'd better, hadn't I, all things considered?'

'You must think I'm an idiot, with your pep talk, Hamer.'

'I do. And you are. And I am not alone in this conviction.'

The woods were drawing darkness into themselves. The lights in the school buildings were a long way off. 'But a solution is in your hands.' Slit trenches had been dug on the edge of a clearing. The air smelled of smoke.

'I don't know what you want,' I said.

'I ask again. Did Captain Carson leave any records, journals, documents?'

'The answer is the same. I don't know. If he did, I haven't got them. I don't even know if they exist. You would know better than me. I imagine you've already looked. Certainly, someone broke into my flat.'

'I'm sure you have lots of enemies.'

'Then it must be important,' I said. My heart thudded. 'People like yourself and the Colonel don't appear on the scene for no reason. Is it connected with the war somehow? Why would such material matter, anyway?'

'I would advise you not to concern yourself with that,' he said.

'Who do you work for, in fact?'

Hamer turned to face me.

'Let us suppose you are telling the truth, and move on,' he said. 'We turn our attention to your friend Rackham.'

'He's not my friend.'

'But you know him.'

'I work in the same school. We have very little contact.'

'But his sister is your friend. You know her rather well.'

'Mrs Rowan is a colleague.'

'Yes, she is. A close colleague of yours. A close, respected colleague.'

'That's enough, Hamer. There's no need to drag her into this.'

'Well, let's hope not,' he said.

'She's got nothing to do with it.'

'That's not for you to say, is it?'

'She mustn't be hurt.'

'Then a solution lies in your hands, Maxwell. You have created a situation in which her being hurt is a possibility, if not yet a likelihood. And after all, this is not the first time, is it?'

We were approaching the lake now. The water was still. The raft was firmly moored at the wooden jetty. We stood and looked at it.

'This is the dreadful spot, then,' Hamer said, using the ferrule of his umbrella to detach a leaf from the sole of his shoe. '"The dreadful hollow behind the little wood". I wonder if, given the choice, Carson might not have preferred a death like Socrates, given the natural resources to hand.'

'I find it hard to believe that Carson is dead,' I replied. 'And we don't know what happened.'

'The inquest found the death to be accidental. Due process was observed. There is nothing to add at this stage.'

'I wonder. I wonder why you and the Colonel turned up when he was dead. I'd never seen you here before then. I'm sure you don't believe in coincidence any more than I do.'

'We attended the funeral of a distinguished member of staff in our capacity as old boys.'

'And I'm the King of Poland.' I did not see the blow coming. I fell to my hands and knees, choking.

'Captain Carson is dead and gone,' said Hamer, quietly, 'and no useful purpose is served by further enquiry into matters which must of their nature remain unknown. You should derive what wisdom you can from the fact. Do you understand me?' I nodded. 'Then for God's sake get up, man. I hate violence. But I can do it. Don't make me do it again.'

Hamer began to walk again, heading around the lake towards the level-crossing gate.

'Now, as to the delightful Mrs Rowan, so troubled by her husband's malaise, so brave in sticking it out come what may, so resourceful – and yet so careless – in her means of solace, you have an opportunity to prevent misfortune or injury befalling her. That will be for the best – for Mrs Rowan, for you, for the posthumous reputation of Captain Carson. For the good of the school, if that idea is not absurd to you.'

'Not entirely,' I said. 'Anyway, does it matter what I think?' Maggie would certainly have something to say about Hamer's instructions regarding her, if I were so foolish as to tell her.

'And for the general good. There is a cause you can serve. That will be something new for you.'

'What is it you want, Hamer?'

'You are investigating Charles Rackham.'

'Not exactly.'

'Then tell me exactly.' The umbrella waited quietly in Hamer's hand.

'Rackham seems to want to harm one of the boys.'

'Which boy is this?'

'David Feldberg.'

'Oh, him. How do you know?'

'Things I've seen. Hints.'

'Not much to go on.'

'I believe it.'

'Schools are full of dislikes and cruelties. That is part of their nature. You might say it's what they're *for*. To temper the steel.' We moved on a little way. 'And why does it matter how Rackham treats Feldberg?'

'Because it's not right,' I said.

Hamer gave me his look of sorely tried patience. 'I think I've dealt with that aspect of things, Maxwell.'

'David Feldberg is a very gifted pupil. Oxbridge material.'

'And he was Carson's protégé. And now he's yours. And at one time Rackham too was Carson's protégé. It's a bit of a web, isn't it?'

'Why should Feldberg suffer?' I said.

'Perhaps he deserves it.'

'Why? What has he done?'

'Need he have done anything?'

'So you're on Rackham's side?'

'I'm a servant of the Crown, Maxwell. That's the only side I'm on.'

The dark was complete now. The faint noise of traffic reached us in the wood. I thought of Carson's letter. So Rackham had a protector, and Hamer and the Colonel were acting for him.

'The question is, which side are *you* on?'

'I'm on the side of a quiet life. I suspect I'm not going to get one. I think Rackham is also doing harm to a friend of mine, Shirley Thorpe, and that he is doing so together with Claes Vlaminck.'

'Well, never mind that. She doesn't matter, obviously. Now, these enquiries of yours into Rackham . . .'

'You're telling me to stop.'

'That would be for the best all round.'

'Why? Is this connected with Carson?'

'That is not your concern. Anything you do know, anything you've withheld – this would be the time to make good the omission.'

'You searched my flat.'

'Do you think so? Perhaps you had a burglar.'

'Nothing was taken.'

'Perhaps you didn't have what the burglar wanted.'

'I have nothing in my possession. Do you imagine that if I had, given this afternoon, I wouldn't tell you? I abhor violence as much as you do.' We had reached the level-crossing gate.

'Which way are you going?' he asked. 'Over the tracks?'

'Back to school.'

'Good idea.' He took out a card and handed it to me. It bore a telephone number. 'If anything does turn up, any materials and so on, ring me up.'

I stepped away and felt the point of the umbrella against my back. I turned.

'This was a warning, Maxwell. Heed it. Last chance.' Saluting with the umbrella, Hamer opened the gate and crossed the track to Percival Street.

I wished a train would silently appear and run him over. Between the bare trees there was a dim light on in Maggie's studio. When Hamer was safely on the other side the signal turned red and, too late, a coal train came lumbering up the line, heading for the docks. I watched its slow passage. When it had gone, the street beyond was empty.

I made my way round the far side of the lake back towards the sixth-form block where the library was housed. Out of the darkness appeared Lurch, wheeling a barrow full of soil, on which rested a spade. He gave no sign of recognition. In fact, he seemed barely conscious.

When I came to the school car park I saw the Bentley. The Colonel was in the driver's seat, reading the *Racing Post* by the interior lamp. He raised his hand in salute as I went by. It was an eloquent, studiedly casual gesture, delivered as though he and I were long acquainted, not friends but certain of where we stood in the scheme of things. He wound the window down.

'Off back to the library?'

'There's always plenty to do.'

'No point playing games in the dark, is there? Pity. Good man. Keep it up.'

As I opened the door of the sixth-form block I heard the engine start, and turned to watch the Bentley pulling away through the gate, down Fernbank, and towards Cemetery Road. Everything seemed insubstantial in comparison with the bluff Colonel and his splendid vehicle.

I went into the lavatory and tried to clean the mud off the knees of my trousers. When I returned to the library Feldberg was sitting reading at the issue desk.

'Is there anything else, sir?'

'No, Feldberg, thank you. You may as well get off.'

'I'd rather stay and read, if that's all right, sir.'

'As you wish. Anyone would think you had no home to go to. Where's your girl, anyway?'

'I imagine she's in the library at St Clare's, sir.'

'Perhaps you should live a little,' I said. 'Take her to the pictures again. Or to a concert.'

Feldberg regarded me tolerantly.

'Who was it who said, "Some people say life's the thing, but I prefer reading"?'

'You've got me there, sir, but I could look it up.'

PART FOUR

TWENTY-SEVEN

I sat in the back bar of the Narwhal, drinking slowly, and tried to draw up a summary of the position. It was early evening and the place was almost empty. Claes was in his usual position over in the snug. I raised a hand in greeting and he smiled in return, indicating that I might wish to join him. I made my way round. Claes's stool was placed against the mirrored partition next to the closed door to the main bar. It did not seem a comfortable position for someone of his size.

'Maxwell, my friend. I was hoping I might run into you.'

'You could have come round into the back bar.'

'Each to his own. It was not urgent.'

'What did you have in mind?'

He produced a book about Degrelle in French.

'I managed to find a further copy after you expressed an interest.'

I had not done this, but I made no objection. 'Thank you, Claes. What do I owe you?'

'Think of it as a gift. A bond of friendship.'

'This is very kind of you.'

'You have the language?'

'Enough, I think.'

'You must tell me what you make of the book.'

'I'll be sure to do that.'

'It is a work of vision.' He nodded as though to persuade me to do likewise.

'What will you drink?' I asked.

'Please, a Snowball.'

'An unusual choice, if you don't mind me saying so.'

'Refreshing, I find.'

I ordered another pint for myself. Stan Pitt was serving.

'Don't normally see you over on this side,' he said.

'Perhaps he is feeling adventurous,' said Claes. 'Perhaps, as you English say, he fancies a change.' Stan gave an unreadable nod, served the drinks and moved out of sight.

'I see that Sir Lewis Allingham will be addressing a meeting next week,' I said.

'The prophet returns,' said Claes, nodding once more, sipping his drink. His grey tongue was yellow now. 'The exile comes home.'

'And do you think you'll be attending?'

'Naturally. All the comrades will be there to pledge themselves to the renewed struggle.'

'Struggle? I thought Allingham was standing for election.'

'The struggle takes many forms.'

'I was wondering about going along. As a historian I am interested in Allingham's writings, in an objective sense.'

'I'm delighted to hear it, my friend. Of course you must attend. How better to develop a sense of the fateful days that lie ahead? Of course you must come.' He was terribly excited, as though injected with amphetamines, or somehow drunk on Snowballs. 'The movement flourishes quietly, awaiting the moment when we will rise up and take back what is ours. We prepare, we sow the seeds, we educate, we train. That is for the future.'

'Some way off as yet, then.' I tried to look slightly unimpressed at this news.

Claes raised a hand and shook his grey jowls.

'But for here and now – well, my friend, I cannot tell you precisely.' There was a click as the door behind me closed. I turned to find Lurch there. 'We put down a marker. A warning. A manifestation of the will. An act which will show our true intent.'

I waited. Let him tell you, I thought. Claes has the vanity of the grandiose and impotent. Let him tell you. Be patient.

'I understand, of course,' I said. 'These things are necessarily confidential. They cannot be my concern. You scarcely know me. But thank you. For now I will read the book and look forward to the meeting.' I made as if to leave.

'It is closer than you think, in all senses,' Claes said. 'I can promise you that. Very close now.'

'Then I shall await developments.'

Claes drained his glass.

'Anyway, my friend,' he went on, 'this happy encounter calls for another drink. What will you have?'

'I would very much like to stay,' I said, 'but I have work to do for school.'

'Of course. We must earn our daily bread. Alas. But I understand. You have made a wise decision about the meeting, my friend. We will talk again soon. And for the other matter, only be patient for a little while.'

Lurch stood aside to let me past. Once out on the chilly street, at a loss, I broke the habit of the a lifetime and crossed the road to the grim and violent Botanical Hotel, where I ordered a whisky and sat watching an elderly woman who came in wearing a Salvation Army bonnet and carrying a collection tin. She took off the bonnet and emptied the tin on to the bar. Clucking her tongue at the tight-fistedness of the infidel, she ordered a port and lemon. I raised my glass to her. We were all at it tonight.

When I left the Botanical there was a Rover drawing up under a streetlight across the road. Claes came out of the pub. The uniformed driver got out and opened the rear door of the car for Claes to get in. I stepped back into the pub entrance. Lurch stood in attendance on the pavement. When the car pulled away I saw for a moment that Claes had turned to talk to another passenger. I recognized Rackham. The car turned the corner and disappeared northwards towards the Plain of Axness. Lurch looked up and down the street and across the road at the Botanical. I moved further back. Seemingly satisfied, he went back into the Narwhal. The fake Salvation Army lady pushed past me into the street.

'They're all liars and bastards,' she said, turning to peer at me. 'Liars and bastards.'

'Looks like it,' I said. 'Here.' I gave her a half-crown. She peered at the coin, unimpressed.

'You don't fool me,' she said. 'You're another one, aren't you?'

'Looks like it,' I said. I thought for a moment she was going to throw her tin at me.

Still unable to face going home, I set off for Shirley's. When I went to ring the bell I found the front door was slightly ajar. I stepped into the hall. There was very faint music from upstairs. If someone was expected, it wasn't me. It would have been easy enough to leave again, but I went quietly up the dark stairs to the top landing. Light was cast by the half-open door of her Shirley's flat. The song was 'Time of the Season'. I'd never thought it was sinister before.

I knocked.

'It's open,' she said. The lamps were covered in silk scarves. Shirley was at the dressing table, leaning towards the mirror as she applied mascara. She turned, alarmed.

'You can't be here, Stevie. You've got to go.' She stood up and her dressing gown fell open to reveal an expensive-looking black bra and knickers. She went over and lifted the needle from the record.

'You shouldn't leave the front door open, Shirley. It's not a very respectable part of town. Anyone might turn up. But I take it you're expecting someone.'

'I'm sorry about the other night, Stevie.' She drew her dressing gown closed and stood with her arms folded. 'But d'you mind if we talk about it later?'

'No, Shirley. I'm here now.'

'No, you've got to leave. I mean, I don't mind if you, you know, while I was asleep.'

'I didn't. Of course not. What do you take me for?'

'Well, that's good.'

'Anyway, Shirley, Rackham won't be coming, not tonight.'

'How do you know? You don't know that.' She went to the window and looked down into the street.

'I saw him being chauffeured away from the Narwhal earlier. He was with Claes.' At this she sat down at the dressing table and tears began to run down her face, smudging the careful mascara. She fumbled to light a cigarette. I looked around and found a bottle of gin, poured some in a glass and handed it to her. She nodded, took a sip and dabbed at her face with a tissue.

'He told me he'd be here,' she said.

'Men were deceivers ever,' I said, bringing over another chair.

'Maybe he's just late.'

'No, he's not. Why does it matter, Shirley?'

'Oh, you know. It's just what happens with me and fellers, as usual, 'cause I'm a daft cow. I'm fookin' soft.'

'Rackham's not usual. Is he?'

'He's not like you. I can tell you that.'

'I hope not.'

Now she was shredding a Kleenex with her fingers. 'He said he'd be here.'

'And did you believe him?'

'Got no choice, have I?' she said in a small voice. 'Look, you ought to go really. Please.' She took a new tissue and went on dabbing at her face.

'Why have you no choice?'

'Never mind. Nothing.'

'Has he let you run out?'

'What are you talking about? Run out of what?'

'Whatever you've been taking.'

'Who says I have?'

'I found the works when I was here the other night, Shirley. After I put you to bed.'

'You had no business looking. It's just occasional. Just for a change. We do it together, me and Charles.' I filed this fact away with the Aleister Crowley book and the grimoire. Worse and worse.

'And then there are those photographs.' For a moment I felt like being cruel. 'I didn't know you were that kind of girl, Shirley.'

'There's a lot you don't know. Anyway, that's all private and personal. Nobody's business.'

'I wonder if Rackham thinks about them in the same way. He took them. He's not in them, is he? What do the other participants think, for that matter? Have you got the negatives? You haven't, have you?'

'It was a mistake. It was supposed to be a bit of fun. It's all a mistake. Stop it, Stevie. Can you just get out?'

'And so here you are, waiting for him.'

'Beggars can't be choosers.' She poured more gin. I poured myself some.

'You need to stop,' I said.

'I know that, don't I?'

'It's not too late. You should get help.'

'It's illegal now. Doctors can't prescribe it.'

'You said you weren't using regularly.'

'I'm not, not really.'

'You could go away and sort yourself out.'

'Where to? What would I live on? I barely earn washers as it is. That's why I started modelling.'

'Yes, I saw you. You were being Olympia.'

'I started at life classes at the art college. Then whatserface, Maggie Rowan, she turned up and asked if I would model for her. She was offering OK money, so why not? Where's the harm? It's art, isn't it. Stephen? What we're all supposed to aspire to. And by the way, yes, I do know what Olympia in the real painting did for a living. And Mrs bloody Rowan got me to make her a dress and then never paid for it, so serve me right, I suppose. And now she's got you too.'

I ignored the last barb. 'And what about Charles Rackham?'

'He turned up at the studio. He was really charming. She put him into the picture too.'

'I've noticed.'

'He was just really interesting. This was in the spring sometime, before you came back.'

'Perhaps I should have come back sooner.'

She shrugged, finished her drink and poured another. 'Charles wrote me a poem. You never did that, did you, Stevie?'

'I'm not a poet.'

'The accomplishments of a gentleman, Charles said, should include the ability to turn a sonnet for his mistress.' She smiled at the phrasing. 'Though what he wrote wasn't actually a sonnet.'

'Was it any good?'

'I've no fookin idea. I couldn't tell what it was about. But it was flattering, like someone buying me flowers.'

'I never did that, either.'

'Nobody did, not till Charles came on the scene. And there was the underwear. Made me feel desirable.'

'I must have bought you *something*,' I said.

She laughed. 'There was the crab sandwich that time at the seaside.'

'You're saying I gave you food poisoning, then.'

'It's the thought that counts.' She came and sat on my knee and wrapped her arms around my neck.

'You can't carry on like this, love,' I said.

'I know. I know. But there's something about him. I think I'm in love with him.'

'Oh, Shirley. Well, you can bet he doesn't feel the same way.'

'I know.'

'He's just using you. Then he'll get bored.'

'Like you did.' She rose and went to the window again.

'I'm sorry. We were kids then. I'm trying to help you now.'

'Well, you're talking about trying.'

'I can give you some money to get away for a while.'

'Some bedsit in Leeds? No, thanks.'

'But you're hurting yourself. You're allowing Rackham to hurt you. He likes hurting people.'

'Perhaps that's why we're suited.'

'There's no future in it.'

'Compared to what? At least when he's here I feel alive.' She lit a cigarette and sat on the edge of the bed. Her mascara was still smeared. She reached for an ashtray resting on a pile of Sven Hassel books.

'Maybe not for long.'

'That's up to me. Are you going to tell anyone about the gear?'

'No, of course not.'

'Then, please, can you go? I know you want to help, but we both know there's nothing you can do. Go back to Mrs fucking Rowan. Tell her I want paying for the dress. It's too young for her anyway.'

'I'm trying to finish with her, Shirley.'

'Makes no odds to me.'

'What's Rackham up to?'

'Well, why don't you ask him? You see him more often than I do.'

'Does he talk about his plans? Does he mention any names?'

'No. Claes is the talker. He can't shut up. He's getting worse. Signs. Destiny. Decisive action. I don't think Charles takes him seriously. He uses him and Lurch.'

'Like he uses you.'

'You can't make me stop seeing him, Stephen.'

'No,' I said, 'I can't, can I?'

TWENTY-EIGHT

I was going to say that the city was a place where nothing happened. That's how the residents would describe it to this day, with resentful satisfaction, as a place dozing among the heavy incurious dullness that Bennett, himself no Wittgenstein, found so widespread among the English. But were these people even English, or some further torpid distillation of it, a tribe remote and foreign even where most at home?

To return to my point: it would be more accurate to say that anything could be going on and it would seem to bring no alteration in the texture of everyday life. In one of his few references to the city in *A Firm Foundation* Carson described it as 'a place of settled habits and steady occupation, content with its maritime tradition and largely unconcerned with the larger dramas conducted elsewhere'. Was this tongue in cheek or despairing?

And now there was a controversial by-election at hand with an extreme right-wing candidate who had fame of a sort. But the streets and the parks and shops and pubs and buses seemed indifferent to the grim excitement this might have provoked. There seemed to be no public realm, no Speakers' Corner, no stern editorial in the unreadably parochial local press (the *Chronicle* was, naturally, edited by an Old Blakean). The election would happen and then it would all go away: after all, everything else had, including the Germans, after they had damaged eighty per cent of the housing stock.

Given that surely unrepeatable precedent, the exchanges in the corner shop concerned more pressing matters. When Mr Pawson, the proprietor of the shop round the corner from my flat, asked a man who came in for cigarettes while I was there whether he'd been to see City at the weekend, he was offering a familiar cue, and the reply came reliably, patina'd with loving and contemptuous familiarity: 'They never fookin come to see me when I'm bad.' And the same exchange occurred a hundred times across the flat and flood-prone city. It was true and not true: you could hear the Saturday roar of the football crowd from miles off, but no one owned up to going to the match. They preferred rugby league, but no one went there either. It was a ghost town whose phantoms appeared in the flesh, seen across wide bombsites and down narrow lanes, greeting one another, calling to their children, standing on the doorstep to watch the rag-and-bone man pass on his horse and cart. Auden wrote of Macao: 'Nothing serious can happen here,' and since the Blitz you might have supposed the same had been true hereabouts. No one had quite managed to reawaken themselves or the city from the enchanted dullness. No one wanted to. But really, as I was to learn, anything might happen. It was simply that almost no one would appear to notice.

By the time we reached Remembrance Day the school was papered with election posters and repapered as soon as Sergeant Risman had torn them down. Boys went about with lapel badges for the main parties. I had outlawed the red-and-black chevroned armbands of the BPP as soon as they began to appear, but they took on a clandestine currency in the middle school, something to wear, something to be part of, a chance to transgress and yet to be on the winning side, or so the wearers thought. The ban was then promulgated by Gammon in assembly as if it had not previously been in effect, so that my control of events seemed to become even weaker than before, like a puppet government awaiting the inevitable takeover. When I complained to Maggie, she observed that Weimar chancellors must at times have felt the same. I was suitably put down for my presumption.

The service itself, taking place in the Main Hall, was marked by a very decent rendition of 'The Last Post' by a bugler out in the quad, and a reading by Rackham of Binyon's famous poem. He read it well, understanding the need to understate it. People were moved. I was moved. My loathing of him grew.

The parties standing in the mock election held their meetings at lunchtimes. It looked as if both the Tories and Labour were bleeding votes to the BPP, with the Liberals, as so often since the war, nowhere. On Friday I made the rounds. Tory and Labour were earnest and colourless, with thinnish audiences of sixth formers occasionally heckling at the gatherings overseen good-humouredly by Major Brand and Tim Connolly. Such Liberals as there were, including the candidate, had evidently gone somewhere else.

When I arrived at the science lecture room where the BPP were assembled there was a crowd of boys in the corridor unable to get in. The doormen, Arnesen and another boy whose name I didn't know, both in cadet uniform, removed their chevrons as I approached, but there was a flicker of hesitation about letting me past.

'Why are you two in uniform?' I asked.

'There's a CCF parade after school, sir,' said Arnesen.

'Don't Queen's Regulations forbid altering the uniform or wearing it to support a political cause?' I had no idea if this was true. 'Give me those chevrons.' The pair handed them over, abashed, not meeting my gaze. 'Who would you rather deal with about this? Me or Sergeant Risman?'

'No contest, sir,' said Arnesen, his grin restored.

Not you as well, I thought. 'Good. Now go away and take this rabble with you.'

When I opened the door, the benches in the high, raked room were packed. The place was in semi-darkness, with the ragged blackouts drawn and tall candles burning in holders on the front desk. It was hot and stank of sweat and the sour gas which haunted the science block. The boys' excited faces leaned down out of the dark as if there must be at any moment a revelation.

Steerman, who was speaking, did not see me, and carried

on ranting into the excited silence about immigration and empire and communism and the coming days. He did not refer to notes. The script was so far beyond the boy's narrow capacities that I knew it must have been written for him by Rackham, who now appeared from the shadows, swirling his gown like an opera cloak, and whispered in my ear. 'If you stop him now, there will be a riot. You don't want that, do you?'

And I was afraid, and I let Steerman finish his oration. When he did so, and the place broke out in furious cheering, I switched on the light.

'The lesson bell has rung,' I lied. 'Hurry along now.' There was a groan of deflation, but as the boys dispersed – and how like *uniforms* their black uniforms looked – they were still talking excitedly, and a number surrounded Steerman, who gave me an insolent smirk as he went off down the corridor. Rackham was nowhere to be seen. Arnesen came past. 'I'm disappointed in you, Arnesen.'

'It's not just me, sir,' he said. 'What about the others?'

'What, indeed? Get a move on.' I went round opening the windows.

Tim Connolly appeared in the doorway and shook his head. 'We can't have this,' he said.

How did he know? 'No, but we seem to have got it.'

'Well, what are you going to do about it, Maxwell? It's getting out of hand.'

'What do you suggest? My hands are tied. The BPP are in until Gammon says they're out.'

'Well, it won't do. It's like being in a madhouse. God knows what Carson would have thought. You've got your work cut out following him, haven't you?'

'Thank you for your support,' I said, and left Connolly to it.

At the end of the day Gammon called a meeting. When I arrived in the Headmaster's office, Connolly was there, with Major Brand and Rackham.

'Mr Connolly has raised some concerns about your handling of the mock election, Maxwell,' Gammon said.

The blame was mine; by implication I was the only begetter of the damned election and responsible for all aspects of its conduct, including what went on in people's heads, especially Rackham's and his acolyte's. Not for the first time, I thought how well suited Gammon would have been to the internal politics of a totalitarian regime. At provincial level he would have been an accomplished performer – until, I consoled myself, he was exiled or summarily strung up when the extent of his dereliction became inconvenient for his superiors.

'I can't say I'm happy about the lunchtime meeting,' I began. 'The stewarding left something to be desired.' Rackham looked insouciant.

'It was like a torchlight rally,' said Connolly. 'They had the blinds in the science lecture theatre closed and the place was lit by candles.'

'You weren't there,' I said, though of course he was right.

'But I was,' Rackham remarked. 'It was certainly theatrical.'

'You mean play-acting?' asked Gammon, who did not much like plays.

'It's not good for the boys to get worked up like that,' said Major Brand. 'Save it for the rugby field.'

'Or the battlefield,' said Rackham.

The Major sniffed and shook his head. 'Teach them the difference between play-acting and what's real,' he said, to no one in particular.

'We shouldn't really have a party like the BPP standing in the mock election,' said Connolly, as if it were only just becoming clear to him. 'They're not really democrats, are they?'

'The BPP exists in the world,' said Rackham. 'It obviously appeals to some voters. Ought we to pretend otherwise? Or when it suits us are *we* not to be democrats?'

'You know what I mean, Rackham. There have to be

limits,' Connolly insisted. He looked at me and I nodded, assuming what I hoped was a sufficiently concerned expression.

'I understand you very well,' Rackham replied, with his infuriating smile.

Connolly shook his head, at a loss.

'Liberalism bares its fangs, eh?' said Rackham.

'We could proscribe the BPP for electoral misconduct,' I suggested.

Rackham laughed. 'Proscribe? Now there's word you don't hear very often. Usually reserved for times of grave emergency.'

'Look,' said Gammon, 'we need to deal with the situation as we find it. We don't need any trouble. The city council would like nothing better than an excuse to incorporate us with the rest in this comprehensive-school nonsense.' Gammon's paranoia meant that all problems were bound up with that threat. I thought the governors might have something to say about it, should it arise, but Gammon was clearly in no mood to listen to such a suggestion. He needed to be right.

'We can hardly *proscribe* the party during the election,' said Rackham. 'What kind of example would that give? If that were going to be done it should have been decided before the campaign began.' Supposing we'd been given chance, I thought, but I kept my impotent counsel. 'But it seems not to have occurred to anyone, because the whole election was unplanned and casually set in motion,' Rackham concluded.

The lie sounded wholly reasonable.

'No, apparently it didn't occur to anyone,' Gammon muttered, glancing at me. He looked at Major Brand for comments. The Major, who, whatever his private opinion, clearly saw himself as unpolitical because a simple soldier, shook his head unhappily and peered out of the window at the dark field.

'But surely there can be no more torchlight rallies,' insisted Connolly.

Rackham conceded this with a smile. The event had

already happened and its excitement and allure could not be undone now. In the course of the afternoon it had become a legend, though I can assure you that you will not find it in the official history.

Connolly had not finished: 'Some of the boys are likely to attend the actual BPP meeting in the town, where the General is to speak. Can that be prevented? Some of them are rather stirred up.'

'You mean ban them from attending?' asked Gammon. 'I wonder. If you'd asked me last year I doubt if I'd have hesitated. Now, though . . . Isn't that a matter for their parents?' An incident taking place off the school premises might be more likely to draw the malign attention of the local council than a meeting a school at lunchtime, surely, but Gammon's other great fear – the parents – took over now.

'Do you suppose that if they want to go they'll actually tell their parents their plans?' Connolly asked.

'Some of their parents might be planning to attend anyway,' I said. Nobody responded to this.

'If it were a matter for expulsion,' said the Major, 'that would be a harsh penalty. They're, well, they're just our boys, after all, and all this is a game to them, an excitement, something out of the routine. In the end, it's up to us to try to make something of them. They may in any case see these BPP types for what they are when they see them in action. I must say I think it's a shame Allingham's involving himself. You'd think he'd have learned by now. Should have stuck to soldiering. Had a lot to offer in that sphere.'

Gammon shook his head. He had come to the end of his competence and no more could be asked of him. The world could not be made to conform, and I should have known that in Gammon at such a time there would emerge an aspect of Pilate. You're in charge, Gammon, I thought. So *be* in charge, one way or the other. Ignore Rackham. Ban the BPP and forbid the boys to attend Allingham's meeting.

But in the end Gammon was an appeaser of whatever

powers presented themselves. As an act of empty rebellion I lit a cigarette, since the Major had started wheezing away on his unlit pipe. But again nobody seemed to notice.

'Up to you, Acting Headmaster,' Rackham said. 'Unless you think you should consult the actual Head, though of course he's unlikely to be available.'

'Whatever anyone thinks about it,' said Gammon, recovering, 'the BPP is a political party with an official candidate standing in the actual parliamentary by-election, and whatever we think of the candidate's political views, he is a distinguished military man with a life of service, and a writer of books, as well as being an old boy, and we do want the boys to take an interest in current affairs.' I had never heard Gammon express such an aspiration before, but its convenience was evident. 'So as long as the boys are not in uniform I think we may have to accept it,' Gammon replied. 'We can hardly allow them to attend BPP meetings here and ban them from the real thing, can we?'

'Quite,' said Rackham. 'In any case, a ban would, I strongly suggest, provoke disobedience on a large scale. We know what happened at the CCF recruitment meeting, Major. Mr Gammon as Acting Head would not be expelling a mere two or three boys, from what I've seen. Bearing in mind his comments about the local council, the consequences of that should be considered before any attempt to exert power in such a way. And their parents, who pay the fees, have some understandable expectations.'

'Then they could warn their own sons off,' said Connolly. 'Perhaps a letter to all the boys' homes—'

Gammon waved this away impatiently. 'The school governs itself or it does not,' he insisted. Connolly began to talk about convening the governors, but Gammon talked over him and Connolly at last gave up a cause that I suspect he knew had been lost before ever he'd opened his mouth. 'Rackham,' said Gammon, 'you've seen the situation at first hand. What do you suggest?'

'That we keep a watching brief. That we have staff in attendance to make sure none of our boys gets into trouble.'

'There might be violence, I've heard,' said Connolly.

'Yes, possibly with the communists from the so-called university and the trade unionists trying to make the whole thing into a circus. All the more reason for our presence to see fair play and good order,' said Rackham.

'Very well,' Gammon said, rising. 'It's agreed.' This was news to me. 'We remain calm. Next week Maxwell and Mr Rackham will attend the BPP meeting, discreetly.' I thought: you have just legitimized my disgrace. 'And let us hope that nothing occurs that any of us shall have reason to regret.' He looked at me as he spoke. 'Thank you, gentlemen.'

In the hall the Major took me by the arm. 'Steady the Buffs, Maxwell. That's what Captain Carson would have wanted.' Steady them your fucking self, I thought. 'And take Sergeant Risman with you,' the Major added. 'The boys know where they are with Risman.' Insult aside, that was the best idea I'd heard for ages.

TWENTY-NINE

Local press coverage was, to say the least, sparing, and a by-election in a safe Labour seat attracted comparatively little national interest. Allingham had fallen from his former prominence and seemed to be viewed as an embarrassment, almost a joke, to be politely ignored if possible. And even though I was under orders to attend, I might have missed the meeting but for a typed note placed in my pigeonhole stating that the venue had been changed from the Assembly Rooms to Axness Hall, which was not even in the same constituency. The organizers seemed to be trying to avoid trouble.

The new venue for Allingham's public meeting had almost slipped out of the city's collective memory, although it was still standing and in use. Axness Hall had at one time been favoured by Moral Rearmament, by visiting American evangelists who'd wandered from the beaten track, and by spiritualist events involving clairvoyants and the like. It was now mostly used for amateur dramatics and gymnastics displays. The place, then, was rather old-fashioned even in an old-fashioned setting. It was also located on the far side of the River Ouse, which divided the city; thus it seemed full of unhappy portent. People from our side tended to avoid going over there. Proverbially you would 'catch summat' if you were foolish enough to cross South Bridge into that slum-terraced back of beyond which so closely and disorientingly resembled our own.

There were exceptions. It was OK to go to the dog track. That was what Sergeant Risman had been planning to do on the evening in question.

'You say this is what the Major wants, Mr Maxwell?' Risman asked, seated at his gleaming desk in his cubbyhole.

'He suggested it.'

When I said that we should arrive separately, he looked at me to indicate that I should have nothing to say on the matter. 'Until this evening, then, Mr Maxwell. Make sure you wrap up warm.'

I keep talking about Allingham as if he were a presence, when really he is scarcely a name now, and very nearly forgotten, so here I insert a brief sketch to enable you to place him a little more exactly. Sir William Allingham (Blake's 1901–8) was a soldier and military theorist, wounded and decorated at Loos and Passchendaele, rising to the rank of general between the wars. His book on mechanized warfare had been a standard work on the topic, carefully studied by Guderian and by the Russians, and tested out at the epic stalemate at Kursk in 1943 with unprecedented bloodiness. I supposed Claes had a copy of this to refer to in his attic operations room when he and Rackham met to correct the historical record. The Wolf's Lair in miniature: did that make me a member of the July Plot?

Allingham also displayed the familiar right-wing lunatic's combination of pastoral idealism, evangelical vegetarianism and anti-Semitism. This would not have marked him out among his peers, but he was slightly too slow, or disinclined, to temper his position on appeasement at the end of the 1930s and spent the war sidelined in Home Command. Churchill had a use for most people, but there were limits. It was said that Allingham escaped internment under Regulation 18b by the skin of his teeth. I suspect that he felt he had been robbed in this regard, denied the taste of martyrdom befitting his class, his rank and his convictions. It also meant that he would always be slightly in Mosley's shadow.

When the war ended he lived in France. His conviction that we should have made common cause with the fascists to save Europe from communism transformed itself into the pan-Europeanism which became the acceptable postwar version of appeasement thinking, though to his grave disappointment he remained a figure on the margins. He talked of the inevitability of a European state. It was said that he had converted to Catholicism under the instruction of the pro-fascist and later excommunicated Cardinal Lefebvre. It was said that his wife, Lady Anne, was even worse than he was.

Allingham was seventy-two years old and now he was standing in the local by-election. As if this were not enough, before the First World War he had been a close associate of Aleister Crowley, and had maintained an interest in the occult ever since. So you might say that Allingham covered the waterfront of right-wing manias with unusual thoroughness. He had the status of a joke but there was still a shimmer of the sinister, a whiff of sulphur, about the tail of his dying comet.

The tide was running steadily as I crossed South Bridge. A barge slipped underneath, heading to join the larger river and then make the journey upstream, the far back of the hinterland's mind. A crewman stood smoking at the forward hatch. I envied him his certain station, his anonymous purpose. He flipped his cigarette into the dark water and went inside, oblivious to the foot-passengers above.

You would hardly have known there was a meeting. There was no sign of any opposition in the street outside. The doors stood open. Tonight's event was soberly advertised alongside recent amateur productions of *Quiet Wedding* and *Rookery Nook*. Inside, on the BPP's poster the party's symbol, a combined sword and crucifix and rose, seemed as anachronistic as the plays.

A trickle of people entered, none of the boys or anyone else I knew among them. Security in the foyer was provided by Lurch and an assistant who looked like a younger, less intelligent relative. The pair loomed for a moment as I entered, but then stepped aside. Lurch, as ever, showed no sign of recognition. His pitted skin was dry and flaking.

Somehow a crowd had got inside, but its members sat quietly minding their own business, reading the paper or talking together in twos and threes. Faintly martial music was playing at low volume. I had expected a greater sense of urgency. Were they all – they were nearly all men, nearly all middle-aged – inured to unglamorous political occasions? Were they awed? Bored? And what was I supposed to do, now that I was here? There was no sign of Rackham.

Claes appeared by the stage. He smiled at me and gestured expansively for me to join him. But seated at the front I would see little. I smiled back, went out into the foyer and found my way upstairs and then to a position near the back stairs and overlooking the stage.

The balcony was scarcely lit, and the heating had not been turned on. It turned out that a group of a dozen or so boys from the fourth and fifth forms had positioned themselves on the opposite balcony, much as they would always try to sit at the back of the class, despite the fact that this and their inability to keep still or be quiet would only make them more conspicuous. They were, thank God, wearing mufti, but they were cackling and shushing each other in a simultaneous attempt to remain undetected and draw attention.

A little further off sat Steerman, with a bored looking Arnesen still in uniform. They couldn't have seen me yet, since their behaviour did not alter. I moved to stand behind a pillar. I was here. I was observing. What was I supposed to do next? Not for the first time, it would seem to depend on Rackham. As yet he was nowhere to be seen.

The music grew in volume. It became a crackly recording of 'Nimrod'. The hall below had just about filled up. The occasion was almost controversial. How soon the music did its fearsome and beautiful work, creating a common sense of loss, of rightful aspiration, of virtue injured but vindicated at the last. Even the boys on the dim balcony had grown quiet, as if unsure what authority laid claim to them like this.

This was larceny, wasn't it? I wanted to shout out an objection, but the music ended and applause broke out as Claes led his guest to the podium. General Sir Lewis Allingham was, as he seemed to have been for half a century, tall, stiff, implacably upright in tweeds, silver-haired, with the polished skin of a netsuke figure. He stood modestly aside while Claes spoke.

'Good evening, friends and comrades. Let me be brief. It is a rare thing to be in the presence of greatness on a world-historical scale as we are tonight with our most distinguished speaker. Sir Lewis Allingham stands in no need of introduction. No, friends, what he needs is justice – justice for his loyalty, his vision and passion.' Applause broke out in a disciplined way. 'In a time of crisis the nation needs, all Europe needs, a leader by example, a clear mind, an honest voice in defence of all we hold dear. I give you General Sir Lewis Allingham.' The applause was sustained and there were cheers and the audience would have gone on but for the single gesture of the hand with which Allingham quieted them as a commander might when addressing a regiment before battle. He gave off a kind of impersonal yet intimate authority. He claimed his auditors' trust as of self-evident right. How could it be otherwise? And he had yet to open his mouth. I reminded myself that the man was a fascist.

'Good evening, everyone. I too shall try to be brief and to resist the temptations to which age is naturally prone, and simply to set the case before you as I see it. This is a by-election brought about by the death of a sitting incumbent – and therefore a part of the democratic routine this country has evolved. I doubt if in the minds of many people such things are significant or even, perhaps, occur at all. A former prime minister and old army comrade was correct when he proposed that people in this country have never had it so good. I say "correct", though only in a limited, material sense. But what I want to say to you here at this meeting in this hall in this city in this *nation*, this evening, is something more than the last hurrah and sunset song of an old man, a simple soldier whose days and duty are all but done. My friends, I assure you I am not doing this for the good of my health.'

More applause. Warm laughter. He continued in this low

key for a few minutes and then slowly his manner intensified. Here it comes, I thought.

'I am here,' he declared, 'to appeal to you to begin a crusade from this evening on to save this great nation whose sons and daughters we are honoured in being, to save it from neglect and contempt and corruption and debasement at the hands of communism and international finance, the hydra heads of the same evil root. Shall England perish?' (*No's and inarticulate lowings from the crowd.*) 'Shall England perish?' (*Louder cries, with much of the crowd on its feet and the boys standing at the balcony, their arms aloft as though in a triumph that had occurred without their noticing.*)

Allingham brought the volume down again with a gesture half of prayer. I saw Claes hovering in the wings. He seemed transported.

'No,' said Allingham, 'England shall not perish until we ourselves are laid upon her burning pyre.'

Uproar. It was like drink, like drugs, like sex, like more than all of them put together. It was a lie, but one so important to the listeners that it had to be true. They screamed and brayed until the building echoed.

'Therefore let us go from here tonight, out into the city and the nation with our crusading determination renewed, our courage refreshed, our vision undimmed, in the knowledge that the service of our beloved England is its own reward. On Thursday next lay down your indelible mark at the ballot, and let us, as one sacred power, speak for England.'

The crowd were afraid that Allingham would stop now, that he would send them back to their glum and half-demolished city and their modest discontents and their unappeased loathing of change, foreigners, immigrants and the rest.

'Need I go on?' he asked. They implored him but with a humble smiling shake of the head he declined the invitation he had so skilfully offered himself. 'Time is short, my friends,' he said, 'and I have said my piece, such as it is. I must away with all the golden lads and girls who home are gone and ta'en their wages. But, my dear friends, my band of brothers, do not forget: take up the flame and fight for England. God save you all.'

Applause rained down. There might have been ten thousand in the hall and not a couple of hundred. Like the boys upstairs, the clerks and salesmen and prison officers and discharged soldiers and dentists' receptionists and off-duty policemen believed in that moment that they had already won.

The cheering and applause showed no signs of dying down when David Feldberg appeared at the end of the front row and raised his hand. I noticed he was alone. Dent, or Dent's father, had more sense, apparently. Claes made to shoo Feldberg away, but the General once more gestured for silence.

'Yes, young man. It is good to see you here tonight. Have you a question?'

Feldberg nodded. 'Yes, General Allingham.'

'Then please ask it.'

'Thank you. My question is this. Why did you say in 1953 that the Jewish Holocaust had been a necessary and inevitable event?'

Allingham's face closed. He seemed to retire from the stage without leaving it, but he directed an unbroken gaze full of blue hatred at Feldberg.

'This is not a matter relevant to this occasion,' said Claes, dismissing Feldberg with a smile. 'This is not the forum for such questions.'

'It's an election meeting,' said Feldberg, evenly.

'Shut up, Feldberg!' shouted Arnesen. He was on his feet, as was Steerman. I shouted at them to sit down. They peered uncertainly across at me.

'I am sure you are too young to vote, young man,' said Claes. 'This is an election meeting. Sit down.' I began to move towards the stairs. There was a pause while the crowd wondered how to act.

'Sir Lewis, please answer the question,' said Feldberg, standing his ground. 'Your statement at the reunion of the veterans of the Nazi Brigade Wallonie in Namur is a matter of historical record, after all.'

Allingham turned and walked off the stage. Booing began from upstairs and spread down the hall. Feet began to stamp.

I ran down the steps at the front of the hall. Before I could get near Feldberg a heavyset man came from nowhere, pushing past me.

'Do not be provoked!' I heard Claes shout.

'I'll give you an answer, you little Jew bastard!' he yelled. There was a low cheer.

As Feldberg turned the man punched him in the side of the head and the boy's glasses flew off. Feldberg staggered and fell to his knees. I saw the glasses land on the floor, where without leaving her seat an expressionless grey-haired woman stamped on them. I tried to get hold of the attacker as he aimed a kick at the dazed Feldberg, but he elbowed me aside and then others were in between us, shouting and kicking. The scene slipped into slow motion. I caught sight of Steerman and Arnesen on the balcony, watching with their mouths open. Next time I looked up they were gone.

'We knew our Marxist friends would not let the evening pass without trying to disrupt the meeting!' Claes shouted into the microphone. 'Do not allow yourselves to be intimidated, ladies and gentlemen.' He glared down at me. I had betrayed a sacred trust, something of that sort. He didn't join the melee. Feldberg was trying to get up, but two or three men were aiming kicks at him and I couldn't get near.

The whole crowd were on their feet now. Some of them were baying incoherently at this example of something that needed to be done, this proof of their deranged contention, this evidence of the injustice they had borne in silence for too long. I noticed others gathering their coats and making for the exit as if nothing had taken place. No one else came forward to help Feldberg. I tried again to break through the encircling mob and took a blow to the back of my head. For a moment I thought I might black out.

Another party intervened and the big man fell as if pole-axed. His companions stepped back. Stan Pitt stood between them and Feldberg, while Sergeant Risman stepped over the fallen man and hauled the boy to his feet. The mob hesitated. This fellow was clearly a bit handy.

'Get yourselves home,' said Stan. The men looked at each other. 'You don't want any trouble. Do you? If so, let's be having you.'

There were no takers. I followed Risman and the dazed Feldberg out through a door by the staircase.

'You're a very lucky boy aren't you, Master Feldberg?' said Risman. 'To have friends like Mr Maxwell to look after you.'

Behind us, music struck up again. None of the crowd tried to follow us down the corridor and there was no one about in the street. Stan appeared a few seconds later, slamming the fire door closed and removing a set of knuckle dusters. He saw my surprise.

'Sometimes, Mr Maxwell,' he said, 'it's Queensberry Rules, and sometimes, like tonight, it's not.'

'The car's round the corner,' said Risman. 'You all right, son?'

'Yes, thank you, Sergeant. And thank you, Mr Pitt.' Feldberg seemed naked without his glasses, but he kept looking over his shoulder as if he wanted to go back and try again. Risman had him firmly by the arm.

'Not tonight, son. Fight again another day, and next time go equipped, all right? You've got some fucking guts, though. Hasn't he, Mr Maxwell?'

Risman was full of surprises. His car, never seen at school even though he and the equally invisible Mrs Risman lived on the site, was a beautiful black Jowett Javelin, the English Citroën.

When we were in the vehicle, he turned and said, 'You're not in the cadets. Are you a Red, then?'

'Not exactly, Sergeant Risman. More of an anarchist,' said Feldberg. His lip was bleeding.

'That's good. Because I hate Reds. Luckily for you I hate Nazis even more. I was there when we liberated Belsen. So there we are, Sonny Jim. Count yourself lucky. But I dare say there'll be hell to pay in the morning.'

We sat considering this information while we drove away into the back streets. For a moment in the mirror I could see people fighting outside the hall. The opposition must have found out the venue at last. A police car rushed past us but its siren seemed to be switched off.

'What will your father say about this, David?' I asked.

'I'm not intending to tell him,' the boy said. 'It would only worry him. Are you going to tell him?'

'I ought to. Do you want to go to the hospital?'

'I'm all right, thank you.'

'You've got a bloody funny way of looking after your old man, son,' said Stan, roaring with laughter while Risman cornered like Fangio. 'You've got balls, I'll give you that. But if you want to keep them, choose your venues wisely.'

I could think of nothing to add. Feldberg nodded and rubbed his jaw.

THIRTY

The local evening paper on Monday carried a report of the fining of three men for public drunkenness and the binding over of two others to keep the peace following 'an altercation' outside a public house in Ferry Lane – the pub opposite Axness Hall. And that was all. The meeting was not reported, the causes not discussed, the politics ignored. But the police had turned up at Feldberg's door at seven o'clock in the morning and taken David into custody. By the time his father had contacted a lawyer, he was rung up from North Dock police station to say that the boy would be released into his hands pending further investigation. When David arrived at school, Gammon, already apprised of the situation, suspended him, and called a meeting at lunchtime.

'The boy Feldberg deliberately tried to cause trouble,' said Gammon. He moved items around the blotter on the Head's desk, as if to align them properly would allow him to occupy the role more convincingly.

'He asked a question at a public meeting,' I said.

'He was deliberately provocative, so I understand.'

'Who says so?'

'There were other boys present.'

'I know there were,' I said. 'As you will remember, I was there, under your instructions, Mr Gammon. I take it you're referring to Steerman, the BPP candidate, and that fool Arnesen.'

'Are you calling Steerman a liar?' asked Rackham.

'I'm not talking to you.'

'Watch your tongue,' said Gammon.

'Feldberg asked Allingham to explain something that is a matter of public record,' I said. 'I was there. Whether Mr

Rackham was present somewhere in the background to observe for himself, I cannot say. But clearly he has an interest in the BPP.'

'You know perfectly well what I mean,' said Gammon. 'The boy went there looking to cause trouble. And he found it. And you failed to prevent it, I might add.'

I was very tired and the room was cold. The low white sky lay on the fields like discouragement. I wondered about pointing this out.

'I didn't see Feldberg until he stood up. He was in fact the last person I expected to be there.'

'Really?' said Gammon, as if the word proved something.

'Well, it seems the boy found what he was looking for,' said Rackham. 'They can't help it. They bring it on themselves.'

'They? Who are they?'

'Levantines. You know what I'm talking about.'

Gammon shook his head.

Rackham continued. 'You didn't help matters when by all accounts you joined in.'

'He was being beaten up,' I said. 'And what were you doing at the time, exactly, Rackham?' I asked.

'Enough,' said Gammon. 'Feldberg is suspended pending further action.'

'His father may have something to say about that,' I pointed out.

'Then he's welcome to make an appointment to discuss it. Or to remove his son from Blake's, should he see fit. He might think that wise.'

'He's an Oxbridge candidate.'

'Very likely,' said Gammon. 'I dare say. But what has that got to do with anything? The boy was arrested. Blake's has its reputation to consider. No one individual is more important than Blake's.'

Bugger Blake's, I thought, but managed not to say it.

'What Feldberg did was bold and, as it turned out, rather courageous,' I said. 'He could hardly have known the audience would turn into to a mob.'

'Nonsense,' said Gammon. 'And you of all people should know that we cannot have favourites, Maxwell.'

'The other boys managed to behave themselves,' said Rackham, smoothing his hair, 'which rather makes my point, don't you agree? I think they were rather shocked. I imagine their parents will feel the same way. As you say, Acting Headmaster, the question is, can we – the school – really afford this kind of thing, given everything else? An example may have to be made. The governors will expect it.'

'Thank you, Rackham,' Gammon said. 'I'll talk to you later.'

'Very well, Headmaster. You know where to find me if you want any more help.'

When Rackham had gone, Gammon turned to me again. 'Are you bent on self-destruction, Maxwell?'

'No. There are other people trying to do it for me. Why does there have to be this air of hysteria?'

'Don't be insolent.'

'What do you want from me, Headmaster?' Like Rackham, I awarded him a title he did not possess.

'From you, Maxwell? Nothing at all. Except that you should go away, a long way away, as soon as possible.' Gammon looked exhausted.

'I'll make the governors give me a hearing. There are things they need to hear. I won't resign.'

'The governors have heard all about you, believe me. No, you will not resign. You will do as you are told.'

'So the wagons have been circled.'

'I doubt if you would understand what this school means to some of us. If it were up to me you'd be gone this afternoon.'

'But then what would happen to the mock election,

Mr Gammon? And in the meantime, what can I tell Mr Feldberg?'

'I shall deal with Mr Feldberg. And you will cease your interference.'

THIRTY-ONE

I knew I should go to see Feldberg and his father after work, but I prevaricated in the school library as though Feldberg might for some reason turn up there despite his suspension. Then I went home.

I was reading when the doorbell sounded. I looked down into the street and saw Maggie standing under the streetlight looking back at me. She raised a carrier bag in her hand and smiled.

'You could have come round, you know,' she said, throwing her coat on the settee.

'I had things on my mind.'

'Best to get rid of them, I find. I'll get some glasses.'

I was not in the mood for drinking. She scarcely noticed. When she had finished the bottle, she stood up and took my hand. 'Come on, soldier. Do your duty.'

'I'm not a soldier.'

'No, indeed. I shall have to make do.'

'You're drunk, Maggie.'

'Every little helps.'

Later I was lying in the dark, wondering how to persuade her to leave, when the doorbell rang again. Maggie stirred slightly but said nothing. I went back to the front window. It was Samuel Feldberg. For a moment I considered pretending not to be in. When I had pulled on a shirt and trousers and reached the door, Feldberg was walking slowly away. I called after him.

'I thought you would come to see us,' he said.

'I was intending to.'

'You might have telephoned.'

'I'm sorry. I was asleep,' I said, as we went upstairs.

'Then I envy your equanimity,' he said. Feldberg seemed to be occupying a dual role as supplicant and judge. Presumably the one cancelled out the embarrassment of the other. If he noticed the wine bottle and the glasses he did not say so. We ended up sitting on opposite sides of the table, as though one of us was there for an interview.

'I'm sorry David has been suspended. I argued against it.'

'Thank you,' he said, then sat waiting.

'I wish there was something I could do.'

'You could surely speak on his behalf again.'

'I have already tried to do that.'

'You might try harder,' he said, with unexpected coldness, though his tone remained even.

'It would do no good, I'm afraid.'

'What are you afraid of, man?' He stood up and began to pace about. 'Supposing you are a man.'

'I beg your pardon?'

'I think we understand each other, Stephen.'

'I have no authority in the matter.'

'Then you must find some. With Captain Carson gone, my son is your protégé now.'

People were always finding me responsibilities I would fail to fulfil. Samuel Feldberg was thirty years older than me and a great deal brighter. What need had he of me? 'David is not the only pupil,' I said. 'I am responsible for quite a number of them.' He looked at me as if I were a stranger who had suddenly sat down uninvited. I reminded myself that, despite the continual traffic it saw, the room was mine.

'He is my only son,' Feldberg said, with heavy patience. 'And he has a gift. It must not be denied or frustrated or allowed to go to waste. Have I to turn to a lawyer for assistance?'

'This is only a suspension, Samuel. His gift will survive.'

'He has been disgraced. It would affect his university reference. And this, this suspension, is a pretext for more. This is malice. I know it. You know it.'

I thought of Hamer's matter-of-fact disposal of David's future. 'It is a temporary suspension,' I said. 'He will be re-admitted after an appropriate interval.'

'You're sure of this?'

I was not sure at all but I saw no way of describing my uncertainty that would not darken Mr Feldberg's mood further. I nodded.

Mr Feldberg continued: 'I might add that your Mr Gammon refuses to see me. He is too busy. Must I go to the school and confront him?'

'I'll look into it,' I said.

Feldberg sighed heavily and turned over a book that lay on the table. 'I am curious to know – why were you at that fascist meeting?' he asked.

'I was sent to keep an eye on any boys who might be there.'

Feldberg laughed.

'In my capacity as organizer of the mock election,' I added, as if it might help.

'Well, your role was an enormous success. First you allow fascists to stand. And then a public meeting ends in fisticuffs. What will be the third thing, do you think?'

'But what was David doing there?'

'He was there to do what you saw him do. He wanted to ask a question.'

'Could you not have prevented him from going? You're his father.'

'I told him not to. I did not lock him in his room. I wish I had, but he should be able to attend a meeting if he chooses. He is a young man, a citizen, and one day soon he will have the vote. It is good that he is not apathetic, no? Yes, it was foolish of him to attend. And where was his friend Dent?' Where indeed, I wondered. 'But David does not lack courage. Should I to lock him in a cupboard and hide him away?'

'It's a complicated matter.'

'Complicated, you think. Sometimes it is foolish to be a

Jew at all, Stephen, whatever we do. David was unwise, but he was not wrong. And he was attacked.'

'He put himself in danger.'

'The danger is always there. You find it, or sooner or later it finds you.'

'Surely it doesn't help to exaggerate.'

Feldberg laughed again. It was a bark of rage. 'Why do you defend these people? He was attacked for asking a question based on the historical record.'

'I don't defend them. I just have to think about the consequences.'

'Consequences? What do you know, Stephen? What have you ever been through, outside of a library? I took David to the police station to complain about the assault he suffered. I was told that there were no witnesses.'

'I was a witness.'

'Then it would seem you don't exist.' He shook his head. 'I have to say I'm not surprised. So? Are you going to go to the police now, when David is suspended, when your involvement in the occasion is obscure, when your superiors are – it is obvious – putting pressure on you? Of course not.'

I could think of no reply.

'For his mother's sake and the sake of David's future I am asking you to intervene on his behalf at school. I had not thought you were such a coward.'

'Then I'm afraid that perhaps you don't know me. But as I have said, I will try.' I no more believed this than he did.

'This Rackham, this Jew-hater, what is his part in this?'

'I'm not sure. He didn't seem to be at the meeting.'

'Think what Captain Carson would have done, Stephen. And do that.'

I had already tried to divine a course of action by this means, but nothing had presented itself. Feldberg could not know that Carson was still more deeply compromised than his feeble deputy and successor had yet managed to become.

Once again I considered telling Mr Feldberg about the account he had left for me.

The bedroom door opened and Maggie appeared. She was wearing one of my shirts.

'Can anyone join the party?' she asked.

Feldberg rose and buttoned his overcoat. 'Mrs Rowan. You must excuse me. I would not normally intrude like this.'

'No need to apologize on my behalf. Mr Feldberg, isn't it?' Feldberg nodded and looked at her impassively. 'And you've come to sue for terms? For young David? After his recent exploits? Very commendable.'

'Exploits. I beg your pardon?'

If Feldberg had not been in the room I might have struck Maggie, but in that case there would have been no provocation to do so.

'And you think Stephen here is your best way of insinuating your wishes into the thinking of the senior staff? Do bear in mind that he is new in the post and it would be underhand to try to manipulate him.'

'I am asking for fair treatment. That is all.'

'I'm afraid you may be barking up the wrong tree. Perhaps you haven't really understood the society of Blake's. I can assure you that slandering my brother won't help. Blake's is really quite close-knit, isn't it, Stephen?' She sat down on the settee, crossed her legs and lit a cigarette. 'But I'm afraid I'm keeping you.'

'Please remember me to your husband,' said Feldberg. 'I have a book that he asked me find for him. Perhaps he will collect it if at some point he is able.' With this he left the room.

I followed him down the stairs. 'I'm afraid I don't know what to say.'

'Then be silent, Stephen. I see that your situation is complicated and that others have prior claims on you. I hope this lady of yours is worth it.'

'I'll telephone or visit soon,' I said.

'What purpose will that serve? You have made what I

assume is your apology. You understand that I cannot say that you will be welcome in my house now.'

He opened the front door and went away up the street.

When I came back Maggie had found the whisky.

'For God's sake, get dressed,' I said.

'You've changed your tune.' She looked haggard in the sour light.

'Do you realize what you've just done?'

'Did you know they've stopped performing lobotomies?'

'What?'

'I didn't know that. I'd been hoping – I mean, I'd been thinking –'

'What the hell are you talking about, Maggie?'

'Stop shouting. It makes you ridiculous. I thought you might understand.'

I took the bottle from her, poured myself a glass and put the remainder out of reach on the sideboard. She began to cry.

'What is it I'm supposed to understand?'

'Robert isn't going to get well. Not permanently. His condition seems to be worsening.'

'I'm sorry to hear that, though I'd guessed it might be the case.'

'Yes. I knew this would be the outcome. Sometimes you just know, and I did.' She dabbed at her face with the shirt-sleeve.

'It's very sad.'

'What? Well, yes. I suppose it is. But you see, I'd hoped that when we got to this stage there would be that option.'

'Option.'

'A procedure. Surgery, for God's sake.'

'You mean a lobotomy?'

She nodded.

'But that would be irreversible.'

'Not now, it won't. It turns out they don't do them any more.'

'Well, it's probably for the best,' I said. I was incredulous.

'Let's not get too fucking Panglossian about it. I mean, what now?'

'Well, I suppose Robert will continue receiving drug treatment and other therapy.'

'No, no. I mean, what now for me?'

'Well, now the facts are clear. That must be something, in a way.'

'Must it? Must it?' She got up and poured more whisky. 'What it means is that he knows.'

'Do you mean about us?'

'Possibly, but that's not the point. But I mean, he knows, some of the time, what's happening to him, and, some of the time, why, and he knows I'm there, and while he knows all this on and off there's no chance of my getting away. That's what I mean, Stephen. If they cut a bit of his brain out there might be a chance, but my punishment is that he knows.'

'I'm sure he doesn't want you to be punished, Maggie.'

'You're right. He doesn't. That makes it even worse. He's so unbearably bloody *good.*' The combination of rage and distress was alarming. 'Why couldn't they just cut a bit out of him? He's no use to anyone, is he?'

'It's too late at night for this,' I said. 'Don't have any more to drink. You need a clear head. Then you'll be able to see what needs to be done.' But she wasn't listening.

'I mean, I don't ask for much, do I? Do I?'

'If all of us were judged on our usefulness there'd be rather fewer people about.'

'Hitler understood about it.'

'Oh, no. That's enough, Maggie. You're drunk.'

'And you're just fucking feeble! Like the rest of them. People make such a fuss. They're like a lot of sheep.'

'Don't say any more.'

'What? My husband, what is he? A parasite, like that Feldberg creature and his little fucking arselicker of a son.' She was weeping now, ugly with grief, the mascara running down her cheeks.

'Get dressed, Maggie. I'll take you home.'

'Fucking Jews. Always fucking complaining. Never enough. Never let a thing rest.'

'That's it,' I said. 'This is impossible. We have to stop seeing each other now. Do you understand?'

She was violently sick.

THIRTY-TWO

I took Maggie's car keys and drove her back to Percival Street. She was incoherent by then. I had to half-carry her up the stairs. When we reached the top floor I struggled to keep her upright while I got the key into the latch. Then the door seemed to open by itself.

'I wasn't expecting you back tonight, Maggie – Oh, hello there.' It was Rackham, bare-chested and wearing pyjama trousers. 'Well, well. What have you done to her? You'd better bring the old girl in. One too many, it appears. So who's to blame this time?' His tolerant amusement woke thoughts of homicide. 'Let's get her through to the bedroom.'

There was a half-glass of wine on the bedside table, next to an ashtray in which a cigarette was burning. Rackham moved a book from the rumpled bedcover and I laid the unconscious Maggie down and moved her on to her side. I turned to Rackham, who now leaned in the doorway.

'What a to-do!' he said, and whistled as though in admiration.

We went back into the living room and he offered me a drink, which I declined. He poured himself a glass and stood at the mantelpiece, where the 'Olympia' imitation had now been placed. He was, in a sense, beside himself. I found myself waiting, as though I needed him to dismiss me.

'Since we're here, perhaps we should talk,' he said.

'Why? What is there for us to talk about? You seem to have it all under control.'

'I think we both know what's happening,' Rackham said. I shrugged. Let him tell me if he would. 'It seems to me very likely that you have something of interest to me. Carson has made you his executor, so it seems a reasonable inference. You are the sort of person that James Carson would entrust something to. He was all alone. You're fairly bright and wholly feckless and he thought you were in need of paternal guidance. He thought the same about me – and it blew up in his face, as it were. Come on, have a drink, Maxwell.'

I shook my head.

'Please yourself.' He sighed and ran his fingers through his hair. I found the gesture exercised a repellent fascination. He moved to sit on the arm of the settee. I remained standing by the door.

'So far, all this business has just been a bit unpleasant. It could be much worse, believe me. I'd never want to hurt Maggie, of course, given the way she's burdened with a husband as mad as a hatter, not to mention her inexplicable involvement with you. But the scandal might have to come out at some point anyway, mightn't it? So there's that to consider. And then there's our little tart Shirley. Olympia.' He turned to look at the picture. 'You've seen her quite recently, I think. With one thing and another I haven't had the time myself. But apparently she's in a bad way, poor love. Selling herself to feed the needle. I mean, where's the future in that? And there's young Feldberg with his bright future ahead of him, or possibly not, and his pretty little friend. All of it comes back to you somehow, and think of the damage that could befall Blake's, which Blake's couldn't possibly tolerate. It's a lot to consider, Maxwell, but we can't go on like this forever. Give me what I need and I'll be out of your hair. Consider the risks.'

'I don't know what you're talking about, Rackham.'

'For God's sake, man. Honestly.'

'Why are you victimizing Feldberg?'

'Who says I am? Can you prove it? Funnily enough, you can't.'

'You must be mad.'

He grinned at this. 'Must I? Maybe you're right. I don't care, though. I've been ever so good for years and years. I did the teaching and I wrote the poems that nobody wanted to read. Much good it did me. I can see you know what I'm talking about. I kept my head down and my nose clean, more or less, but now I'm bored with it. I thought: this can't be all there is. I needed excitement, a project . . . So give me what I want and I may just go away.'

'You need other people to suffer,' I said. 'I don't understand that.'

'Well, I should say it has its points. But the thing is, Maxwell, I really don't care. I might do anything at all at any time if it occurs to me, supposing you don't give me what I need. I can't be touched.'

'How would I recognize what you're looking for?'

'You already know. It's written all over you.'

'I'm at a loss.'

'Well, don't be. Bring me what I want. Give it to me. Or you'll have to take responsibility for what happens, since clearly I won't. And you haven't got the guts for that, have you?'

'What are you going to do, Rackham?'

'Eeny meeny – I'm spoilt for choice. Would you rather wait and see? But best not wait too long. Shall we call it a night, Maxwell?'

'I think it was you who killed Carson,' I said.

'Would you like me to break down and confess under the weight of a lifetime's accumulated guilt and self-loathing, you having tipped the balance? What makes you think I did kill Carson?'

'Who else would want to?'

He smiled and shrugged. 'According to you, I have no motive.'

'Look after Maggie.'

'I'll see to her. I always have done so far, one way or another. She's my sister, after all. And as for what we've been discussing, be quick.'

I could have taken Maggie's car to get home, but instead I

crossed the railway line into the grounds of Blake's. The grass glittered with cold. I made my way down through the birch wood to the edge of the lake. 'Lake' was too grand a word for the body of water in question. But it seemed demeaning for someone like Carson to drown in a pond. Whereas in my case it would be a wholly suitable location. I stood on the wooden jetty. It was salted with frost. The raft was firmly moored now. The water was full of stars.

I walked on and tried to derive some conclusions by measuring my situation against the setting, but there seemed to be no proper match. I could leave, simply up and go – the 'elemental purifying act' admired by the poet. I would have to break off relations with Maggie when she was sober anyway, though tonight might leave no need for such formal niceties and adult recognition and acceptances. I wanted to lie down and go to sleep there and then. There was David Feldberg and his father. There was Shirley. There was whatever in God's name Rackham was hoping to achieve, and there was Hamer always in the offing under his black flag. And Claes, and Carson's papers, and the accursed mock election, and my own complete unreadiness to cope with any of it.

Answer came there none.

As I made my way alongside the groundsmen's barn-like corrugated hut I heard a mechanical rattle nearby. I realized the sound was familiar. When we were in the cadets there was weapons training – load, strip and reassemble a Lee Enfield .303. I could probably still perform the procedure myself. This reverie was combined with the conviction that I was about to die. I would not even hear the shot that killed me.

But nothing happened. I tried to work out the source of the noise. One window of the shed was faintly lit. When I peered in I saw Lurch, sitting on a metal chair and cleaning a rifle, contentedly absorbed in his task, while Claes watched with a connoisseurial air, drinking what looked like a Snowball.

THIRTY-THREE

The day of the election was cold and dry. I had set off for the polling station at the nearby primary school before I realized that I was not registered to vote. I passed Smallbone escorting his mother to the ballot. She gave me a smile that managed to be a glare, while Smallbone offered a philosophical shrug. There were, of course, a lot of older people about. The future would have to depend on them.

At the gate of Blake's Sergeant Risman emerged from the Porter's Lodge, where he and his invisible wife lived. We fell into step. He was wearing a steward's armband of his own immaculate devising.

'I'm surprised they haven't sacked you after the other evening, Sergeant.'

'I was acting on instructions, Mr Maxwell. I saved the daft little bugger's arse, and I expect the Major put in a good word for an old soldier like me. Bad business about the lad, though. Suspended? Stupid little bastard, but at least he's ready to get stuck in. Will they have him back?'

'Not if Rackham gets his way.'

Risman sniffed. 'I see. But you're still with us, then, I take it, Mr Maxwell?'

'More or less. For the moment.'

'Then it's not finished, is it, this business?'

'I don't know, Sergeant.'

'Steady. Say not the struggle naught availeth, sir. That's Kipling, that.'

'No, it isn't. But thank you. Is the Memorial Hall set up for the voting?'

'All done last night. I'm just going for another look round. Mind how you go. It's really not over yet. I can smell it.'

The plan was that the boys could vote at break or lunchtime, with the results to be declared by the end of school. During morning registration my form exuded an air of studied indifference combined with fevered watchfulness. Everyone would know about Feldberg by now. Someone had chalked odds on the board. The BPP was at evens along with the Conservatives. Someone else had added Feldberg at 1000/1 plus a swastika. I rubbed it out.

'Sir?' said Arnesen.

'What is it? You're on very thin ice.'

'Not like Feldberg, though.'

'I wouldn't be too sure,' I said, more confidently than I felt.

'My father says the election should be cancelled.'

'Oh, yes? Why does he say that?'

'Because of the situation. You know.' The others looked on intently.

'Which election are we talking about?' I asked.

'This one, here, I mean, not the other one outside.'

'Well, that's a relief. Anyway, Arnesen, democracy has to be seen to take place.'

'I suppose so, sir. That's what people say. But actually, why?'

'Because otherwise we would start behaving like wild animals and end up eating each other.'

The bell rang.

'I wouldn't mind eating Mrs Rowan,' he said, *sotto voce*, but I pretended not to hear.

'Remember to vote,' I said, as the group dispersed.

At break I went over to the Memorial Hall to observe the turnout and conduct of the proceedings. I suspected this election would be more popular than the real thing. Boys were already crowding into the covered entrance that led from the field, the quad and the Main Hall, and once through the double doors they were being directed to two voting booths built, with characteristic noises of ill-done-to complaint, by Renwick.

Inside, Tim Connolly was overseeing events in his anxious, kindly way. The candidates stood about with their rosettes among groups of their supporters. The press had not, of course, been invited. The election was in that sense not really taking place.

To my discomfort, Maggie and Rackham were also present. They seemed as normal as they ever seemed, though Maggie was very pale. They did not acknowledge me or speak to each other, though they stood side by side.

Cold, pale light fell on the proceedings through the high windows, faintly tinted by undistinguished religious scenes in stained glass. The Memorial Hall had stood only since 1920, in honour of old boys killed in the First World War, but it had been purpose-built to look Victorian and thus to claim a yet older heritage, as if somehow (and this is the English device) it had always necessarily and rightly been there. A good place to hold a mock election, I thought, sourly. The flats for *Ruddigore* were finished and in place with their Gothic turrets and shadowy gateways, ready for the cancelled production. The piano had been moved back on to the stage.

'It seems to be going well,' I said to Connolly. He looked as if he expected disaster at any moment.

'So far, so good,' he said, without conviction. 'As long as no one tries to pull some stunt. Those BPP lads of yours, for example.'

'They're not my lads, thank you very much, Mr Connolly. And I think justice would be summary if anything were to happen.'

Connolly looked startled at this, perhaps imagining drumhead courts martial and hangings, the thieving Bardolph dancing on the air over the field of slaughter. At that moment, as a group of smirking BPP supporters filed past I could see the appeal of such procedures.

Major Brand appeared, accompanied by Sergeant Risman, and stood giving off his (I now felt) endearing air of myopic goodwill.

'So where's Gammon?' I asked.

'Called away, apparently,' Connolly replied. 'Probably just as well. The other day he looked as if he was going to have a stroke. So. Let's just try to get through the day unscathed, shall we?'

'Let's keep it moving there, chaps,' said the Major to the queuing boys. 'Make your mark and don't hang about. Not long to the bell.'

Arnesen was in the queue. 'Not very democratic, sir,' he said.

'Don't want to overdo it, do we, Private Arnesen?' said the Major. Arnesen smiled.

I am not sure who was the first to notice when the piano burst into flames. Certainly there was a pause while everyone looked at this unexpected development. Then Risman was shouting, 'Fire! Evacuate the building now!' He hit the alarm by the door. The bell began to sound, and the boys began, at first slightly unwillingly, to exit the hall. Connolly had got hold of a fire extinguisher and was trying to make it work. Risman seized it from him and mounted the stage.

I seemed unable to move. I wondered if somehow I had known that this would happen. I watched Risman aiming foam at the piano, while the flames ran swiftly up the black-out curtains over the stage and began at appalling speed to scurry for the wings and the ceiling. Now there was thickening smoke. Rackham stared at the blaze critically, as though to satisfy himself that it met the requirements of the occasion.

'I said OUT!' shouted Risman. 'All of you. Mrs Rowan, Mr Rackham and the rest – get going.' Connolly passed Risman a second extinguisher but it was too late. The fire had spread hungrily and ignited the painted flats. I took Maggie by the arm. She looked as if she barely recognized me.

'Come on, old girl!' said Rackham. 'Time we were gone.' He pulled her away from me. I turned back. Now I could hardly see.

'Leave it, Sergeant!' I yelled from the door.

'I'll be right behind you. Now fook off out it and pardon my French. Is there anyone backstage?' he yelled. 'If anyone's in there, get yourself out now. The place is going up!' For a moment I saw Risman as he lingered on the stage and gestured fiercely at me to go.

When I got into the entranceway smoke was running along the ceiling. It became difficult to breathe. I heard panes of glass bursting nearby.

Outside, the crowd of voters had spilled on to the field, swelled by the rest of the boys still milling about at the end of break, while masters struggled to get them into form groups in the correct fire-assembly positions along the Spion Kop try-line. Rackham and Maggie were nowhere to be seen. Renwick, in his brown carpenter's overall, stood hands on hips on the parterre outside the Headmaster's office, staring and purple-faced as smoke appeared through the roof of the Memorial Hall.

'So one of your little conchie communist bastards has set fire to my piano,' he said. 'I wonder which one? I hope you're pleased with yourself, Maxwell. Resign, man. Do it today. And why not shoot yourself while you're at it? I said you'd be nothing but trouble.'

'Renwick, no one who played your damned piano thought it was any good,' I said. 'Like playing a piece of two-by-four, according to Feldberg.'

'Feldberg? What do you expect from his sort?' Renwick wandered away, still chuntering.

Sirens approached, and two fire engines appeared on the field to ragged cheers from the watching boys.

'Maxwell,' said Gammon, materializing out of the air at my side, 'what have you done now?'

'Me, Headmaster? Nothing. But someone seems to have set fire to the Reichstag. Risman's still in there.'

'Then why have you left him behind?'

'That's not what happened.'

Gammon looked as if he was about to start stamping his feet.

Firemen were moving the watching crowds to a safer distance. Water began to play over the smoking roof of the hall, and mechanical ladders were extended.

'Well, is everybody else safely out of the building?' Gammon asked.

'We should know in a minute,' I said. 'As I was about to say, Sergeant Risman stayed behind to check.'

'Of course he did. Of course he did. That's what Risman would do.' Gammon was beginning to jabber. I realized that he was on the brink of hysteria. Major Brand approached.

'As far as we know, everyone's out,' he said. 'Risman did a check in there, thank God. Luckily it seems that no one was having a crafty Woodbine backstage. So anyone missing from the count had been marked absent at morning registration.'

'Thank the Lord for that.'

Now Risman appeared from the smoking doorway with the two cardboard ballot boxes under his arms. He came and placed them at my feet.

'You'll be wanting these,' he said, and bent over to cough.

'Thank you, Sergeant Risman,' said Gammon. 'But clearly the election must be cancelled.'

'Right you are, Mr Gammon. If you say so.'

'We could re-ballot,' I said, hoping he would reject the idea.

'Don't be ridiculous. There are other priorities,' hissed Gammon.

'It gives a bad impression if we abandon the election,' I said.

'And a worse one if the place burns down!' Gammon was shouting now.

'Headmaster,' said the Major, 'so do we send the chaps home? We can't have them just hanging about.' To close the school would feel like treason for Gammon. But he nodded, and the Major went off to give the instruction. Low, uncertain cheers followed from the boys.

'This is unprecedented,' said Gammon. Now he seemed distracted.

'I would think so,' I said.

'Apart from the stray bomb that hit the fives courts during the Blitz, but that doesn't really count.'

'One for the history books,' I offered.

Gammon seemed to wake up at this. 'The police will have to be called, again.'

'I'm sure Inspector Smales will clear things up to your satisfaction.'

'Get out of my sight,' said Gammon. 'As far as I'm concerned, Maxwell, all this leads to your door.'

I picked up the boxes of ballot papers. 'It certainly looks that way.'

Gammon may have wanted me out of his sight, but when he was finally allowed back into the building he summoned the usual members of staff for a post-mortem concerning events in the Memorial Hall.

'I always thought that it was unwise to hold the mock election. But Captain Carson insisted,' said Gammon. I forbore to point out that Carson was dead. 'I've been on to the newspaper. They've agreed to be restrained in their coverage. Fortunately, the damage is not irreparable.'

'Renwick is very upset about the piano,' said Connolly.

'Perhaps now is his chance to build one worth playing,' said Rackham. Connolly looked at him in horror. I found myself struggling not to laugh.

'Is there something amusing you, Maxwell?' asked Gammon. His eyes seemed to bulge unhealthily, as if they might explode from his face. Again I had to suppress my laughter.

'Your Reds did us all a favour,' said Rackham.

'My Reds,' I said. 'Where are they? Who are they?'

'It's obvious, isn't it? They didn't put up a candidate, and they decided to wreck the election. Revolutionary tactics.'

'Why go to the trouble?' I asked. 'It's not a real election.'

'It's a real building that's just been burnt down,' said Rackham patiently.

'That's a bit far-fetched, isn't it, Rackham?' said the Major. 'I mean, these are our chaps you're talking about.'

'Our chaps? If you say so. Have you considered that perhaps not all our chaps are really our chaps at heart? Our colleague Maxwell here is certainly compromised by association.'

Not only was Rackham amused, he was also terribly excited. Disasters and conflagrations, Auden claimed, have a special appeal for poets, and Rackham was living proof. What he lacked in talent he made up for in affinity.

'I'm advised by the authorities that the fire was started deliberately with some kind of timing device attached to a petrol bomb,' said Gammon, struggling to maintain control of the proceedings.

'Well, whoever it was didn't learn that in the cadets, I can assure you,' said the Major. 'That's jungle stuff. Or Jerry during the house-fighting in 'forty-five.'

Rackham shook his head.

'That may be what we are supposed to conclude. Easy enough to find out how to do it if you know where to look, though.'

'Your pals at Vlaminck's probably have the knowhow,' I said. 'Let's not forget about the firebomb at the medics' hostel.'

'What are you talking about, Maxwell?' Gammon shouted.

'That sounds like the wild accusation of a desperate man,' said Rackham. He didn't want it to stop. As far as he was concerned this was life.

'What's this about Vlaminck's?' said Connolly. 'It's out of bounds to the boys.'

'Enough!' Gammon said. 'We need a clear view and a course of action.'

'What does Inspector Smales have to say?' I asked.

'Investigations are continuing,' Gammon replied, as if it were not my business.

'Well, I know where I'd look,' said Rackham.

'I'm sure the Inspector knows what he's doing,' Gammon snapped. 'He will also be keeping me informed about the Feldberg situation.'

'Let's hope so,' said Rackham. 'People will think Blake's is going to pieces. The eyes of the city are upon us.'

'Surely, Acting Headmaster, there's no reason to associate Feldberg with the fire. He wasn't even here,' I said.

'Well, exactly,' said Rackham. 'He wouldn't be, would he?'

'Maxwell, if there is anything you want to say that would help the investigation into this serious threat to life and property,' Gammon said, 'it behoves you to own up to it now.'

'If I knew anything, Acting Headmaster, I assure you I would certainly feel beholden.'

Gammon was pale and sweating despite the chill in the office. He sat down and turned the chair to look out of the window. A fire engine was turning, leaving ruts on one of the rugby pitches. 'You may go, all of you,' he said.

'What about Feldberg?' I asked.

'I have heard enough about him,' said Gammon.

'How long is he to be suspended?'

'Indefinitely.'

At the gates later on I found Arnesen hanging about.

'Have you got a lift?' I asked him.

'They let me ring from the office, thanks, sir. My mum's coming in a bit.'

'Good. Don't forget there's still homework. See you tomorrow.'

'Will that be when we start eating each other, sir?'

'You'll have to wait and see.'

'Yum yum.'

'Don't be stupid. Somebody could have been killed.'

'That's war, though, isn't it, sir?'

THIRTY-FOUR

Low down on page six, the evening paper reported a small fire in the grounds at Blake's.

The CLOSED sign was showing but Mr Feldberg was there in the shop. He seemed to have aged in the exertion of self-control.

'You are too late,' he said. 'David is not here. He's gone.'

'Where?'

'If I knew that I would go there. That policeman, Smales, was here again asking for David. He said it was in connection with a fire at the school.' Mr Feldberg held up the newspaper. 'He stood there as though I should abase myself to him.'

'What did you tell Smales?' I asked.

'Only what I knew. That David is not here. I told this Smales, but he didn't believe me. In fact I wondered if he would find a way to arrest me too. David went out this morning and hasn't come back. It is not like David to do that. I invited Smales to look around the shop and the flat. He asked for a list of other places where David might have gone. It was a short list – the library, the record shop where he works on Saturday mornings, and the home of Rachel's parents. They've been on the telephone three times now. She cannot be found either. Her mother is terrified. She has rung the police but they say she has not yet been missing for long enough to investigate.'

'Why would David run away?' I asked.

'How can you ask that? He would not run away.'

'What if he were to feel threatened?'

'Then I believe he would try to meet the threat face to face. You saw yourself what happened at Allingham's meeting. He's not a coward.'

'No, but discretion might be wiser sometimes. In any case, his enemies won't meet him head on.'

'I don't understand why he should have enemies of this kind.'

'You told me yourself that his presence would itself be a provocation.'

'Yes, but a provocation to insult. To whispers. To the petty resentments of cowards. Like men at golf clubs. Like your policeman Smales. This Smales said that it seemed to him David had been looking for trouble and that he'd found it. If ever Smales acts in this matter, I think it will mean it is too late.'

'Smales is not my policeman. He suspects me in the death of Captain Carson. He sees what he wants to see. And, like a lot of people here, he wants a quiet life.'

'Oh yes? And you imagine I don't?' Mr Feldberg stared out towards the dim arcade. We could hear the entrance gates were being closed and padlocked for the night.

'Someone tried to wreck the mock election by setting fire to the Memorial Hall. The vote had to be abandoned. David is suspended until further notice.'

'Your Mr Gammon has already informed me. He wishes me to withdraw David from the school. I told him I have a lawyer.'

'I'm sorry. I did what I could to get the decision changed. But I was in the minority.'

'If you say so.' We went through into the shop. He gestured me to a chair near his desk. 'This is a game of some kind. And you think David is involved in this? You know him. Why would you think so for a moment?'

'I promise you I wouldn't for a moment think he had anything to do with the fire. Apart from anything else, it would be wholly against his best interests.'

'And why would the police think it?' The questions came steadily and with the same careful intensity.

'Perhaps because it seems like a simple explanation. But

Samuel, I've got something more to tell you. Rackham is trying to make David a scapegoat.'

'For what, in God's name? A scapegoat? You must explain this! How do you know?'

'He as much as told me.'

'Why would he tell you such a thing?'

'It's a long story.'

'Tell me.'

'I should have told you the rest before, but it seemed mad, despite the source.'

'Never mind how you felt. What is the source? Tell me now.'

I described Carson's letter. Mr Feldberg listened as though recognizing in its entirety something that had always been there.

'I'm sorry. I should have told you about the letter before.'

'Yes, you should, Stephen. And why didn't you?'

'Last time I came to the shop it was to tell you, but then I saw you and David and Rachel. You were teasing and joking, like families do. I couldn't think how to begin. And I couldn't face it. The letter wasn't proof, though I believed it.'

'And setting your beautiful sensitivity aside, were you also afraid?'

'Yes.'

'That's how it works.' Mr Feldberg got up and walked about, his back to me. 'And is your Mr Rackham all-powerful now, so that he can instruct the police?'

'As things stand he seems to have influence in the school and with those associated with it. When he claimed to have protection he was telling the truth. It's not certain who guarantees his safety. But a man called Hamer, from the Security Services, I think, has warned me off pursuing Rackham. He threatened me.'

'This Hamer, has he taken David?'

'That I don't know. I suspect not. He wasn't very interested in David.' I would not repeat Hamer's comments. 'I think if anyone has taken David and Rachel it is Rackham. And Claes Vlaminck. He was talking about taking action, making an impact.'

Mr Feldberg nodded. 'Of course. Remember what I said about Vlaminck? And the fire at the school is his doing?'

'I think so. Or that of his accomplice. It's the school,' I said. 'Everything comes back to Blake's. Its task is to survive. That is all it is for. Everything is subordinate to that.'

'I know the English are mad, Stephen. I've lived among them long enough. How else are they to be explained? But are you now telling me that they are evil? That a boy could be sacrificed to a school? And his girlfriend too? Here and now? Is that what you're saying?' He got up again and began to draw the blinds.

'I don't know what I'm telling you. I don't understand it myself.' Which was not quite true. 'It's like a tribe.'

'Believe me, I know about tribes.'

'I mean that the school is not for anything other than itself. It might seem to represent money and patriotism, but if by some strange process those values and loyalties were taken away in the world outside, the school would simply recreate them more fiercely. It's like Ulster. No one here really wants them or understands them, but they insist.'

'I hope it's not like Ulster. It's more English lunacy, this tribe of yours. And is it yours?'

'I'm a half-breed.'

'So who will help me if you won't?'

'Of course I'll help. That's why I'm here now.'

Feldberg shook his head. 'And yet, Stephen, you must forgive me if I wonder whether you can be trusted. Trouble came when you came. Captain Carson made a misjudgement – a second misjudgement, I should say – when he took you in. Captain Carson is dead. No good deed goes unpunished, eh?'

'I'm sorry if it seems that way to you, Samuel, but it seems you have no choice. I am all there is, plus Smallbone.'

Mr Feldberg sighed.

'Smales won't help,' I said. 'As I told you, he's following the only line of enquiry he can imagine. Anything else would be disastrous from his point of view. And Gammon has been given a convenient explanation for what's going on, and he is afraid because he is the Second Master and will never be the Head if things go on like this, and he cannot separate his own interests from those of the school. As you can see, he's not alone in that. David is a very small element in the picture as far as he's concerned.'

'An element. He is my son. He's lost somewhere in this accursed city. I could go to the newspaper,' Feldberg said, vehemently but without conviction.

'What could you actually tell them at present? That you suspect a conspiracy? Even if you had more solid information the result would be the same. Because this is a backwater, a very large one, but still somewhere nothing is permitted to happen. You've read the paper. You know what it's like.'

'Yes, yes, Stephen, but I must do something. You are sure Rackham and that, that *creature* Vlaminck are behind all this?'

I nodded.

'But why do they try to destroy David? He has done them no harm. Of course, I know the answer. Then these men will know where David is. And yet no one acts against them.'

'Rackham has a protector. Someone important. Carson didn't know who it is. Rackham knows something of value, something dangerous to this person. If Rackham is indulged in this way, allowed to cause trouble, he will continue to keep the secret to himself and his protector will not be put at risk or exposed.'

'Would you make a bargain with this lunatic?' asked Mr Feldberg.

'No, but for me there's nothing at stake. He has to be stopped. He's out of control now. Even his protector must see that.'

'But would they care? I promised David's mother I would

guide and protect him. And now this. If ever I desired power, it's now. Come with me.'

He led me through the back of the shop and down into the cellar. He switched on the light. In a corner was an old wardrobe. He opened it and removed a section of the floor and took out a shallow wooden box, which he carried to a table. When he opened it I saw a pistol and several magazines of ammunition. He took the pistol out and offered it to me. I shook my head.

'I can see you're surprised, Stephen. I was a soldier. Soldiers collect things. As souvenirs if possible, but in case of need. A Browning semi-automatic from a dead German in the Falaise Gap. I suppose he had it from a dead American officer in turn.' He sighted down the barrel of the gun at me.

'Don't do that,' I said.

'It's not loaded yet.'

'Sergeant Risman taught me that there is no such thing as an unloaded weapon.'

Mr Feldberg shifted his aim and pulled the trigger. There was a hollow click.

'The Sergeant's right, of course.' He returned the box to its hiding place but he inserted a magazine in the pistol and brought it back up the stairs with him. He placed it in the pocket of the overcoat on the rack near his desk. 'David would have stayed in the cadets but I made him leave, to have more time for his work. There was no war taking place, I thought. Clearly I was mistaken.'

'You mustn't think of using that, Samuel.'

'There are other people involved in this who have no difficulty with violence, Stephen. They seem to enjoy it. They set the rules of engagement. You can go out the back way now. Let me know what you find out. I will do the same. Now you're under an obligation to me, as well as your beloved Captain. You should forget any ties to Mrs Rowan.'

THIRTY-FIVE

I had to try. I went to a phone box in the marketplace. The light had been smashed and it was hard to read the number. The phone rang several times before it was picked up.

'This is Stephen Maxwell,' I said.

'I warned you, didn't I?' Smales replied.

'It's not me I'm worried about.'

'Sounds as if you should be. Who else is going to employ you now? Ran an election and got the school burnt down. That'll look interesting on an application form.'

'I'm ringing about David Feldberg.'

'Where is he?'

'I don't know.'

'Then get off the fooking line.'

'Don't hang up. He's in trouble.'

'He will be when I get hold of him.' Smales laughed.

'I mean in danger.'

'Ditto.'

'I think Rackham and Vlaminck have got him.'

'Oh yes? Where? We should pop round. Where have they got him?'

'I don't know.'

'Then how do you know they've got him?'

'They must have.'

'Oh, right. And have you any evidence?'

'Rackham wants to hurt him.'

'And can you prove that?'

'Not exactly, but—'

'Then get off the fooking line.'

'Hamer's involved.'

'Never heard of him,' said Smales, and hung up.

I set off walking back through town to the Narwhal. On the way I passed Claes's shop. There were no lights on. I knocked at the side door. There was no reply.

The Narwhal was quiet, not long before closing. I rang Smallbone and told him to bring his van and meet me there.

'It's late, Maxwell. I've got a busy day tomorrow. There's a stamp fair in Harrogate.'

'Harrogate will have to wait. It's urgent, Bone.'

'It's always bloody urgent with you, isn't it?'

He turned up a few minutes later.

'I heard about the fire,' he said. 'Someone's dropping heavy hints. I dare say Gammon didn't notice. Too busy sacking you.'

'I'm finished, yes, but they can patch up the Memorial Hall. An old boy, one of the estate agents or trawler-owners, will write a cheque. Anyway, something more serious has happened,' I told him. 'Something else.'

He looked awkward at this. 'Oh, yes?'

'David Feldberg is missing, with his girlfriend.'

'That's very interesting timing. I see.'

'What do you see, Bone?'

'I see trouble coming my way with big boots on. I need to be out at church when it knocks.'

'Why?'

'Because you won't let the authorities deal with it.'

'Smales won't help me. Quite the contrary.'

'So you'll drag me into it somehow, Maxwell. Even though there's nothing you can do, is there?'

'I can't simply do nothing. I've told Feldberg's father I'll help. He's alone otherwise.'

Bone shook his head. 'You don't really know why the lad's run off. Do you? You might end up making things worse. Anyway, the girl might simply be up the duff.'

'I think the pair of them have more sense than that. They have a lot to look forward to. I don't think he has run off.'

'I would, if I was in the shit like that. Gretna Green or

maybe our old friends the Foreign Legion.' Bone stared into his glass.

Don't let me down now, I thought.

'Tell the police,' he said woodenly.

'They know as much as they want to. Smales is looking for David in connection with the fire.'

'Can you blame him? It looks very bad. You could understand him starting it.'

'There's no reason to think that, except prejudice. It would be completely out of character.' Bone raised a hand in apology. 'I think it's Rackham,' I said. 'First he got him suspended—'

'Or you might think David did that for himself.'

'It was just a question at a public meeting.'

'Context, Maxwell, context, as Carson would have been swift to remind you. The lad didn't have to go there, did he?'

'It was pretty courageous. No one else stood up like that.'

'Or bloody stupid. Lacking in circumspection.'

'You have to give him credit for caring.'

'All right. Suppose I do. What bloody good has this caring done?'

'So then the piano bursts into flames and everyone thinks he's responsible?' I said.

'Well, you've got to admit it isn't very promising. Most people would draw the obvious conclusion. My mother's a good barometer of public sentiment. I know what she'd say.'

'You don't really think it's him, do you, Bone?'

He shook his head. 'Probably not, no.'

'What would you do, then?'

'Me? I wouldn't do anything. You don't know the whole of what's involved, or who. But I know you, Maxwell. You'll go blundering in. You could end up in the shit – I mean, deeper in the shit.'

I stared at him.

'OK, well, as I say, I'd just tell the authorities,' he said.

'There's no other approach. That's what the citizen's meant to do. Hand it to the experts.'

'Experts like Messrs Gammon and Smales. But I've told you – it suits them to blame him. It covers the school.'

'I sometimes think that bloody place has replaced the world.' Bone finished his pint. 'I knew I should have stayed in and watched *Top of the Form* the night you first came back. I just don't like it when you lure me into doing the right thing. So what now?'

'We need to try to find David and Rachel.'

'Well, where would you suggest we start? It's late.'

Lurch must have been listening. He appeared from behind the screen in the snug, a pint of mild tiny as a shot-glass in his giant hand. He took a sip, put the glass down, all the while staring impassively across, then took two paperbacks from the pocket of his parka and held them up to show the covers. A Sven Hassel and a Georgette Heyer. Then he finished his pint and produced a scrap of black lace and wiped his mouth with it. He gave a slow nod and a graveyard smile, put the books and the lace away in his pocket, finished his drink and went out.

'Reddit,' said Bone.

'He was trying to provoke me,' I said.

'How? By claiming he can read? I bet his lips move when he wipes his arse.' Bone finished his pint. In the bar Stan called last orders. 'Time for one more?'

'Shirley was reading those recently.'

'Maybe they swap. Maybe Lurch likes a bit of romantic fiction in return.'

'Oh, shit.' I put my coat on and moved towards the door.

'You're on your own if you take a swing at him,' said Bone. 'I want that understood in advance.'

'Shut up, Bone. Where's the van? We need to get moving.'

When we got out on to the main road Lurch was nowhere to be seen. Bone's knackered blue Bedford van was parked round the corner. The frost made it reluctant to start. He pleaded with it tenderly and then nursed it back over the main road. We left it next to a bombsite a couple of streets from Shirley's flat over the old pub. As we approached, the building was in darkness. There was no one about.

'Very select round here,' said Bone. 'If you're a grave robber.'

'No sign of Lurch.'

'He's probably gone home. He must live somewhere. Under a big stone in the churchyard, for example. Anyway, how would he know you'd be in the pub?'

'Because it's a fair bet I will be. Or because he was following me.'

The front door was locked this time. I rang the bell three times. No reply.

'We'll have to get in there,' I said.

'Oh, no. I draw the line at breaking and entering. I think I'll go back and wait with the van.'

'I need you here.'

'I'm no good in a fight. Neither are you, come to that. Me mother would kill me if I got arrested.'

'Look, Bone, listen. Claes and Rackham have been using Shirley. They've got her addicted.'

'You what?'

'And I think they're prostituting her.'

'Are you making this up?'

'I wish I was.'

Smallbone stared out at the dark street.

'But you're talking about Shirley. I mean, she's a nice girl. Everyone knows that. I mean, she's not some tart off the docks. She's Shirley.'

'Claes and Rackham don't care about that. She's in danger, Bone.'

'Can't fookin have that. Right you are, then.'

We went over the double gate into the delivery yard, Smallbone wheezing from the effort. There were no lights showing at the back. The kitchen window was unlocked and we struggled inside, scrambling over the taps and the sink. Our attempts at silence should have raised the dead.

The whole place smelled of damp and wood-pulp paper. It seemed empty, somewhere made futile by neglect and disuse, like many another in those parts. A fire extinguisher stood by the door. It seemed unlikely to be required. The building itself seemed to have forgotten that anyone had ever been there.

'Try the cellar. I'll have a look upstairs,' I said.

'I don't like this,' Smallbone said. He sighed and opened the door off the hall. He found a light switch and went gingerly down. When he was out of sight I began to climb the stairs.

The two first-floor rooms and the bathroom were, like the corridors, piled with books and magazines. As I reached the attic landing I saw a faint light. The door of Shirley's flat was slightly ajar. I stopped to listen. Nothing. I crossed the landing and pushed the door open.

There was a lamp on the floor, masked with a paisley scarf. A television was playing silently. In the faint blue-grey glow I saw a figure lying on the bed. It was Shirley, naked, unconscious.

On the television screen beyond the bed – I couldn't help but look – was the City Hall, with the Mayor was silently announcing the result of the West End by-election, relieved to have got it out of the way in record time yet again. The turnout was impressively low. The victorious candidate came forward. Flashbulbs went off. There was a shot of his defeated rivals. They looked sheepish, like people who'd waited too long for a bus that wasn't coming – except for Allingham, who looked noble, philosophical and altogether elsewhere, like one for whom defeat was simply confirmation of the final victory to come, where it mattered, in the confines of his head.

'Shirley.' She was facing away and didn't stir. 'Shirley, wake up, love.' I knelt down and nudged her shoulder. She made a far-off noise. I shook her and turned her to face me. Beside her lay the Sven Hassel books and the syringe. She was still breathing, just. I got up to switch the main light on, but when I reached the door it slammed into me. As I fell backwards I saw Lurch coming in, with something in his raised hand. There was a movement behind him, then the sound of a heavy impact, and he staggered and collapsed on top of me.

'Maxwell? Are you all right?' Bone asked. The light came on.

'What did you hit him with?'

'The fire extinguisher.' Lurch seemed to be unconscious. I struggled out from underneath him. 'I heard him come in when you'd gone upstairs, so, you know, I followed him. He had a wire. A whatsit, a garrotte. Look.'

'Jesus!'

'There's no one else here as far as I can tell,' said Bone. 'We need to be gone. Shit, look at this place. What's up with Shirley? Where are her clothes?'

'Help me get her downstairs. She needs a doctor.'

'Well, she can't go anywhere like that. Is that a needle? Bloody hell, Maxwell. I'm not happy about this.'

I found a nightdress under the pillow and slid it over Shirley's head. She seemed unaware.

'Lurch is bleeding, look,' said Bone. 'Big gash on his head. So what do we do about him?'

'Don't tempt me. Leave him. We need to get Shirley out of here.' I wrapped her in the counterpane.

We carried her down to the front door. Bone slipped out to get the van. I sat at the bottom of the stairs holding Shirley. Her breathing was faint and her skin was clammy.

'Shirley, you stupid cow,' I said. 'Whatever are we going to do with you?'

Bone seemed to be taking a long time coming back with the van. Then I heard noises from upstairs. Lurch was coming round, it seemed. He was in a hurry, crashing blindly into obstacles before getting out on to the landing. There was a scuffling, followed by a dull, contained bang and a sudden brightness from upstairs, then a scream and a splintering noise. I went back into the hall and looked up as Lurch fell into the narrow stairwell and stuck there like a missile, his burning head visible above us, his mouth open in a gurgling scream. Smoke wreathed around him. His feet drummed against the panelling above him. The light brightened as fire took hold and he stared blindly down in agonized rage. Time to go.

I carried Shirley out into the street and closed the door as quietly as I could. Bone was just pulling up at the kerb. Light was playing at the windows of the house now, as though the glass would shatter in a moment or two. I pushed Shirley on to the front seat and squeezed in after her.

'Get a move on, Bone. The house is on fire.'

'What?'

'Get fucking going, man. Go the back way on to the park by the Convent. We need to get her to the Infirmary.'

'What the hell are we going to tell them?' asked Bone as we drove away down the dark terraces.

'We can't tell them anything. We'll just have to leave her in the entrance.'

'Christ, Maxwell. I knew something like this would happen. Is she awake?'

'Not really.'

'She's not . . .'

'Not yet.'

'Ask her what happened.'

'Shirley. Are you there?' I said. She didn't respond. 'I'll take her into Casualty, Bone. Just get us there as fast as bloody possible.' We drove along the edge of the park, fearing to be stopped by one of the police cars that lay in wait for unwary drinkers trying to go home the back way. Shirley would take some explaining. Steam pipes here we come, I thought. We went past the Convent and Carson's house and stopped at the main road. There a police car went past with its siren on and a couple of girls went dawdling over the zebra crossing.

'Lurch must have set the bomb at Shirley's as well. But he was too late to get out. He was trapped. I saw him. His head was on fire,' I said.

'You couldn't have helped him. Too dangerous. Anyway, it was only Lurch's head.'

'There was no time, but I didn't want to help him anyway, did I?'

Bone looked at me curiously.

'Why did they want us to go there, though?'

'To get us out of the picture. We were all supposed to go up with the house.'

'I said something like this would happen.'

'I'm sorry, Bone.'

'Now you're sorry,' he said. 'You're a shithouse, really, aren't you, Maxwell, my friend?'

We arrived at the side gates to the Infirmary and waited while an ambulance pulled away. Then I carried Shirley to the entrance and placed her in a wheelchair and pushed it through the swing doors into the dim reception area. There was no one about so I rang the bell on the reception desk. A nurse appeared.

'Overdose, I think,' I said, and ran outside again. The van was already moving as I got back in.

'Is she all right?' Smallbone asked. 'I mean, she will recover, won't she?'

'Your guess is as good as mine.'

'Well, she's got to. I mean, you know. She's Shirley.'

We pulled into a deserted pub car park and sat smoking Smallbone's cigarettes.

'Now what?' he said. 'Should we just go to the police and explain?'

'What would happen? They'd arrest us.'

Smallbone shook his head unhappily.

'You can go home if you want,' I said. 'There's no need for you to get any more mixed up in this. I'm grateful.'

Smallbone laughed and rested his head on the steering wheel. 'Mixed up? It's a bit fookin late for that, isn't it?'

'As you say, I'm a shithouse.'

'Setting that aside for later recriminations, supposing there's going to be any later in our case, what with all these fookin nutters poncing about in the neighbourhood, we still don't know where Feldberg and the girl are.'

'Rackham and Claes can't stay here now, can they? The bomb at the school, the bomb at Shirley's, even Smales would have to take an interest, whether he liked it or not.'

'So they get out?'

'And take Feldberg and Rachel with them.'

'Why take them? What use would they be any more?'

'Maybe they're already dead.'

'Did I mention you're a shithouse?'

'Maybe they're still planning to get rid of them.' It was midnight, then a quarter past. Eventually, it came to me. 'The boat. They could use the boat.'

'Boat? What boat?' said Smallbone.

'Maggie has a boat. Rackham uses it too. Quite a fancy seagoing motor yacht. I saw Rackham setting out in it one afternoon.'

'That could be a tactful way of leaving. Without making a splash. As it were. Fuck. Sorry.'

'I think what Lurch nearly managed to do to us and Shirley was a diversion, Bone. Rackham and Claes are on the move now. They've got to be. They've had the election – Labour won, by the way. And the fire at the school. And they've dropped the lad in it. It's what Claes called a manifestation of the will.'

'That fucking prat,' said Smallbone.

'So they might as well get going and while they're at it they can deal with David and Rachel.'

'But if they've left, what can we do?'

'Suppose Lurch was meant to go with them? They'll be waiting for him. We need to find a phone box.'

'You said no police.'

'I'm going to ring Samuel Feldberg. And then Risman. Then we're going to Blake's.'

THIRTY-SIX

We drove to Fernbank, parked the van in the dark between streetlights and climbed over our second fence of the evening. I took the torch from the glove compartment. The night was still and cold with some low mist on the field. We followed the path through the wood, pausing to listen where it turned at the creek. Under the freezing fog the tide was coming in, but *Lorelei* could not have set sail yet. We crossed the rugby pitch below the level of the towpath until we reached the steps. Someone had left the gate open at the top.

There was a light showing on *Lorelei*. The vessel moved slightly at its mooring as the black water flooded into the creek.

'We need to get closer,' I whispered.

'And do what?'

'Get on board somehow.'

'After you, Claude.'

Lorelei shifted again.

'Stay here and keep watch.'

'You don't know who's on the boat, do you, Kemosabe?'

'I'm betting neither Claes nor Rackham's there at the moment.'

'You're betting? Daft sod.'

'There aren't any lights showing in the cabin.'

I went along the jetty and lowered myself on to the deck. There was no noise from below. Nothing moved on shore and I could no longer see Bone. I opened the hatch and went into the cabin. There was a further hatch leading down to the sleeping quarters. I opened it and could see nothing.

'David,' I said. There was a faint stirring, like an animal turning in its sleep. I risked turning on the torch. There were two figures on the floor of the cabin, bound and hooded. One of them moved slightly.

'It's Stephen Maxwell,' I whispered. 'I'm going to get you out, but we need to be very quiet.'

I removed the hood from the first figure. It was David. He was gagged with gaffer tape. I removed Rachel's hood. She too was gagged. I pulled the tape from David's mouth.

'Remember,' I hissed, 'be very quiet.' I removed the tape from Rachel. She coughed as if she had been choking. I put a hand over her mouth and listened. Nothing.

I went back to the cabin and found a knife and came down again and cut the tape on their wrists and ankles.

'We're going to get off the boat in a minute. Don't worry. It's all right now. Get your breath back.' I could feel Feldberg staring at me. 'Can you stand? Rub your ankles to get the circulation back.'

I went up to the cabin and looked out. Claes appeared on the shore and walked a few paces down the jetty, then stopped to look back at a noise. A running figure came after him down the bank and on to the jetty. As Claes turned at the sound, the runner struck him. Claes wavered on the edge of the jetty before toppling backwards into the mud with a cry. The runner came nearer along the jetty.

'David? Rachel?' It was Mr Feldberg's voice.

'We need some help,' I called. Feldberg came down into the cabin followed by a breathless Bone.

'I never saw him coming,' said Bone.

'Neither did Claes.'

We helped David and Rachel on deck and then up on to the jetty.

'Help me,' said Claes. He lay waist-deep, half-tilted back, in the mud at the shore end of the jetty. A notice warning people not to walk there was just out of his reach. He seemed to be stuck. The water ran more quickly now. He moaned and clutched his shoulder.

'Samuel, why don't you and Smallbone take David and Rachel to Casualty?' I said. 'I can deal with this.'

'Help me!' said Claes.

'I would stay, if it weren't for the children,' said Mr Feldberg.

'They were going tie weights to us and throw us into the sea,' said David. He had his arms round Rachel, who was sobbing. 'They told us that was what they would do.' He was furious as well as terrified.

'You're safe now,' I said.

'You think so?' said David. 'Where is Rackham?'

'Never mind him. He can't hurt you.'

'No, no, I want to hurt *him*. I want to kill him.'

'We can't do that,' I said.

'There is no "we", Mr Maxwell, is there? I can do it, though, if I can get hold of him.'

'You need to think about Rachel. She needs you now. Go with your father. I'll be there soon.'

'Why, what can you do, Mr Maxwell? After all this? Nothing.'

'Enough, David,' said his father. 'Think of Rachel. Go with Smallbone. I'll be with you in a minute.' The boy nodded reluctantly and the three moved away over the embankment and out of sight.

'Maxwell!' said Claes from below. 'Quickly, my friend. I need assistance.' He sank a little.

'Do not help him, Stephen,' said Mr Feldberg.

'I could get a rope from the boat,' I said.

'No,' said Mr Feldberg. 'Not after this. Remember, I am armed.'

Claes's face was white and moon-shaped against the dark. His tongue protruded from his open mouth. Suddenly he sank a little further. It was like watching something being swallowed by a snake. He thrashed with his hands under the shallow water, and then they seemed to be trapped in the mud and only his head and shoulders remained visible. 'Get me out! There is no time to waste.' He cried out in horror, knowing what must happen. 'I beg you!'

'You could have killed Shirley,' I said.

'Do not let me drown like this!'

'What about Shirley, Claes?'

'Quick now!'

Only the head remained above water. His voice had taken on a hysterical gargling quality. The breath was being forced out of him by the weight of the mud. He opened his mouth once again and the thick black water began to fill it. He gave a choked groan and swallowed as if he meant to drink the creek dry. His nose vanished below the surface and his wide white eyes continued to gaze at me in disbelief. Then he was gone.

For a time bubbles could be heard breaking the surface.

I walked with Feldberg back down to the field. David and Rachel were holding on to each other.

'What now?' said Smallbone.

'Go back to the hospital,' I said. 'See if Shirley's OK.'

'Where are you going?' said Bone.

'There's something I have to collect. I'll join you when I've finished.'

Mr Feldberg showed no signs of moving.

Bone said, 'It would be best to take Rachel and David to the hospital, sir.'

'I'll come with you,' Mr Feldberg said. 'But I need to talk to Stephen a moment. I'll be there shortly.' Smallbone ushered the pair away into the wood.

'What about the police?' I asked.

'No police,' said Mr Feldberg. 'If it happens that the creek gives up its dead, then what happened to Claes was a tragic accident. The kind of thing that happens when you ignore warnings not to trespass in dangerous places. Here.' He held out the gun.

'I don't want it.'

'It's not a matter of what you want,' he said. 'Take it. I'm going to see to the children. You have business to settle. You have a debt, first to the Captain and now also to me. Redeem yourself.'

I took the gun. We went our separate ways across Majuba field.

At Percival Street I could no sign of Risman. As I went up the stairs I could hear music. It clarified itself into 'The Way You Look Tonight'. I tried the door of the flat. It was unlocked and I stepped inside. Rackham and Maggie were dancing slowly, after a fashion. He was bare-chested and Maggie wore his shirt. I could tell she was drunk again. After a few moments Rackham saw me and stopped. Maggie looked round groggily. He removed the stylus from the record and she flopped on to the settee.

'You're full of surprises, Maxwell,' said Rackham.

'Give the boy a drink,' said Maggie.

'A drink's not what he wants, by the look of him.'

'Well, I'll have one.' She reached down for a bottle on the floor and slopped wine into a glass.

'So what have you got to say for yourself, Maxwell?' Rackham asked. He leaned against the dresser.

'Claes is dead, Rackham. And so is Lurch.'

'This is a bit bloody gloomy,' said Maggie. 'Let's have the music on again. Have a drink, Stephen, for God's sake. Standing there like a eunuch in a cathouse.'

'David Feldberg and the girl are safe.'

'It sounds like a busy night,' said Rackham.

'And the police will be on their way.'

'I very much doubt it.'

'You mean that ghastly Smales person?' said Maggie, and snorted. 'Christ! Talk about the great chain of being.'

'I'm going to collect my picture and leave you to it,' I said.

'You carry on,' said Maggie. 'You're welcome to it.' I went through into the studio, moved the picture and took the envelope from under the floorboard and put it in my coat pocket.

When I went back into the living room carrying the picture, Rackham was holding a carving knife.

'I've told you before, Charles,' said Maggie in a high, petulant voice, 'what you get up to elsewhere is your business, but you can't carry on like that in my house.'

'Shut up, you stupid bitch,' said Rackham matter-of-factly. 'You're not in charge of anything.'

'Oh, Charles, don't.' Out of nowhere Maggie began to weep in great gasping sobs. 'You mustn't hurt me, you know that. Don't be hateful. Don't, darling, please.'

'I'm warning you, you old whore.' He struck her across the face with the flat of his hand. She howled.

'Leave her alone, Rackham,' I said.

'You shouldn't have interfered,' he hissed. 'You should have stayed right away from Blake's. Sticking your nose in to help your little Jew friend. You're as bad as that old queen Carson. I'm sick of the lot of you. Now tell me where it is.'

'Where what is?'

'Carson's journal. I know he kept one.'

'Then you know more than I do.'

'Do you want me to cut your tongue out?'

'Then how will I tell you anything?'

'Tell me and you can go.'

'I can't help you. You belong in a madhouse.'

'I'm bored. I'm bored. I want to get on to the next thing. Tell me.'

I shook my head. He came towards me. Maggie screamed and flung herself at him. He threw her off. I got in one blow of my own before the door opened.

'Put that down, Rackham,' said Hamer. Risman appeared behind him.

'Or what?'

'Or Sergeant Risman will shoot you.'

'I doubt it. You can't touch me. You must know that.'

'So you haven't heard? Goodness me, you really haven't, Rackham?'

'What's that?'

'The case is altered, I'm afraid. Your defender, your special friend, is dead. It was recent. Your protector is gone and you are alone.'

'Put the knife down, Mr Rackham,' said Risman. 'Be a good gentleman now and come along easy. Best thing all round.'

'Maggie needs medical attention,' I said.

'Rackham, think of your sister,' said Hamer.

'She can go to hell. I want safe conduct.'

'Then give me whatever Carson wrote. He must have written something. Writing was all he could do.'

'Maxwell knows where it is,' spat Rackham.

'Maxwell?' said Hamer.

'I can't help.'

'All right, Risman,' said Hamer. Risman produced a pistol. 'Let's be sensible. I can read you the Official Secrets Act, Maxwell. Defence of the Realm, all the rest of it. But if you want to walk out of here, just help me. The story's over anyway. For God's sake, where is it?'

I reached into my pocket and took out the envelope. Maggie flew at me brandishing a bottle. Risman caught her and took the glass from her hand. I handed the envelope to Hamer.

'And this is all of it? The only copy of all of it.'

'You have my word as a gentleman,' I said.

'Don't be funny. You might not be out of the woods yet yourself, Maxwell.' He folded the envelope and pocketed it. 'Well, now. What a to-do.'

'You've got what you want,' said Rackham. 'So we'll call it quits. *Lorelei* is to rendezvous with a Belgian freighter. I join it and sail to Antwerp. If I can get there, I'll be gone. Into Europe. I'll just disappear. Maggie is supposed to bring *Lorelei* back.'

'Yes, you'll be gone,' said Hamer.

'We'd better be off, Mr Hamer,' said Risman. 'Time's getting on if we want to catch the tide.'

'Very well, Sergeant. Maxwell, you and Mrs Rackham had better come along for the cruise.'

'Best put some clothes on, ma'am, eh?' said Risman.

THIRTY-SEVEN

It was dark on the river, a few lights showing on other vessels taking the tide, then, coming up to northwards, Axholme lighthouse signalling the final southward curve of the estuary out to sea.

We sat in the cabin. Rackham was at the wheel, with Risman stationed behind him. Hamer was reading over Carson's document. Though we were in motion, everything seemed suspended. Hamer had ordered Maggie to sober up and make coffee. She had gone unwillingly below.

Now the wind from the south-east freshened as we passed through the mouth of the estuary. The boat, for all its solid size, rolled a little where the sea and the river's tide met. Surf churned at the bows and then calmed again. Ahead of us, I made out something large, the wrong shape for a ship.

'Kite Island,' said Rackham automatically. Hamer looked up.

'It looks manmade,' he said.

'It is,' said Rackham. 'It's a fort built to keep Napoleon out. Then it was a naval prison.'

'And now?'

'Just seagulls, I should think.' We came within fifty yards of the huge stone plinth on which the fort stood. It stank of guano. A few lights showed but there was no one home. Soon the fort slipped past into the darkness, its lights ghosting awhile in the chilly dark.

Maggie came unsteadily from below with a tray of mugs and a brandy bottle.

'No milk, I'm afraid, gentlemen,' she said. She put down the tray. 'Drop of brandy to warm you up.' Risman declined the brandy.

Hamer stood up and looked past Rackham at the chart spread out on the map table.

'What's next?'

'The sea. The last sandbars. Then the floor drops away at Fletcher's Hole.'

'Then that's where we want to be.'

'The rendezvous is further on,' said Rackham, turning to look at him.

'Yes,' said Hamer.

'I have plenty of money,' said Rackham. 'If that's the issue.' He remained calm.

'I'm sure you have. It isn't.'

'Just let Charles go,' said Maggie. 'Please. It's all over now.'

'Almost,' said Hamer.

'There's something you need to know, Maxwell,' said Rackham. 'It will change the complexion of things. Shall I tell him, Hamer?'

'Up to you.'

'Maxwell, you want to know why I killed Carson.'

'Tell me, Rackham,' I said.

'I didn't kill him,' Rackham said, with his thin smile. Hamer put Carson's envelope back in his pocket.

'Get on with it.'

'Carson had warned me to confess what happened during the war, or he would expose me. He knew I had an eminent protector, but now he said he was too old to worry on his own account, that he had to make up for his own cowardice, and that he would give me chance to atone for mine, and so on, all very tidy and virtuous and feeble. He gave me the weekend to think it over. I arranged to meet him on the Sunday evening after the exercise, discreetly, in the woods, to tell him what I'd decided. If he saw a need for caution about this arrangement, he clearly didn't care. I watched from a safe distance as Risman did his rounds at the end of the exercise and then I went to the rendezvous point.'

'The jetty.'

'And Carson turned up, still in uniform – very apt – to hear my decision. And as arranged, Hamer came along and hit him on the head and put him in the water, and there we had it, the awful accident.'

'Take the wheel, Mrs Rowan,' said Hamer. 'Are we there yet?'

'Yes,' said Maggie, 'but what are you going to do?'

'Circle awhile,' said Hamer.

'Hamer, is this true?' I asked.

'It is. We'd got to the point of no return. Carson couldn't be relied on.'

'And you let me think Rackham killed Carson.'

'Well, Maxwell, I rather think that's an assumption you made for yourself.'

'So really, your enemy is Hamer,' said Rackham, amused. 'You've been barking up the wrong tree, Maxwell, you idiot. So what do you want to do with him, Hamer?'

'Go below and bring up the stuff, Rackham.'

'Tell Risman to do it.'

'I'm telling you.' Rackham disappeared down the steps.

'This calls for an apposite quotation, doesn't it?' said Hamer. 'Something from Bacon, perhaps.'

'Why does anyone have to die?' said Maggie.

'That doesn't sound like Bacon to me,' said Hamer.

Rackham reappeared with rope, gaffer tape and the hoods. He went below again and returned lugging two buckets full of concrete. As he turned to close the hatch behind him Risman moved forward and hit him on the back of the head. Rackham fell to the floor.

'Hands first, Maxwell,' said Hamer, passing me the tape.

'Stop this!' Maggie screamed. She let go of the wheel. Risman moved closer behind and cocked the pistol.

'Best not, ma'am,' he said. 'Got to let things take their course. Cut the engine now.' The sound from below died, and we drifted in the dark. Maggie was weeping.

'I won't do this,' I told Hamer.

'But you wouldn't like harm to come to anyone else, would you, Maxwell?' Hamer replied. 'Young David, or Rachel?'

I taped Rackham's hands behind his back. As I worked on taping his ankles he began to regain consciousness and kicked out.

'Hamer, I told you I would disappear!' he said.

'And that's what you're going to do,' said Hamer. 'Tape over his mouth, Maxwell. Then the hood. And tie a bucket round the ankles. Get him to the side.' Rackham was thrashing blindly by now, making muffled animal cries.

'Please!' yelled Maggie. 'Don't hurt him. Tell me what you want and we'll do it.'

'Over he goes,' said Hamer.

I shook my head.

'As you wish. You lack stomach, Maxwell. That's hardly a surprise. Sometimes I wonder if you're really a Blake's man at all.' Hamer raised Rackham's legs and tipped him into the water. Maggie collapsed, screaming.

Rackham did not resurface.

'For God's sake stop the caterwauling, 'said Hamer. 'Pull yourself together. You're going to repeat the process with Mr Maxwell.'

'No,' sobbed Maggie.

'Oh, do come on. You're only delaying the inevitable.'

'Let her be,' I said.

'Be practical, Maxwell. Or do I have to kill her as well?'

'You're going to do that anyway.'

'Very well,' said Hamer. 'Risman, get hold of the woman.'

Risman passed the gun to Hamer. As Hamer moved towards me, raising the gun to strike, Risman was suddenly at his side. I didn't see the knife, but I saw a wide grin spread across Hamer's throat and he fell forward, clutching the spurting wound and making a gargling noise.

We stood and watched him bleed out.

Risman retrieved the envelope from Hamer's coat and handed it back to me. 'There you are, Mr Maxwell,' he said.

'Now we can stop playing pass the fookin parcel.' He turned to Maggie. 'Pardon my French, Mrs Rowan. Right, ma'am, you need to get Mr Hamer ready for his swim. Quick as you can, ma'am. You only need to do the bucket, of course.'

She stared at him.

Soon it would be Christmas.

Epilogue

2010

Tomorrow it will all begin again at Blake's. Autumn term. As I have put it in my volume of history, 'Blakeans, wherever they may be around the globe, cannot hear the word "September" without a quickening of anticipation at what adventures the new term will offer. They know what a gift they have been given, and are ever-generous in their support.' Is that too much?

There were, for a while, other women, and once or twice vague thoughts of a future sketched themselves out, but somehow never became a reality. There would not be a wife, there would be no children. Something I cannot quite come at in myself seems to regard this as a fitting outcome. It was bound up with Maggie. Even at her worst she attracted me like no other. There has been loneliness, but I have learned to conflate it with a desired solitude, like that of some self-sufficient antiquary of an earlier time, moving steadily from relic to relic as if the past could be appeased. I wrote a textbook on the 1939–45 period, but then found myself feeling I had written enough, although somehow a 'literary' reputation continued to attach itself to me in the school. Hence the commission to write volume two of the history – which I find I have, not unhappily, neglected in order to try to complete this account of things.

How fine it is, to speculate at leisure. Not that there is any other urgent matter in prospect. Once again I find that times and places fold in on themselves, resistant to the simple sequence you and I should both prefer. Bear with me now. One thing is clear to me: the past – every morning on waking

I discover with alarm and excitement that my life is now mostly the past – is more substantial and beguiling to me than anything else, despite what it holds. Each day I write looking out between the bare plane trees on to a setting I have known for fifty years, but the place is not what it was. Mere persistence has earned me the right to say that.

And soon it will be November once again. Fog, frost, churned-up rugby pitches, the ghosts of masters past stalking the touchlines and delivering their ferocious exhortations to the troops. The dead men seem like old children now, and I am almost of their party, walking through the woods and down to the lake to join them, or setting sail on that last foggy night from the creek on *Lorelei*.

Since my retirement, as well as pottering in the library, I enjoy the privilege of sitting up on the balcony during the Service of Remembrance. Usually nowadays the bugler makes a decent fist of 'The Last Post' and the boys manage a respectful silence, though now the great conflict must seem very remote to them – the faint report as though of another age, as indeed it is. There are discussions, I understand, about whether Blake's will continue to hold a service, but I think it will be a few years yet before the staff and governors feel easy about renouncing such a ritual.

What rituals do we have to offer in its place? There is something called a Prom, an American-derived event, a dance held jointly with St Clare's, with whom it is planned to amalgamate before long. This Prom, which involves a great show of expense on costumes for the girls, is to take place in the Carson Performing Arts Centre. So be it. *Ruddigore* was never staged. Now there is talk of *Evita*.

After the events of this narration I came to feel, rather surprisingly, that I should involve myself in the Cadets, so I applied to the local Territorial unit and a while later joined Risman and other colleagues in their military activities at Blake's. I have not been entirely able to account for this sense of obligation. True, it followed in Carson's footsteps and

Major Brand's, and it helped, I suppose, to embed me more firmly in the life of the school, but at the bottom there is something irrational and tribal – and weirdly satisfying – in this assertion, and acceptance, of belonging.

When we returned to shore, steered by Maggie, who had ceased to speak, the envelope seemed more like a fetish than evidence. I called Hamer's number. Colonel Dennison replied. A doctor was called for Maggie and she was admitted to hospital for psychiatric assessment. The papers ran respectful obituaries of a senior member of the aristocracy who had spent much of his life abroad while loyally serving the nation in various unsung capacities.

Risman and I went to see Gammon. The conversation was cordial. Gammon was accommodating. After a day or two it was discreetly announced that Rackham had decided to leave in order to devote himself to his literary work.

I was tidying up in the library after lessons a few days later when Colonel Dennison appeared.

'A moment of your time, if I may, Maxwell.'

'Please come in.'

'I believe you have something for me.'

'Give me a moment,' I said. I went to the Special Collection case and retrieved the envelope from its hiding place among the works of Allingham, Carson and Rackham. I returned and made to hand it to the Colonel. He shook his head.

'Fine evening for a walk,' he said.

After a time we came to the lake, and the jetty where the raft was moored. It was a clear starry December night and our breath made clouds.

'No more ambushes, I hope, Colonel.'

'Not my line, I'm glad to say.' A breeze silvered the dark water. 'I think it's time to call a halt.'

'What would that require?'

'Whatever Carson gave you.'

'And in return?'

'Nothing. No further action.'

'No more Hamer.' The Colonel smiled.

'No, no more Hamer. Seems to have dropped off the radar. Gone native.'

'I dare say.'

'The trouble with chaps like Hamer,' he began, and I thought, The trouble with chaps like Hamer is chaps like you, and all the other chaps. 'The trouble with chaps like Hamer is they risk a loss of perspective. Engage too closely. Forget what's really at stake.'

'And what would that be, Colonel?'

'Continuity in change. Stability.'

I took out the envelope.

'I have your word,' I said.

'Of course you do, Maxwell.'

'I hope you mean that, Colonel,' said Risman, emerging from among the trees. 'We've had enough bullshit here at Blake's. There's the future to consider.'

Dennison gave his gouty grin.

'Then, Sergeant, you have my word as a fellow soldier,' he said. I handed Dennison the envelope. 'This is it? All of it? You swear?'

'It's all I've got,' I said. He looked at me for a few moments.

'I think we've all got the same interests at heart,' he said. 'At least I hope so. Chap has to be able to rely on something.' He went off round the lake towards the railway crossing.

'Where is it?' asked Risman.

'I don't know what you're talking about,' I said.

'Good.' He stared at the lake. 'Hamer showed up and thought I was his man. Colonel Dennison thought I was his man. But what I serve is the school, and now we'll say no more about any of it. And wherever you haven't got whatever it is you haven't got, I hope it's safe.'

I'm out of it these days, of course, though I see the manoeuvres in the woods from my study window. I think of

Risman, long gone now, with his mixture of self-possession and atavistic loyalty. He never did speak of the events of that winter night again, though I wanted him to.

Rackham was forgotten with surprising speed. Poetry, after all, was not what Blake's was about. Maggie, on the other hand, seemed to recover quite quickly from her breakdown, but the drink took an ever more serious hold and within a year she was discreetly asked to resign. We no longer met. She had private means, of course, but occasionally Smallbone and I would spot her in some pub in town, sometimes in rough company and sometimes alone. Her husband, whom she apparently visited more often than before, died of a heart attack, and soon afterwards Maggie was found floating in the fish dock with a high level of alcohol in her blood. The verdict was misadventure. For obvious reasons I had doubts about attending the funeral. It was perhaps a good thing that in the end I did, as I was almost the only mourner. The other one was Gammon.

Afterwards he chose to walk with me across the park to Carson's house. I was going for a look round while deciding whether to sell it.

We paused by the plant house and stood by the pond. It was frozen, with waxed bread wrappers, discarded by those who came to feed the ducks, trapped in the ice.

'I shall be going in the summer,' Gammon said.

'I see.' Would it have been too much to cheer? To push him on to the ice.

'Connolly will be taking over for the time being while the governors decide on a permanent replacement for me.'

'I see.'

'I shall be taking up an appointment in Hunslet. Pastures new.'

Not in Hunslet there aren't, I thought. 'That's Milton,' I said.

'What is?'

'"Tomorrow to fresh woods and pastures new." It's from

"Lycidas", where Milton mourns his dead friend, his friend who drowned.'

Gammon wrestled with this crux for a time. We walked on and reached the road. Carson's house stood opposite. In order to relieve Gammon of the burden of response, I said: 'And I take it this will be a promotion for you.'

'I shall be concentrating on geography,' he said. I had never seen Gammon miserable before. He had a wizened and pathetic look.

'It's a large field,' I said.

He looked for a moment as if about to issue a rebuke, but remembered himself. 'You mustn't think I knew,' he said, almost imploringly.

'Knew about what?'

He hurried on. 'There were others much better informed than me. My only concern, Maxwell, my only concern was for the school.'

'If you say so, Gammon. You must excuse me now. I have to go and look at the late Captain's house.'

'I acted for what I hoped was the best. I hope there are no hard feelings. We are colleagues, after all.'

'Yes, we are, aren't we?'

As to Smallbone, on the evening after the sea voyage I went to see Shirley in the hospital, and I found he was there before me, reading to her from, for some reason, *Ivanhoe*. At first she seemed to be asleep, but she opened her eyes and glanced from me to Smallbone and back. With gratitude and relief I recognized the goodbye look.

'Maurice has been ever so good,' she said. Smallbone, of course, did not ordinarily permit the use of his Christian name.

'I can imagine.'

'I'm sorry, Stevie, about before. I lost track of where I was.'

'Let's not worry about it. As long as you're here, with Maurice to look after you.'

Bone gave me a dark look: caught red-handed being kind.

When his mother died a couple of years later, Smallbone sold the stamp business. He and Shirley moved to the seaside and, naturally enough, opened a bookshop. I went up to see them not long after they opened. Shirley was pregnant. They wanted me to be the godfather, and of course I agreed, and was there at your christening, Eleanor, in a church overlooking the grey North Sea.

And then, as sometimes happens, neither entirely by intention nor accident, we lost touch. I don't imagine you know very much about me, if anything. By now you'll have heard more than enough.

For years, ten, twenty, I waited for the blow to fall. It never did. Perhaps the matter was no longer considered of interest, no longer a story. Well, we shall see about that.

Percival Street and Maggie's house were demolished under compulsory purchase and made into a carpark for the new Infirmary. I liked to watch the building work from the railway-crossing gate. The city was not, it seemed, wholly immutable, though the trains still ran along the line beside the woods and then across the bridge over the creek, where, after its last night-voyage, *Lorelei* remained moored for a long time, until one day I noticed it was gone.

I returned the pistol to Mr Feldberg and told him I hoped that my debt was paid. He agreed, but we were never quite on the same terms as before. David went on to Cambridge and read PPE rather than history, and later married Rachel, who specialized in paediatrics. Afterwards I lost track of him too for many years, until one evening I was watching the television news and he was interviewed as a representative of the Israeli government's team during some phase or other of the always-doomed negotiations with the Palestinians. He was, of course, intelligent and articulate. He was also cold and implacably intransigent. I was not surprised.

And this manuscript is yours, Eleanor. When I die, it will be sent to you with the copy I made of Carson's document (of course I was lying: what would you expect?) to reach you at the university. Do with it as you see fit.

Evening falls over the fields and the woods and where manoeuvres continue. I, though, seem to have finished. There is the bell of the lightship on the incoming tide, far downriver. Out beyond that lies the place where some of the bodies are buried.